**"This i**
**away the**                                    **"**

Dennis Ryland nodded. "What are its range and area of effect?"

Wells exchanged looks with Jakes and Kuroda, then said, "From an airborne platform at twenty miles' range, you could zap a major city with two bursts in about five minutes."

"Good," Dennis said. "That's very good. Will the people on the ground feel anything?"

"Not a thing," Jakes said, rejoining the conversation. "They won't know what's happened till they go to use their promicin powers—and find out they don't exist anymore."

Dennis imagined Jordan Collier's smug little smirk turning into a look of horror. The thought put a smile on Dennis's face. "How long until we have a working prototype?"

Jakes shrugged. "Once you give us the sample? Maybe two or three days, barring any mishaps or interference."

"Excellent," Dennis said. He picked up a phone. "I'll tell my crew to bring it down." He punched in a Haspelcorp number that would connect him directly to the crew in the jet. As the line rang, he told the scientists, "Work quickly. We might need this sooner than we thought."

"Don't worry, Mister Ryland," Jakes said with a beatific smile. "Soon, the world will be completely back to normal."

# OTHER *THE 4400* BOOKS

# THE 4400.

## PROMISES BROKEN

### DAVID MACK

Based upon *THE 4400* created by
Scott Peters and René Echevarria

Pocket Star Books
New York   London   Toronto   Sydney

Pocket Star Books
A Division of Simon & Schuster, Inc.
1230 Avenue of the Americas
New York, NY 10020

**◉CBS** CONSUMER PRODUCTS

First Pocket Star Books paperback edition November 2009

For information about special discounts for bulk purchases, please contact Simon & Schuster Special Sales at 1-866-506-1949 or business@simonandschuster.com.

The Simon & Schuster Speakers Bureau can bring authors to your live event. For more information or to book an event, contact the Simon & Schuster Speakers Bureau at 1-866-248-3049 or visit our website at www.simonspeakers.com.

Cover design by Alan Dingman

Manufactured in the United States of America

10  9  8  7  6  5  4  3  2  1

ISBN 978-1-4165-4323-7
ISBN 978-1-4391-6065-7 (ebook)

For those who show us that, together,
we *can* change the world

These all died in faith, not having received the promises, but having seen them afar off, and were persuaded of them, and embraced them, and confessed that they were strangers and pilgrims on the earth.

—Hebrews 11:13

# Part One

# Strangers and Pilgrims

# ONE

Naked and shivering, Roger Keegan awoke bound to a chair. He sat in the center of a pool of harsh incandescent light, but the room around him was pitch-dark. His feet were flat on the cold concrete floor. Metal handcuffs bit into his wrists, which were secured behind his back. All he could smell was ammonia.

*Looks like a cellar,* he thought. *Am I still at the casino?* He had come to Las Vegas for a few days of well-earned vacation: some cards, some strippers, maybe some surf-and-turf. Somewhere between his six Cuervo-and-Cokes at the Mirage and his visit to a nearby gentlemen's club, something had gone very, very wrong.

A door creaked open in the darkness, but there was no light to draw Roger's eye. Footsteps were answered by crisp echoes as they drew closer.

Roger swallowed in a futile effort to expel the sour taste of metabolized booze from his tongue, which was coated in a vile paste. Squinting, the forty-two-year-old middle manager saw three dark figures step into the ring of shadow just outside his circle of light. Two looked like men; the other had the appealing curves of a woman.

The man on the left lit a cigarette, illuminating his brown face with a flicker of orange flame. Then he flipped his lighter shut, and all that remained was the red pinpoint at the end of his cigarette. Roger winced at the pungent aroma of tobacco. Whatever the man was smoking, it was harsh and bitter.

"So," said the man in the center. "This is him?"

"Yes," the woman replied. "He's been prepared."

Throwing fearful looks at each member of the trio, Roger said, "Wait a second, there's gotta be a mistake! I'm just a sales rep! My name's Roger Keegan, I don't—" The clack of a round being chambered into a semiautomatic pistol cut him off.

"We should get started," said the man in the middle. He and his two compatriots stepped into the light.

They were attired in casual business clothing—suits without ties for the men, a simple gray skirt-and-jacket ensemble for the woman. She was pale and blond, and held an odd-looking device with a syringe and a needle. Roger didn't recognize her or the black man with the cigarette. Standing between them, however, was a man with a graying beard who looked familiar.

It took Roger a moment to dredge the man's name from his memory. Then it came to him. "Holy shit!" he exclaimed, eyes wide with disbelief. "You're George Sterling! Is this a movie?"

The famous Hollywood producer-director ignored Roger and extended a hand to his male colleague. "Let's get on with it."

The black man handed Sterling the pistol. He and the woman stepped back as Sterling released the weapon's safety and looked at Roger.

"You're a lucky man," Sterling said. Then the movie mogul lifted the gun, pressed the muzzle to his own grayed temple, and pulled the trigger.

The shot resounded off the floor and walls as the left side of Sterling's head vanished in a pulpy red spray.

His body went limp, fell face-first at Roger's feet, and landed with a meaty slap. The pistol tumbled from his hand and clattered across the floor.

Blood spread in a swift tide around Roger's bare feet. Trembling now with fear and adrenaline, he shouted at the blond woman and the black man, "What the hell's going on?"

They didn't answer him. The blonde stepped forward, kneeled beside the dead Hollywood titan, and jabbed the needle of her gadget into the base of his skull, into his spinal cord. She tapped a touchpad on the side of the device. A moment later, a shimmering silver fluid began filling the syringe behind the needle, drawn up and out of Sterling's neck.

Roger yelled, "Who are you people? What is that?"

"You'll find out soon enough," the black man said, stepping behind Roger's chair.

The blonde removed the needle from Sterling's neck, stood, and walked toward Roger. "Hold him," she said.

Her cohort wrapped one muscular arm around Roger's throat and jaw. With precision and force, he twisted Roger's chin and immobilized his head.

"Stop!" Roger begged. "Please, don't do this!"

The woman met his plea with a cold smirk and icy blue eyes. "What is it you think we're about to do?"

"I . . . I don't know," Roger said, too scared even to guess.

Stroking his cheek, she asked, "Then why be afraid?"

While he was still concocting an answer, she jabbed the needle into the nape of his neck. Piercing agony traveled down his spine like an electric jolt. Then a searing heat flowed into him, purpling his vision and filling his head with vertigo.

He felt himself scream, but he heard only silence.

Jakes hadn't felt any fear as he'd pulled the trigger. This death would be merely an interlude, and a brief one at that.

Putting a bullet through his brain had still hurt, though.

He inhaled sharply as he felt his consciousness take root in a new form. This body's senses were sharp. He caught the competing fragrances of cheap cologne and expensive perfume.

His eyes opened, and he saw his fellow agents of the Marked. "I'm all right, Wells," he said to his male colleague.

They were each two or three bodies removed from who they had been in the future, before their identities had been encoded into nanites for their perilous undercover mission into the past. When they had first hijacked new personas, they had agreed to call one another by their new names, to maintain their covers and avoid confusion. With so few of them left, however, there was no reason not to revert to their true names.

Pleased by his new voice, he asked, "How long did it take?"

"Less than two minutes," Wells said. He glanced at Kuroda, who put away the nanite-transfer device. "The upgrades to the bonding process worked better than we'd hoped."

Jakes nodded. "Good. Then you won't mind untying me."

"If we must," Wells joked. He stepped behind the chair and removed the handcuffs from Jakes's wrists.

While his comrade untied the rest of his restraints, Jakes massaged his new wrists, scowled at the glare of the light above his head, and wrinkled his nose at the lingering bite of sulfur in the air. He looked at George Sterling's bloody corpse. It galled him to give up an identity that had blessed him with such vast wealth and influence, but it was for the best.

The Marked had recently suffered brutal setbacks in their covert war against the 4400—people abducted from far-flung parts of the world over the course of nearly six decades of the late twentieth and early twenty-first centuries, taken by agents of the future determined to alter the shape of things to come. Injected with the neurotransmitter promicin, which gifted them with extraordinary paranormal abilities, the 4400 had been returned en masse on August 14, 2004, in order to avert a catastrophe that would end the world as they knew it.

In other words, the returnees had been changed and sent back to erase the past and topple the future's last bastion of stable civilization, which the Marked were sworn to defend.

Unfortunately, the war had turned against the Marked. An assassination squad—sent by Jordan Collier, the charismatic leader of the rapidly spreading promicin movement, and led by the ex-military telekinetic returnee Richard Tyler—had killed seven of Jakes's fellow agents.

It was likely a matter of simple luck that Jakes had escaped Tyler's attack on Wyngate Castle, the opulent redoubt that George Sterling had built with his movie-industry millions. If not for a secret passage Jakes had added to the estate, he, Wells, and Kuroda would likely be dead.

They were now the last three agents of the Marked. They alone remained to save their future from Collier and his quasi-religious promicin movement.

As his bonds fell away, Jakes stood. "That's better," he said. Kuroda handed him his clothes. He dressed quickly, then walked toward the exit. Wells and Kuroda followed him. "I wired what's left of Sterling's fortune to the Caymans with the rest of our assets," Jakes said. "We can use that as startup capital."

Kuroda picked up her briefcase, in which she carried the new nanite-transfer device. "I still don't see how we're supposed to do anything posing as these *nobodies*," she said.

"Impersonating people in high places worked for as long as it could," Jakes said. "Now we have to lie low."

Wells was dismayed. "How does that help us? We've already missed our window of opportunity against Collier."

"Maybe," Jakes said. "Maybe not." He opened the door to the dimly lit stairwell, where the air was hot and stuffy compared to the cool confines of the subbasement. "That's why we have to make a new friend—one who wants to stop him as much as we do."

Over their trudging footfalls, Kuroda said, "You've already made contact with this 'new friend,' haven't you?"

"Yes, I have," Jakes said. Even though his new body was relatively young and physically fit, the heat in the stairwell had rivulets of sweat running down his back as he climbed one switchback flight after another, back to the main floor.

Laboring up the steps behind him, Wells protested, "It's still too late. The date for the calamity came and went."

"I know," Jakes said. Pushing open the door to the ground level of the hotel under construction, he squinted against the glare of the late-afternoon sun. Wind like a gust from a furnace whipped his brown hair from his face. "But all that means is that Collier prevented the disaster he knew about." He permitted himself a malevolent smirk. "It's time to give him one he won't see coming."

# TWO

## JULY 21, 2008

HARBOR ISLAND WAS BURNING. Crimson flames filled the late-dusk sky with black smoke that stank of oil.

The huge, man-made wedge of land at the mouth of the Duwamish River was an industrial maze of fuel refineries, smelting plants, and shipping yards. It also housed Seattle's largest reserves of gasoline and aviation fuel, and was one of the few parts of the city that had not fallen under the control of Jordan Collier in the months since he had renamed Seattle as Promise City, his safe haven for the world's promicin-positives.

Tonight it was a battlefield.

Moving down a street flanked by searing walls of fire and twisted, burnt machinery, National Threat Assessment Command agent Tom Baldwin held his Glock 26 steady in a white-knuckle grip and advanced toward the fray. At his side was his partner, Diana Skouris. Ahead of them and leading the way was an NTAC tactical strike team equipped with full combat gear and M4A1 assault rifles. Roving searchlights from a helicopter high above them swept the path ahead.

The strike team sergeant lifted a fist and signaled the two plainclothes agents to hold up. Tom and Diana kneeled but kept their semiautomatic pistols at the ready as the strike team fanned out across an intersection blocked by smoldering debris and gutted cars. With one sweaty hand, Tom adjusted his bulletproof vest, which was a bit snug in his armpits.

Blades of lightning flashed from the sky. Blinding white strikes hit three members of the NTAC team, who fell in smoking heaps. Their comrades opened fire, filling the air with the angry stutters of a fully automatic barrage. Tom doubted they even knew what they were shooting at.

Everyone hit the deck as a flash of detonation filled the street in the distance: another fuel tank had exploded. The shock wave almost knocked the fillings from Tom's teeth. A reddish-orange fireball roiled into the night sky.

Tom reached out and put a hand on Diana's shoulder. He shouted over the clatter of rifle fire, "You okay?"

The slender brunette nodded, then hollered back, "We're sitting ducks out here!"

He nodded, then pointed to a clear route through a parking lot. "That way!" They scrambled off Lander Street, crossed Thirteenth Avenue, and jogged east through the lot toward Eleventh Avenue.

A handful of men and women dashed up the road in the distance ahead of Tom and Diana. In the flicker of firelight, Tom saw that they wore the uniforms of Promise

City peace officers, a newly formed law enforcement entity composed of promicin-positive former Seattle cops as well as civilian volunteers. They answered only to Jordan Collier, which rubbed Tom the wrong way, but they were Seattle's best defense against rogue p-positives.

A figure of smoke appeared in the peace officers' midst. It solidified into a black-clad young man, who plunged a knife into one officer's upper back. As the rest of the slain officer's comrades turned to face their attacker, he transmuted back into smoke and vanished.

More lightning lanced from the overcast sky and hammered the peace officers. Tom lifted his arm to shield his eyes from the painful flash. Thunder rolled in its wake. As he lowered his arm, he saw that Diana had done the same. They resumed running toward the besieged Promise City cops.

Motorcycle engines growled. A wave of kinetic force that shimmered like heat radiation leveled the few remaining peace officers. Moments later, three Suzuki sportbikes roared down the road, heading south, away from the acres of erupting fuel tanks.

Tom stopped and raised his Glock. Diana did likewise. They aimed and fired multiple shots at the escaping cyclists.

The rear and middle riders twitched and tumbled off their bikes, which toppled and skidded as the wounded terrorists landed hard on the asphalt.

Their last shots missed the first rider, who sped away into the canyons of stacked, multicolored shipping containers that dominated the southern and eastern parts of the island.

"C'mon!" Tom shouted, holstering his Glock and

sprinting for the downed bikes. Diana stayed with him, pacing him at a full run. They reached the closest bike, whose engine had stalled. "Help me," Tom said, sliding his hands under the bike. Together they pushed it upright. Tom climbed on and quickly restarted the engine as Diana hopped onto the seat behind him.

He kicked the bike into gear and twisted the throttle. The engine roared, and the motorcycle laid down a strip of rubber as Tom launched it down the road. Wind slammed against his face and forced him to squint as he accelerated.

Diana wrapped her left arm around Tom's waist and used her right hand to activate her walkie-talkie. "NTAC-Five to NTAC-One," she shouted over the wind noise. "One hostile on a rice rocket, southbound on Eleventh! Agents in pursuit! Over!"

Their field command team squawked back in reply, *"Copy that, NTAC-Five. We have eyes on the prize. Over."*

Tom kept his eyes on the distant figure ahead of them. The escaping rider was headed toward the West Seattle Bridge, which passed over Harbor Island without providing access to it. Police vehicles had closed off either end of the bridge, and their blue and red lights flashed brightly against the dimming sky.

NTAC snipers stood on the bridge with their weapons aimed over the guardrail as they watched Harbor Island and waited for targets to reveal themselves.

Another rippling disturbed the air ahead of the escaping suspect and made the bridge seem to waver like a mirage. Then the effect struck half a dozen of the elevated roadway's concrete supports, which shattered as if they had been made of eggshells. Broken metal and stone collapsed into dusty rubble, and the roadway buckled and plunged to earth with a deep groan of distressed steel and a deafening thunderstroke of impact.

The suspect veered right onto Spokane Street and vanished into the spreading gray cloud of smoke and haze.

Shouting over Tom's shoulder, Diana asked, "Where the hell's he going?"

"Who knows?" Tom said, skirting the edge of the spreading cloud and searching for any sign of the suspect.

Keying the walkie-talkie again, Diana snapped, "NTAC-Five to NTAC-Seven! Get down here and blow this shit clear! Over!"

*"Copy that, NTAC-Five. Over,"* replied the chopper pilot. Seconds later, the black helicopter swooped low ahead of Tom and Diana. Its rotors kicked up enough wind to clear away the dirty fog and pounded out enough noise to drown out the engine of their sportbike as Tom twisted the throttle fully open. On the other side of the now bifurcated West Seattle Bridge, the suspect was racing away toward the Harbor Island Marina.

"NTAC-Seven," Diana shouted into the radio, "suspect is at the marina! Repeat, suspect is at the marina! Put a light on him, but keep your distance! Over!"

*"We've got him, NTAC-Five,"* replied the chopper pilot. The helicopter's harsh white searchlight beam zeroed in on the escaping suspect as he boarded a speedboat docked in a slip at the marina. The young man turned and glared upward into the beam. Then a focused ripple of distortion

followed the light back to the helicopter—and shredded it in midair. It tumbled out of the sky, a firestorm of broken metal and burnt bodies.

Tom swerved left and narrowly avoided getting pinned under the mangled aircraft as it slammed to the ground and rolled over a dozen cars in the marina's parking lot behind him. One vehicle after another exploded into flames, turning the lot into a fiery automotive graveyard. Shrapnel pattered across the ground on either side of Tom and Diana as they raced out of the lot and down the ramp to the marina's outer slip.

The speedboat's engine growled to life, and the suspect severed the mooring lines with a quick burst of his disruption power. Tom squeezed the brake handle, and the sport-bike skidded and fishtailed across the dock. Diana was off the bike before it stopped moving, her Glock already clearing leather as she shifted to her shooting stance.

As the bike halted, she opened fire on the boat, which sliced its way through the dark water of the Duwamish. Tom drew his Glock and joined his partner's futile barrage. Diana's weapon clicked empty. Tom's pistol ran out of ammo a second later.

Then a white frost stilled the river's churning surface, and the boat's spreading wake stopped in mid-ripple. The icy change overtook the speedboat, which struggled for a moment through a thick slush, then came to a stop with a sharp crack of splintering fiberglass as the surface of the Duwamish froze solid for half a mile in every direction.

The young man in the boat turned and looked back in alarm, then staggered backward and collapsed.

Looking over his shoulder, Tom saw a pair of Jordan's uniformed Promise City peace officers on the shore. One had his hand on the now frozen surface of the water. The other was still looking through the scope of her sniper rifle. Its wide muzzle had been modified to fire darts. Tom figured the darts must be loaded with the concentrated sedative and promicin-inhibitor that could render p-positive individuals unconscious and temporarily suppress their extrahuman abilities.

Diana noted the peace officers and holstered her weapon. "I guess we ought to go say thank you," she said, sounding not very enthused about the idea.

"I guess," Tom said. He holstered his Glock as they walked back across the dock to shore.

In the two minutes it took Tom and Diana to walk over to the peace officers, reinforcements arrived. A platoon of NTAC strike forces, dozens of Seattle cops and Promise City peace officers, and six NTAC agents—led by both incarnations of their colleague Jed Garrity, whose two selves had come to be distinguished by the colors of their neckties, one red, the other blue—raced one another across the ice sheet, all vying to be the ones to make the arrest.

The only people not in a hurry to reach the boat, it seemed, were Tom, Diana, and the two peace officers who were actually responsible for stopping the suspect's escape.

"Nice work," Tom said with a friendly nod to the duo. "I'm Tom Baldwin, and this is—"

"We know who you are," the raven-haired woman said in a dry British accent. She glared at Tom with striking green eyes.

Tom and Diana exchanged apprehensive looks. In the years since the 4400 had returned, NTAC had been chiefly responsible for policing them, and Tom and Diana had been at the center of many of the most tumultuous events involving the returnees. Consequently, both agents had attained a measure of notoriety—or, in some circles, infamy.

As usual, Diana remained calm in the face of hostility. "We just wanted to say thanks, is all."

The muscular, crew-cut man offered her his hand. "Any time," he said. "Jim Myers. This is my partner, Eva Lynd."

"A pleasure," Diana said, briefly shaking his hand.

Tom said, "If you don't mind my asking, how'd you guys get here before us? I thought Jordan agreed to let NTAC defend the city's fuel reserves."

"And you've done such a brilliant job of it," Eva said, casting a sour glare in the direction of the inferno at the north end of the island.

Glossing over Eva's verbal jab, her partner, Jim, replied, "We got a tip about the attack."

"From who?" asked Diana.

Jim shrugged and shook his head, prompting Eva to frown and roll her eyes in disgust. "Just tell her," Eva said. "She'll find out when she checks our phone logs." Jim aimed a pointed stare at her, but she ignored him and continued. "It was your future-telling daughter, Maia," she said to Diana. "She warned us about the attack an hour ago." Grimacing at the swath of destruction, she added, "Not that it made much difference."

Eva and Jim turned and walked north, away from the

shore and from Tom and Diana, who stood and watched them go.

Tom felt the tension in his partner's silence and knew that Diana was seething over Eva's revelation. He waited for her to snap. It didn't take very long.

"How many times have I told Maia not to talk to Jordan's people?" she asked rhetorically, her voice pitched with anger.

"I know," Tom said, trying to sound sympathetic.

"How many times, Tom? How much clearer could I be? I *told* her not to talk to Jordan, or to *any* of his people in Promise City, not even that girl Lindsey she hung around with."

He knew that playing devil's advocate would be risky, but he tried anyway. "Look, it's not like she's a traitor, Diana. She was just trying to help." He lifted his chin toward the boat trapped in the ice. "And maybe she was right. If Jordan's people hadn't been here, that guy would've gotten away."

Diana took a deep breath. Closed her eyes.

Exhaled slowly. Opened her eyes.

When she spoke, her voice was calm—which made the fury behind her words all the more frightening.

"Tom, I know that what you're saying makes sense. You're right: without Jordan's people, we'd have lost the suspect. But right now, I don't give a damn about that. What I care about is that my daughter did *exactly* what I told her *never* to do." She took another breath, then added, "I'm going home now, Tom. And when I get there, I'm going to have a *very* long talk with Maia."

# THREE

JORDAN COLLIER STOOD at the window of his seventy-sixth-floor corner office. He stared southwest, across Elliott Bay, at the raging inferno that had engulfed Harbor Island. It had been ablaze for nearly an hour, growing brighter as the sky dimmed. The conflagration was mirrored on the rippling water.

There was a knock on his office door.

"Come in," he said.

The door opened and closed. Footsteps followed.

Reflected in the window was Kyle Baldwin, one of Jordan's top advisors, walking toward him. "You asked to see me?"

"I did," Jordan replied, his tight-lipped frown barely masking his fury as he turned to face the towheaded younger man. "What happened down there?"

Kyle stopped in front of Jordan's desk and bowed his head. "You're upset about Harbor Island."

"Yes, I am," Jordan said. "People died out there tonight, and there was no reason for it." He picked up a single-page report and waved it angrily. "You didn't even consult me before sending our people into NTAC's territory. You knew the island was under their jurisdiction, Kyle. What were you trying to do?"

"Save their lives," Kyle said. "We had a reliable tip that a bunch of fifty/fifties with a grudge were going after the fuel tanks. I thought if we moved fast enough, we could prevent the attack." He paused as Jordan pivoted and made a show of looking out the floor-to-ceiling window at the burning spectacle in the distance. Rolling his eyes, Kyle added, "I know we failed."

Jordan tossed the paper onto his desk, then settled into his chair. He ran a hand over his dark beard while he recovered his composure. "Most of NTAC's agents are p-positive, Kyle, just like us, and they're trained to handle situations like this." Dismayed, he clenched his fist. "The real tragedy is that all those people died for nothing. So what if they blow up the fuel? We have people who can transmute fluids into anything we want: drinking water, gasoline—"

"Promicin," Kyle interrupted.

That drew a scowl from Jordan. Pointing a finger, he continued. "We're not going there, Kyle. This is not the time. We're surrounded by the U.S. military, and we've got rogue p-positives all over the city. The last thing I want to do right now is start a war with the government."

"You've already got a war with the government," Kyle shot back. "One that they started."

Exasperated, Jordan got up and walked to a wooden cabinet that housed a small selection of premium liquors and some lowball glasses. "I think you and I have different definitions of *war*. I'd call our current situation a standoff."

Jordan opened the cabinet's front panel, which flipped down to provide a shelf, and he chose a glass.

"Sure, Jordan, but for how long? You think the Army's gonna wait forever while we plot our next move?"

"Provoking them won't buy us more time." The self-styled leader of the Promicin-Positive Movement opened a bottle of twelve-year-old Glenmorangie Quinta Ruban single-malt scotch whisky and poured himself a generous measure.

One perk of having rechristened the now exiled Haspelcorp's former headquarters (which previously had been known as the Columbia Center, the tallest building in Washington State) as the Collier Foundation building was that Jordan's new base of operations had come fully furnished and generously stocked with luxuries.

Pushing the cork stopper back into the bottle, Jordan continued. "In any event, we've moved beyond guerrilla tactics. Diplomacy is our true show of strength. Only from a position of power does one have the option to negotiate." He sipped the amber-hued liquor and savored its forceful overtones of port.

Kyle stepped closer to Jordan as he replied, "Great. While you're busy negotiating, the Army's gearing up to blow us off the face of the Earth. We need to start thinking in terms of 'divide and conquer.' If we put promicin in the water of six or seven major cities, we'd force them to split their focus."

"And we'd probably kill forty or fifty million people," Jordan said, wondering when his youthful shaman had become so hawkish in his worldview. He carried his drink back to his desk. "Not exactly a recipe for winning hearts and minds."

"So what? You knew before you started giving it out that

promicin would kill half the people who took it. When nine thousand died last year, you called it 'the Great Leap Forward.' So, what's the matter? Fifty million too big a number?"

"The problem," Jordan replied, his tone sharp with wrath, "is that no one was ever supposed to be *forced* to take promicin. Your cousin Danny's viral ability was an accident, not part of the plan." He set down his glass. "Did it ever occur to you that maybe we could build a future in which those of us who are gifted with promicin could live in peace with those who aren't?"

Kyle turned and paced in front of Jordan's desk, shaking his head in bitter denial. "Dream on, Jordan. Regular people hate us. They're terrified of us. They want us dead."

"Some do," Jordan admitted. "But only because people tend to hate what they fear, and fear what they don't understand." Settling back into his chair, he added, "I refuse to believe that mass murder is the solution to that problem. Our war isn't with the people of the world, Kyle, or with their governments. The war we have to fight is the one against prejudice."

The young man let out a derisive huff. "If you say so."

"Yes, I *do* say so. And I expect you to abide by it."

A sullen look conveyed Kyle's grudging surrender.

"You can go," Jordan said, gesturing toward the exit.

Kyle walked quickly, clearly eager to be away from Jordan. He yanked open the office door. It rebounded off the wall with a dull thud as Kyle made his ill-tempered exit.

As the door slowly drifted shut, Jordan reclined his chair and sipped his scotch. He wondered, not for the first time in recent months, whether Kyle might soon go from being an asset to a liability. When the young man had come in search of him the previous year, he had proved his value as a visionary. Kyle and his invisible-and-inaudible feminine spirit guide, Cassie, had helped Jordan and his followers navigate the difficult path toward their goal of transforming the world and fulfilling Jordan's prophecy of a better future for humanity.

Alas, in the months since they had transformed Seattle into the promicin-friendly redoubt known as Promise City, Kyle had started ignoring Jordan's agenda of diplomacy in favor of heavy-handed and sometimes violent tactics.

Jordan wondered how much of this recent turn was Kyle's will, and how much of it was Cassie's—and whether there was any distinction to be made between them. So far, Jordan had been able to keep his hotheaded senior advisor under control, but he feared that this tenuous grace period would soon end.

His office door began to click shut when it was pushed open a crack. After a quick, soft knocking, his assistant, Jaime Costas, poked her head in. "You have a visitor, Mister Collier. One of the people on your short list for the leadership council."

Beckoning his invitation, he said, "Okay."

Jaime pushed the door open.

His visitor stepped into the doorway.

Jordan's jaw went slack. He blinked in surprise. Put down his drink. Stood and greeted his guest with a gentlemanly nod.

"Please, come in," he said, his heart swelling with hope. "It's an honor."

# FOUR

Diana Skouris pushed open the door to her apartment and tugged her keys from the lock. Telegraphing her mood, she slammed the door behind her and stormed across the living room. "Maia!" she yelled, her voice reverberating off the walls. "Get out here!"

She was beyond upset, past angry, and deep into irrational fury as she pulled off her jacket and flung it onto the sofa. There were so many things she wanted to shout at her adopted daughter that she didn't know where to start. After all the years they had been together, and all the risks Diana had taken and sacrifices she'd made to protect Maia, she felt as if she had a right to expect more respect from the girl than this.

*Dammit, I've told her a hundred times to steer clear of Jordan and his people,* Diana fumed as she shrugged off her shoulder holster and set the weapon on the kitchen counter. *All the 4400 have ever done for her is put her in danger— so why is her first loyalty to them and not to me?*

That rhetorical question nagged at her as she opened

the refrigerator and took note of the leftovers available for that night's dinner—which Maia might or might not be allowed to have.

The apartment was quiet except for the hum of the fridge. Diana heard no sounds of movement coming from Maia's room.

It didn't surprise her that Maia was in no hurry to come out and face the music, but after all the stomping, screaming, and sulking that had followed Diana's fiat that Maia cease all contact with Lindsey Hammond—her friend and fellow teen 4400—she at least expected to hear Maia defiantly drowning out her commands with Frank Sinatra music.

*She's probably either spooked or sulking,* Diana figured. She let the fridge door close, then walked toward Maia's room. "Maia? I'm serious: you need to come talk to me."

There was no response.

Diana stepped through the door into her daughter's room. Maia wasn't there. The bed was made, and through the open closet door it was obvious that many of Maia's favorite pieces of clothing were gone. Also absent was Maia's diary, which contained her alarmingly unerring visions of the future.

*Oh, my God.* Fear washed through Diana like ice water in her veins. Though her little girl was now thirteen years old and no longer required a sitter to stay at home, Diana had remained afraid that someone might try to take her. Everyone from the 4400 to the government to random kooks seemed to have an agenda for "the girl who could see the future."

Her heart raced and her breaths came short and shallow

as she searched Maia's room for clues. No sign of a struggle, no note. That was good, but Diana was still panicking. She felt her pulse thudding in her temples. It was a battle to keep her mind clear as a hundred terrified thoughts welled up at once from the darkest corners of her imagination. Images of Maia trussed up, or gagged, or drugged unconscious in the back of a van.

She felt light-headed almost to the point of vertigo as she lurched out of Maia's room and bounced around her home like a silver sphere in a pinball machine, ricocheting off the doorjambs and walls, weaving from her own room to the bathroom and back down the hallway, to the kitchen and then the living room.

Then she saw it, on the floor in front of the television.

A handheld digital video recorder. There was a pink adhesive note affixed to it. A single cable linked the device to an input jack on the side of the high-definition flat-screen TV. Diana hurried to the camera and picked it up.

The Post-it had a two-word message, scrawled in Maia's distinctive block capitals: PLAY ME.

Pushing past the dreadful, sinking feeling in her stomach, Diana grabbed the remote off the coffee table and turned on the TV. As soon as the screen powered up, she saw that the display was already set to the auxiliary input. She activated the digital camera; the screen flickered blue and showed a zeroed time code. Diana took a breath and pushed the PLAY button.

A blurred picture flickered onto the screen, then sharpened into focus. It was Maia, sitting on the living room sofa, exactly where Diana was sitting watching the tape.

"*Hi, Mom,*" Maia said in the recording. She pushed a lock of her honey-blond hair from her face and continued. "*Since you're watching this, you've probably figured out that I'm not home. I decided to leave and go stay with Lindsey at the Collier Foundation.*" Diana muttered vile curses under her breath as the video kept rolling. "*I know that you know I told Jordan's people about Harbor Island, and I know you're coming home to yell at me some more, and I'm sorry, but . . .*" The girl rolled her blue eyes. "*I'm sick of it, okay? So I'm leaving, which I know you're also mad about. But don't bother being mad at Lindsey, because this wasn't her idea, it was mine.*" She glanced away from the camera for several seconds as a guilty look played across her innocent face. Then she looked back with a remorseful expression. "*I love you, Mom, but that's where I have to be. I'm sorry. Bye.*"

Maia leaned forward and reached toward the camera. A moment later, the recording stopped. There was a burst of snowy gray static on the TV, followed by a blue no-signal screen.

Diana pressed STOP and turned off the TV, then sat with her face in her hands for minutes that felt like hours.

Conflicting emotions swelled inside her, competing for space: her rage at Maia's defiance faced off against her fear for her daughter's safety; her failure to control Maia's willful behavior filled Diana with shame; and the sense that she had lost her daughter's respect left her frustrated and bitter.

Most galling of all, there was little that anyone could do to help her bring Maia home against her will. Despite the girl's legal status as a minor, there was no way that Jordan would permit Diana or anyone else to remove any 4400 against their will from his sanctuary at the Collier Foundation. Unless she could persuade Maia to come home of her own free will, Diana would have to accept that she had lost her to Jordan and his quixotic mission to spread promicin around the globe.

Her face felt feverish, flushed with anger at her helplessness. She got up, walked to the kitchen, and turned on the cold water in the sink. Cupping her hands under the cool torrent, she gathered a double handful and splashed it on her face, then patted a few more palmfuls on the back of her neck.

She had just begun to recover some semblance of calm when her phone rang. After drying her hands and face with a clean dish towel, she answered the phone. "Hello?"

*"Diana? Tom. Meghan wants us both at The 4400 Center, pronto. I'll pick you up in about ten minutes."*

"Why? What's going on?"

*"It's Jordan,"* Tom said ominously. *"He just called a meeting."*

# FIVE

HALF OF TOM'S ATTENTION was on his driving, and the other half was on Diana's ranting.

"I'm serious, Tom, I've had it with Maia," she said, sounding even more irate than she had just a couple of hours earlier on Harbor Island. "Running away is one thing, but running into the center of the bull's-eye? Is she crazy?"

He cocked his head and allowed himself a thin, wry smile. "Sometimes I think we're all crazy for staying here."

Diana said nothing; she just stared out the window at the busy nightlife in Capitol Hill. It was a warm summer night, and the sidewalks bustled with people. A balmy breeze carried faint aromas of cigarette smoke and fresh coffee into the car.

The neighborhood—a curious mash-up of low-cost, apartment-style condos and some of the city's most elegant mansions—had long been the heart of Seattle's counterculture. Back in the nineties, some had called its plethora of coffeehouses and bars the birthplace of grunge music and fashion. Even now, after Jordan's takeover of the city, this tight-knit community had hardly changed. Tom had never been comfortable hanging out in this part of Seattle, but he admired its resilience.

Tom steered his NTAC-issued sedan left off East Galer Street, past the southeast corner of Interlaken Park, along the tree-lined stretch of Crescent Road, and down the driveway of The 4400 Center. Four years earlier, the postmodernist white concrete building had been the Collier Museum, a modest but well-regarded repository for modern art. After the return of the 4400, Jordan had converted it into a safe haven and gathering place for the returnees. Backed by meticulously groomed gardens and flanked on three sides by the park, the Center was a much-needed quiet oasis in the city. In the wake of Jordan's usurpation of the local government, it also served as "neutral ground" where he and NTAC representatives could meet.

Another generic-looking four-door sedan was parked at the Center's entrance. One of the two incarnations of Agent Jed Garrity stood beside Meghan Doyle, the director of NTAC's Seattle office, who in the year since her arrival also had become Tom's not-so-secret girlfriend.

The blond woman stepped alongside Tom's car as he pulled into a parking space and shut off the engine. As he and Diana got out of the car, Meghan's demeanor was strictly business. "Still no word from Collier what this is about."

"What a shock," Tom deadpanned. As the four NTAC personnel walked across the brick driveway to the Center's front entrance, Tom nodded to Jed, his longtime colleague. "Hey, J.R."

The initials were short for Jed's nickname, "Jed Red." After the previous year's viral promicin epidemic infected him, he had manifested an unusual 4400 ability: a copy of himself.

At first, no one at NTAC had known what to make of Jed's doppelganger; some had mistaken his second self for a simple clone. But after one of the Jeds was killed during a field op several months ago, an exact duplicate of the slain Agent Garrity had appeared many miles away, leading NTAC's think tank director, Marco Pacella, to hypothesize that Jed's ability was to always have a protected backup of himself. If something bad happened to him, a new copy sprang into existence somewhere safe. Jed had called it "a strangely useless ability." Marco had called it "the ultimate insurance policy."

These days, the only way to tell the two identical but separate copies of Jed Garrity apart was the color of their neckties: one wore only red ties, and the other wore only blue. But no one at NTAC liked saying "Jed Red" because of the rhyme, and "Jed Blue" had spawned one too many "Jet Blue" jokes. So they now went by "J.R." and "J.B."

As the front door of the Center opened ahead of them, releasing a surge of clean-scented, cool air from inside the building, Tom noticed for the first time how badly he himself smelled. Between the mayhem on Harbor Island and the paperwork that had followed, he'd had no chance to shower or change his clothes, which were filthy and rank with sweat.

The Center's chief executive, Shawn Farrell, stepped outside to meet them. "Thanks for coming on such short notice," the trim, fair-haired young man said to Meghan. Shaking Tom's hand, he added, "Good to see you, too, Uncle Tommy."

"Likewise, Shawn," Tom said.

"Let's head in," Shawn said, motioning for them to follow him into the Center. "Jordan and his people are waiting."

Inside, their steps echoed on the polished stone floors of the main concourse. As they followed Shawn to the first-floor conference room, Tom was struck by the fact that his nephew, who physically was only twenty-one years old (he was twenty-four if one counted the years he had been missing during his abduction to the future), carried himself with the measured calm and dignified air of a much older man. Just a few short years earlier, it would have been impossible to get Shawn to dress in anything other than jeans, T-shirts, and sneakers; now he looked at home in a tailored Armani suit and custom, handmade Italian leather brogues. The crucible of responsibility had forged him into a true leader of the 4400 community.

*Susan would be proud of him,* Tom mused, before the memory of his sister's untimely death in the fifty/fifty epidemic cast a pall over his moment of filial pride in her son.

Shawn pushed open the double doors of the conference room. A long table of dark wood stretched ahead of him and the NTAC agents. On Tom's right, standing at the middle of the table, was the casually attired Jordan Collier. Past him were two advisors: Tom's son, Kyle, and, to Tom's surprise, the telepath Gary Navarro. With Tom and Diana's help, the black former baseball player had gone into exile a couple of years earlier, to escape a life of forced service to the National Security Agency. This was the first time Tom had seen Gary since the night he left.

Standing behind Jordan was his new executive assistant, a pixyish woman in her mid-twenties named Jaime Costas. At Jordan's left was another face Tom hadn't expected to see this evening: Maia Skouris.

The thirteen-year-old whispered something to Jordan as the NTAC team filed in and moved to stand opposite them, on the other side of the table. A moment later, while everyone else was still sizing one another up, Jordan waved Shawn over to him, passed along another whispered confidence, then stood silently as Shawn circled the table with a hangdog look on his face.

Tom overheard as Shawn leaned close to Diana and said softly, "I'm really sorry about this, but I'm afraid I need to ask you to wait outside."

Diana shot a deadly look at Shawn, who raised his hands and backed away from her, his demeanor contrite. Then she turned her seething glare at Maia, who made a point of sullenly averting her gaze. It was painfully obvious that this embarrassing moment had been the girl's doing.

"Fine," Diana said, giving free rein to her contempt.

As she turned away, Tom stopped her with a gentle touch on her arm. He lowered his voice. "I'll talk to her for you."

"Don't bother," Diana replied. She left the room in fast, angry strides and let the door slam shut behind her. Its impact echoed inside the conference room, a lingering memory of anger.

Meghan put her focus on Jordan. "What do you want?"

"First, to apologize for Harbor Island," Jordan said.

Tom folded his arms across his chest and nodded in the direction of Diana's exit. "You're off to a great start."

Nonplussed, Jordan continued. "Promise City's peace officers have been reminded that NTAC has jurisdiction over Harbor Island—"

"What's left of it," J.R. cut in.

Jordan paused, then resumed. "Tonight's crossfire was the result of a miscommunication, for which I take responsibility."

"Funny," Tom said, fixing his stare on Maia, who looked back at him with her own unblinking gaze. "I thought it was the result of someone giving you an unauthorized tip."

Kyle spoke up. "It doesn't matter where the tip came from, Dad. What matters is that we were trying to save lives."

"Right," J.R. replied. "Is that why your people were using deadly force out there? To save people by killing them?"

"I never told anyone to use deadly force," Kyle said. "I only said they should protect themselves."

Tom turned his ire at his son. "This was *your* decision?"

"We're not here to lay blame," Jordan said, holding up a hand to halt the brewing dispute. "What matters now is that we work together to keep the people of Promise City safe, and prevent conflicts like this from happening again."

Meghan nodded, but she frowned her suspicion. "And how do you propose we go about doing that?"

"The Russians call it *glasnost*," Jordan said. "Openness. We'll share Maia's precognitive warnings in exchange for an open discussion about the U.S. government's intentions toward Promise City, and toward promicin-positive persons around the world."

Rolling her eyes and heaving a disgusted sigh, Meghan said, "That'll never fly with Washington, and you know it."

Looking at Meghan but speaking to Jordan, Gary interjected, "What she means is, Seattle NTAC's out of the loop. Washington's keeping them in the dark, so they have nothing to offer us."

Tom swallowed a mouthful of curses aimed at the telepath. Instead he clenched his left hand into a fist behind his back.

Meghan turned and walked toward the door. "We're done here," she told Jordan. "Next time you want to meet, leave the mind reader at home." J.R. fell into step behind her as they made their exit. Jordan and his team moved in the opposite direction, toward a different door that led to another part of the Center.

"Wait for me outside," Tom said to Meghan, then slipped past her and Jed to circle around the table and catch up to Maia. He stopped the teen just before she reached the door. "Maia, hang on a sec," he said, trying to sound diplomatic.

Maia turned and stood facing him in the doorway. There was a hardness in her eyes, and her face had begun to mature from the roundness of a child's visage to the slender countenance of a striking young woman. She asked in a flat voice, "What?"

Behind her, Jordan, Kyle, and Gary all were watching and listening. Tom did his best to ignore them. "I know you and your mom are having problems right now, but I really don't think running away's gonna help. Do you?"

"Yes, I do," she said, and started turning away.

He gently grasped her shoulder. "Wait," he said. Then he saw the three men glaring at him, and he let go of her. Maia looked back and waited for him to speak. "C'mon," he continued. "Your mom's worried about you. And yeah, she's ticked off, and I can understand if maybe you don't want to come home tonight . . . but would you at least talk to her before she leaves?"

Maia seemed to consider the idea for a moment. Then her eyes once more turned cold and unforgiving. With a disdain beyond her years, she said, "There's nothing to talk about." Then she stepped through the door and didn't apologize as she let it close in Tom's face.

*That could've gone better,* he berated himself. He bowed his head, breathed a despondent sigh, and wondered what he was going tell his partner. *Hey, don't feel bad, Diana— now we* both *have kids who work for Jordan Collier.*

# SIX

## JULY 22, 2008

DENNIS RYLAND, executive vice president of Haspel Corporation, stepped out of his private jet into the retina-searing glare of morning sun on white salt flats. The twin turbine engines of the Gulfstream G650 desecrated the silence of the Nevada desert with their steadily falling whine.

Just a few months shy of his sixty-sixth birthday, Dennis felt as if the sun were burning away precious years of his life in the seconds it took him to descend the jet's folding stair ladder to the runway. The temperature had just hit 112 degrees Fahrenheit, and the arid heat cooked the sweat from his face before it could escape his pores.

Inhaling the scorching deep-desert air, he recalled one of his favorite lines of classic cinema dialogue, from David Lean's epic *Lawrence of Arabia*. Asked why he liked the desert so much, Peter O'Toole had replied with his trademark dry delivery, "Because it's clean."

The tarmac radiated heat through the soles of Dennis's shoes. He quickened his step and cursed the protocol that demanded he wear a suit and tie even in this circle of hell.

A sultry breeze tousled his still-dark but subtly graying hair as he reached the door of a sand-blasted wooden shack with a patchwork roof of corrugated tin and rusted sheet metal. To a casual observer, the tiny ramshackle building might look as if it were in danger of being carried away in the next dust storm. That impression was entirely by design.

He opened the rickety wooden door and stepped into the sweltering shade of a vestibule barely large enough for two people to stand in. The outer door closed behind him.

For a moment, there was only the feeble illumination of daylight peeking in through the gaps around the door. Then a panel slid open on the wall in front of Dennis, revealing the glowing green pad of a hand scanner—the first of three biometric security measures he would have to satisfy to gain entry to Haspelcorp's secret, off-the-books weapons research laboratory. He put his hand on the pad and waited.

The device hummed as a bright, horizontal beam traveled up and down, reading his palm. A vaguely feminine but essentially neutral-sounding synthetic voice declared through a hidden speaker, *"Prepare for retinal scan."*

This was his least favorite part of the procedure; the emerald-colored light always left him seeing spots for a few minutes afterward. He took a breath, stared into the circular retnal scanner for his requisite semi-blinding, and forced himself not to blink.

When it was over, the synthetic voice said, *"State your name and clearance code for voiceprint authorization."*

"Ryland, Dennis. Authorization code Whiskey-Tango-Foxtrot, three, one, six, seven, six." He'd chosen his code himself. The words were a juvenile display of veiled contempt for his masters; the digits were the date of his daughter Nancy's birth.

*"Voiceprint and clearance code authorized."* The security panel went dark. A series of magnetic locks behind it released with dull thuds and clacks. Then the wall swung away from him, admitting him to a short passage that led to a tiny elevator.

As soon as he entered the climate-controlled corridor, his face became drenched with perspiration. Now that the air around him was pleasantly cool, he realized how over-heated he felt. Dennis took a handkerchief from his jacket pocket and mopped the sheen of sweat from his face and the back of his neck.

He got into the elevator and pressed the button for the secure sublevel. The doors closed, and the lift descended with a soft hum and only the slightest vibration.

It took half a minute to complete the descent. The lab was three hundred feet underground and shielded by the latest defenses and counterintelligence technologies. Finally, the lift slowed and stopped with a gentle bump. The doors opened.

Dennis stepped out into a wide-open space. Brightly lit and immaculately clean, its work areas were partitioned behind four-inch-thick panels of AlON—aluminum oxynitride, a clear ceramic polymer optically equivalent to glass but strong enough to be used by the military as a form of transparent armor for windows on tanks and aircraft.

Occupying much of the lab's space were many of the most advanced automated research and fabrication devices ever invented. Haspelcorp had made a cottage industry of buying up promising patents from struggling inventors and then sequestering the fruits of those labors in places such as this.

Everywhere he looked, machines were hard at work. Flashes of blue-white light and showers of sparks danced on the edge of his vision. Motors whirred, hydraulics gasped, and generators purred, low and steady. Robotic arms moved parts from one space to another, milled tiny components to exacting specifications, and shaped the microscopic details of new microchips. Screens of data scrolled nonstop across huge computer monitors. Odors of ozone and hot metal filled the air.

*And to think,* Dennis mused behind a thin smile, *three months ago this lab was empty.*

Haspelcorp had been on the verge of dismantling the lab before Dennis had intervened. In the aftermath of the scandal that had erupted after Haspelcorp had been revealed as the original source of the promicin that Jordan Collier stole and distributed illegally around the world, the Department of Defense had revoked many of the company's most lucrative defense research contracts. Without them, this lab had seemed to have no purpose; its maintenance had become just another liability on the company's balance sheet.

Officially, the lab was still inactive. The only people who knew that it was back in business were Dennis and the trio of scientists who now had exclusive access to it. They had come to Dennis two months earlier with a proposal so stunning and so tantalizing that if he had refused to back them, he would never have forgiven himself.

They had said they could rid the world of promicin.

Forty-eight hours later, after a flurry of clandestine meetings and classified memoranda, Dennis had installed them here, in this lab, with all the resources of Haspelcorp secretly at their disposal. Today he intended to find out what, precisely, his generosity had bought.

At the center of the sprawling subterranean space, the three white-coated researchers were gathered around a large, ceramic work table, on which rested a cylindrical device. The top half of its casing had been removed, revealing a complex amalgam of wiring, circuit boards, and shielded components. Myriad tiny parts and precision tools littered the table.

The chief scientist looked up as Dennis approached. He intercepted Dennis and extended his hand. "Mister Ryland! Thank you for coming. Did you bring the samples from LHC?"

He shook the man's hand. "Yes, Doctor Jakes. I did."

Noting that Dennis had come empty-handed, Jakes arched an eyebrow and flashed a wry, mischievous smile. "Are you hiding them some place I don't want to know about?"

"They're still on the plane," Dennis said, releasing the younger man's hand. "Before I turn them over, I think we need to talk a bit more about this project of yours. Starting with how you were able to tell the team at the Large Hadron Collider how to make an element that before yesterday was only a theory."

"That theory has been the basis of my entire career,

Mister Ryland," Jakes said. He walked back to the work table and nodded for Dennis to follow him. "And a generation of scientists before me devoted their lives to unraveling its secrets. Most of the work had been done before I got involved. Metaphorically speaking, I'm just lucky to be standing on the shoulders of giants."

Standing at the table with the three scientists, Dennis eyed with suspicion the humming, high-tech gadget they were building. "Fine," he said. "But I don't think you appreciate the position you've put me in. A discovery like this can't be swept under the rug. The folks at CERN are going apeshit over this, and it's already on the radar at Homeland Security. Getting that sample and the antimatter out of Switzerland cost Haspelcorp nearly a billion dollars. Keeping it quiet cost *another* billion. So before I give it to you, I need to know why you want it."

Waving his hand over the half-finished invention on the table, Jakes said, "To make this functional."

"Explain it to me. In simple words."

Jakes nodded to his blond female colleague, Doctor Kuroda. Dennis assumed that "Kuroda" was her married name, even though he had never seen her wear a wedding ring, which wasn't unusual for people working in precision fabrication labs such as this.

Kuroda rested her hands on the device. "We need that element because, when bombarded with baryogenic radiation, it emits high-energy alpha particles. Because it's a superdense and stable element with both closed-proton and closed-neutron shells, it can serve this function for up to several months. The radiation it emits will break down the monoaminic bonds in promicin without affecting other organic tissues."

Dennis massaged his forehead to stave off his impending headache. "I asked for small words," he said.

The third scientist, an African-American man named Wells, replied, "This is a neutron bomb for promicin. It takes away the powers but leaves the people unharmed."

"That I understood," Dennis said. "What are its range and area of effect?"

Wells exchanged looks with Jakes and Kuroda, then said, "From an airborne platform at twenty miles' range, you could zap a major city with two bursts in about five minutes."

"Good," Dennis said. "That's very good. Will the people on the ground feel anything?"

"Not a thing," Jakes said, rejoining the conversation. "They won't know what's happened till they go to use their promicin powers—and find out they don't exist anymore."

Dennis imagined Jordan Collier's smug little smirk turning into a look of horror. The thought put a smile on Dennis's face. "How long until we have a working prototype?"

Jakes shrugged. "Once you give us the sample? Maybe two or three days, barring any mishaps or interference."

"Excellent," Dennis said. He picked up a phone. "I'll tell my crew to bring it down." He punched in a Haspelcorp number that would connect him directly to the crew in the jet. As the line rang, he told the scientists, "Work quickly. We might need this sooner than we thought."

"Don't worry, Mister Ryland," Jakes said with a beatific smile. "Soon the world will be completely back to normal."

# SEVEN

"I DON'T CARE if they were made with a 4400 ability or not," Tom Baldwin said as he entered the office he shared with Diana at NTAC. "These are the best fat-free doughnuts I've ever had."

He set two napkin-wrapped chocolate doughnuts and a paper cup of office-brewed coffee on his desk, then opened a drawer and took out a small plastic container of ubiquinone pills. The "U-pills," as they were commonly known, were a natural dietary supplement that could ward off the airborne version of the promicin virus. Though there hadn't been any reported cases of fifty/fifty since the Danny Farrell incident the previous year, Tom was taking no chances, especially since the now deceased NTAC scientist Abigail Hunnicut had tried to replicate the virus months earlier, as a prelude to a new pandemic. He popped one pill into his mouth and washed it down with a swig of coffee.

At the facing partner desk, Diana sat slouched in her chair—something she had rarely ever done in the years she and Tom had worked together. She stared at the room's back wall, her mien dour. Tom knew what was bothering her, but he hoped he might be able to change the subject. "Want a doughnut?"

Her voice was barely more than a mumble. "Not hungry."

"How 'bout a cup of coffee? You caffeinated yet?"

She kicked her plastic trash can across the empty space beneath their desks. It bumped to a halt against his leg. He looked down and saw four empty, coffee-stained paper cups. A strong aroma of slightly scorched java wafted up from the can.

"Guess so," Tom said. Figuring that maybe not talking would be the wisest course of action, Tom settled into his chair, powered up his computer, and took a bite of his doughnut. He chewed all of three times before Diana spoke.

"Dammit, Tom, how could Maia *do that* to me?"

He forced himself to swallow his partially masticated mouthful, washed it down with a swig of too-hot coffee, and sighed. "I don't—"

"I mean, she was always such a good kid, y'know? Sweet, polite, thoughtful, trustworthy." Diana shook her head in confusion, so Tom nodded his in sympathy. "And mature! There were times she seemed more grown-up than my sister April."

He had to roll his eyes. "Most people are more grown-up than April."

She conceded the point with a sideways tilt of her head. "True. But I expected better things from Maia. And all of a sudden she was angry and withdrawn all the time. She wouldn't talk to me. She got stubborn, too. Willful. Defiant. Now this? Siding with Jordan against me? Running away to Promise City? I just don't get it, Tom. What the hell happened?"

It all felt so familiar to him that he had to grin. "It's called becoming a teenager, Diana. You're now the proud parent of a thirteen-year-old. My condolences." He handed one of his pastries between their monitors, over the divide between their adjoining desks. "Have a doughnut."

The simple but heartfelt gesture struck a humorous chord in Diana, and a crooked smile of amusement brightened her face as she accepted the doughnut. "Thanks," she said.

"All part of the service," Tom replied.

He took another bite of his doughnut, determined to enjoy it this time.

An alert flashed on his computer screen. A loud, guttural alarm noise crackle-squawked from his speakers. It was a warning that high-priority signals relevant to national security had just been intercepted by NTAC's new Internet data filters. Across from him, similar noises and flashes of light indicated that Diana was seeing the same thing. Outside their office, echoes of the alarm filled the junior agents' cubicle farm.

*Goddammit*, Tom brooded, choking down another unsavored bite of his breakfast. He and Diana scrambled into action, trying to call up the flagged signals for hands-on analysis.

There was nothing there.

"Diana, do you have any intercepts on your screen?"

"No, nothing." With each peck on the keyboard and click of the mouse, her forehead creased a little bit deeper with concern. "I thought I had something on the internal channels, but when I tried to follow it, it came up 'Not Found.'"

"Same thing just happened to me," Tom said. His frustration mounted as he chased digital ghosts through NTAC's high-tech signals surveillance system.

One of the Jeds leaned in through their office door, his blue tie swinging like a pendulum beneath his head. "Did you guys just get that intercept alert?"

"The alert, yes," Tom said, his fingers flying over his computer keyboard. "The intercept, not so much."

"Same thing out here," J.B. said.

Meghan shouldered past J.B. and wedged herself into the doorway beside him. "Sorry," she said, and he nodded his acceptance of her curt apology. To Tom and Diana she said, "What the hell's going on?"

Eyes wide with frustration, Diana looked away from her screen to answer Meghan. "Something tripped a bunch of red flags on Homeland Security's servers, but there's nothing in the logs. It's either the biggest glitch the system's ever had, or something weird just happened."

"What about our automatic backups?" Meghan asked.

Tom shook his head. "Nothing ever got that far. Whatever set off the bells, it got wiped before our system had a look at it."

Looking in over Meghan's shoulder, J.B. asked, "Now what?"

A devious look played across Meghan's face. "Maybe we don't have a record of that data, but I'll bet the NSA does. I'll call in a favor with an old pal, see if we can get our hands on the original intel." She knocked on the wooden doorjamb for luck, then slipped away to her office.

Tom, Diana, and J.B. traded wary glances in the moments after Meghan's departure.

Diana broke the silence. "Isn't it illegal for the NSA to share internal surveillance with us?"

"Back to work," J.B. said, too smart to try to answer that question. He stepped away and walked back to his own office.

Still awaiting an answer, Diana looked across the adjoining desks at Tom, who picked up his doughnut and coffee. "Don't look at me," he said. He bit into his doughnut and added through a mouthful of chocolate, "I just work here."

# EIGHT

Maia Skouris found it hard to concentrate on what her tutor was saying, because she kept finding herself distracted by visions of the woman bloodied and dying in someone's arms.

"I'm sorry," Maia said. "What was the question?"

The tutor, Heather Tobey, frowned in mild reproof, then repeated her query. "What is the Ninth Amendment to the United States Constitution?"

A teacher by profession, Heather was one of the original 4400. She had been gifted with the ability to nurture others' innate talents to their full potential. It was sometimes a slow process.

As Maia looked at the score she had just received on her humanities test, however, she had to conclude that she had no hidden talent for understanding U.S. history.

"The Ninth Amendment," Maia began, then let her voice trail off to buy herself time to think. "It . . . uh . . . outlaws alcohol?"

Heather's frown became a scowl. "No," she said. "That

was the Eighteenth Amendment. We're still on the Bill of Rights." Softening her countenance, she said in a coaching manner, "Even the framers of the Constitution knew they couldn't think of everything. And they didn't want that to be held against other people. So how did they safeguard against that?"

Searching her memory, Maia found the first half of the answer, which she blurted out in the hope of shaking loose the rest of the answer. Quoting the text, she said, "'The enumeration in the Constitution, of certain rights, shall not be construed to . . .'" As she paused to dredge up the end of the sentence, another horrific vision momentarily filled her sight.

*Shadows dance in a darkened room lit by scarlet flames. The floor sparkles with shattered glass and is sticky with blood. Smoke lingers, thick and sharp. A dull roar muffles distant voices full of fear and sorrow. Then comes a heartbreaking sound: a young man weeps. Heather is cradled in his arms; the light in her eyes fades, blood pours from her mouth and seeps from ragged wounds in her chest and stomach . . .*

"Go on," Heather said. "You can finish it."

It was eerie, the sensation of talking to someone she had just seen at death's threshold, but Maia had experienced this too many times before to let it show. Fixing her mask of calm, she said simply, ". . . 'shall not be construed to deny or disparage others retained by the people.'"

"Excellent," Heather said. She started gathering up her books and papers. "We're out of time today, but if you'd gotten that question right on your test, you'd have earned a B-minus instead of a C-plus." Loading her things into a satchel, she continued. "But I'll tell you what. If you can write me a two-hundred-word paper on why the Ninth Amendment is important, and give it to me tomorrow, I'll raise your grade on the test to a B." Heather stood and slung the satchel at her side. "Deal?"

Maia nodded. "Deal."

"Great," Heather said. She walked to the door of Maia's suite, and Maia stayed a few paces behind her. The tutor opened the door, and as she stepped out she smiled and said, "See you tomorrow!" With a friendly wave, she made her exit.

Waving back, Maia forced out a smile of her own, then closed the door behind Heather and locked it.

Pressing her back to the door, she heaved a sigh of relief. It was never easy foreseeing the death of someone she liked, and she had witnessed far too many—more than she had ever said, and more than she ever would admit. She was only thirteen years old, and already she felt as if she had a lifetime of secrets.

She trudged in heavy steps across the residential suite that Jordan had made available for her private use. Located on an upper floor of the Collier building, her apartment was much larger than the one in which she had lived with Diana, and it was more expensively furnished. There were lots of glass tables and pale leather upholstery and stainless steel and polished granite. Everything was gleaming and perfect. She even had a king bed to herself.

Her accommodations' luxuries didn't end with the suite itself. Twenty-four-hour room service was a phone call away, a housekeeping staff tended to her dishes and her laundry, and until she had moved in she had never known how many satellite television channels there really were.

All that Jordan had asked from her as a concession was that she accept private academic tutoring from Heather, so that her education wouldn't stagnate. Maia had protested that it was summer and that school could wait until the fall, but Jordan had held his ground and made it a mandatory condition of her residency at his headquarters.

She drifted into her kitchen and opened the refrigerator, driven partly by a mild appetite and partly by boredom. A pale-green Golden Crisp apple caught her eye, and she plucked it from the shelf. Biting into the firm, slightly tart fruit, she let the refrigerator door thud closed. She ambled back into the living room and collapsed onto the couch with her snack.

An uneasy feeling nagged at her. When she thought of Diana, her heart swelled with resentment. After all that Maia had done to prove herself to her adoptive mother, and to everyone else, it filled her with rage to be treated like just another kid.

*At least Jordan and his people treat me like an equal,* she thought bitterly. But there was no denying that she missed her home. Most of all, she missed her mother. Being treated as an equal was a pleasant change, to be sure—but it wasn't the same as being loved.

An idle thought gave her a twinge of guilt: Who could have loved her more than her real parents? Ethan and Mary Rutledge had been dead now for decades, but for Maia it had been only four years since she'd last held her mother's hands and felt the warm safety of her father's embrace.

Maia's friend and fellow returnee Lindsey Hammond had introduced her to another 4400, whose ability had enabled Maia to see and touch her dead parents again. Even knowing that they were an illusion, a mental or physical trick of some kind, had not made the experience any less powerful or moving. Seeing them had brought her to the edge of tears. Walking away from them to go home to Diana had pushed her over that edge.

She'd gone home after that encounter feeling racked with guilt. After all the love and devotion that Diana had shown her, was it fair to compare her to people who were dead and gone? Was it right to long so badly for another afternoon in the company of illusions when she had abandoned Diana in an empty home?

Her loneliness and her yearning for what she'd lost was too powerful to resist. Maia got up from the couch and walked to the closest phone, which sat on an end table near the window. She would call Lindsey and ask her to arrange another meeting with the 4400 who summoned the shades of the dead.

As she lifted the phone's handset from its cradle, another vision seized control of her senses.

*A warship, on the water but close to land, fires a missile. White smoke blooms like a flower, then smudges the sky as the rocket hurtles away, a low-flying blur.*

*It darts and twists between the buildings of a familiar cityscape. Then it finds its mark, zeroing in on the top corner of a building. Impact.*

*Fire and thunder. Screaming. Bodies.*
*Jordan vanishes in a wall of white flames.*

The vision ended, leaving Maia in cold sweat. Her finger trembled above the phone's keypad. She had been told what to do if a moment such as this came to pass.

She pressed the red emergency button at the bottom of the keypad and hoped that her warning would arrive in time.

# NINE

KYLE BALDWIN ENTERED the Collier Foundation's de facto "crisis center," a conference room on a protected sublevel, shadowed by Cassie—his promicin ability personified as a redheaded vixen from his subconscious, an advisor whom only he could see or hear.

Palming sweat from his forehead and back through his close-cropped dirty-blond hair, he announced his presence to the four people who had answered his urgent summons: "Listen up." The others turned to face him. He recited what Cassie had told him to say. "Maia says we've got a missile inbound. It's coming from the water, so it's a good bet it was fired from a ship. Job one is stop that missile. Let's huddle up."

He sensed Cassie looming behind his shoulder as he draped his left arm over the shoulders of Lucas Sanchez, a dark-haired and mustached gestalt telepath in his mid-forties, and rested his right arm on the back of Renata Gaetano, a young Italian woman with long, dyed-blond hair and a pear-shaped figure. Renata, who had acquired her skills months earlier during what Jordan called "the Great Leap Forward" and the rest of the city called the fifty/fifty epidemic, was an electrokinetic with a knack for controlling and destroying electronic equipment and systems.

On her right was Hal Corcoran, another willing recipient of the promicin shot. Just shy of his sixtieth birthday, he was a heavyset man who had been robbed of his eyesight by diabetes. In what seemed to Kyle like an expression of karmic justice, the man whose eyes were hidden now by opaque black glasses had acquired the ability of remote viewing; his particular skill enabled him to visualize large areas and then home in on targets of interest, even those moving at great speeds.

Completing the circle was Kemraj Singh, a slightly built young man from Pakistan. One of the original 4400, Kemraj was a powerful hydrokinetic. As he clasped his dark hand around Lucas's, he closed his eyes. Kyle did the same, and Lucas put his gift to work.

Participating in gestalt telepathy was one of the oddest sensations Kyle had ever known. Everyone in the circle became part of a group mind, linked by Lucas's ability. The first feeling of connection was physical. Each member of the circle became aware of the others' breathing. Within seconds their respiration had synchronized. Five minds became one. Thoughts passed instantaneously from one person to all of the others. Yet within the merged persona, distinct voices remained.

"Find the missile," Kyle whispered, knowing that he would be heard even if he didn't speak aloud.

Hal was the first to reach out, casting his special vision high above Promise City. Turning west, the cloudy sky was reflected on the cobalt waters of Elliott Bay. Hurtling forward, they raced away from the city, over West Seattle, and out into the sparkling beauty of Puget Sound.

Against the cerulean surface of the water, Hal spied a swiftly moving white contrail. He fixed his focus on the nose of the missile that was speeding toward them. "There," he said.

"Got it," Renata replied. Kyle felt her mind reach out to the missile and make contact with its sophisticated electronic guidance systems. As she prepared to coax it toward a fatal dive into an open patch of Elliott Bay, Cassie's breath was hot on the back of Kyle's ear as she whispered to him, "Stop her."

"Stop," Kyle said. From past experience, he knew the others could neither see nor hear Cassie, even in the gestalt link.

As if seducing him, Cassie continued. "Don't waste this opportunity, Kyle." He turned his head to see her smirking at him, leading him to wonder what sinister plan she was hatching.

Through Hal's remote sight, the skyline of Seattle heaved into view, growing larger by the second. "Kyle . . . ?" he asked.

Renata added, "What do you want me to do, Kyle?"

Cassie stroked one fingernail down the center of Kyle's back and cooed, "Say it with me, Kyle." The next moment, he heard his voice speaking in synchronicity with hers, as if he had become her puppet. "Let the missile buzz the city," they said in unison. "Then turn it back at the ship that fired it."

He couldn't believe the words that were coming out of his mouth. His feelings of shock and hesitation were mirrored on the faces of the others in the circle.

"Do it," he and Cassie said.

Focusing her thoughts, Renata took control of the missile. Kyle felt it bow to Renata's commands, and she guided it through a wide turn over the city that was daredevil-close to the taller buildings downtown. Then it was on a return trajectory, streaking across Elliott Bay, flying so low that Hal could see its blurred reflection on the water's surface.

Kyle spoke more words as Cassie put them into his mouth. "Renata, keep the missile on target. Hal, find the ship it came from." At the speed of thought, Hal projected his sight across Puget Sound, and followed the missile's dissipating contrail to a U.S. Navy warship. "Kemraj," Kyle/Cassie said, "move all the water away from its propellers—hold it steady."

Cassie directed Kyle's focus to a specific point on the ship's hull and told him what to do. "Hit the deck near the forward gun," he said to Renata. "And scramble their defenses."

"Okay," Renata said with obvious reluctance.

Everyone obeyed Kyle's orders. There was nothing left for him to do but sit back and watch—and listen, horrified, as Cassie giggled with malicious glee.

# TEN

THERE WERE NEARLY thirty officers and enlisted personnel in the combat information center of the U.S. Navy guided-missile destroyer U.S.S. *Momsen*, and the ship's executive officer, Commander Alim Gafar, was convinced that not one of them knew what the hell was going on—himself included.

"Somebody give me a SITREP, goddammit," he said, raising his voice above the buzz of nervous chatter that filled the dimly lit compartment. Confused faces looked up from illuminated tables and banks of eerily glowing computer monitors.

Lieutenant Carrie Wright, the tactical action officer, halted in her mad back-and-forth dash between the main battery gunnery liaison and the radar supervisor. "We lost control of the Tomahawk, sir," she said. "It's still active, but we can't get a fix on its position."

"If it's still active, it hasn't hit the target," Gafar said. "Use the override and put it in the drink."

Wright shook her head. "Override failed, sir. No response."

From behind Gafar, the radar supervisor called out, "Found our bird, sir! Bearing nine-six, CBDR and hugging the waves!"

The report sent a chill through Gafar: CBDR was an acronym for Constant Bearing, Decreasing Range. A collision course.

"Collision alarm!" Gafar said. "Fire control, abort that missile now!"

"No response, sir!" an ensign replied.

A palpable wave of anxiety swept through the CIC. Gafar knew he would have only seconds to act. "Arm the CIWS," he said, pronouncing the acronym "Sea-Whiz."

The Phalanx Close-In Weapon System was a deck-mounted autocannon designed to blast incoming missiles and aircraft to shreds. He had never expected to have to turn it against one of his ship's own Tomahawk cruise missiles.

"Targeting," reported the antiaircraft gunnery liaison, a first-class petty officer whom Gafar knew only by the nickname Kiwi. "Six seconds to range . . ."

Gafar stood and waited, placing his trust in his CIC team. Firing the missile had not been his choice; the order had come directly from the president to the *Momsen*'s commanding officer, Captain McIntee, who in turn had given it to Gafar. Knowing who their target was, he hadn't expected anything good to come of this decision, but he certainly hadn't expected this.

With no warning he was standing in total darkness, listening to the long, dwindling whine of computer drives spinning down. "Somebody crack a light!" he called out.

"Ensign Monroy, pass me the sound-powered phone and patch me through to one-MC."

Flashlights snapped on in the sepulchral gloom and slashed through the darkness.

The communications officer adjusted the durable emergency communications device and passed the handset to Gafar, who said, "Bridge, Combat."

Captain McIntee answered, *"Combat, Actual. Go ahead."*

"Captain, we have total power failure. Aux Fire Control needs to target the CIWS."

*"Negative,"* the captain replied. *"All sections are dark, and we're dead in the water. We—"* Over the line, Gafar heard another officer shout, *"Visual contact! Inbound bogey!"*

"Brace for impact!" Gafar bellowed across the CIC. "Away DC and fire teams! Go watertight! Move!"

Everyone followed him as he ran for the exit and scrambled into the passageway to secure the hatches and warn the damage control and firefighting teams to prepare for the worst.

A bomb blast roared through every deck and compartment on the *Momsen*. The ship heaved violently under Gafar's feet, then rolled to starboard. Within seconds, he smelled the sulfuric tang of cordite and the pungent stench of leaking oil and burning fuel.

He was shouting orders, but no one was listening. Men were on fire, and the corridors reeked of charred flesh. Toxic smoke stung his eyes, and a string of secondary detonations confirmed his fear that the missile had hit the ship's ordnance supply.

Stumbling forward, he strained to see the overhead through the black cloud that roiled above him. Panicked crewmen slammed into him and continued on, ignoring his warnings that they were running into a deadly blaze.

Another blast turned everything white for a moment, then gave way once more to flame-licked shadows.

The *Momsen* groaned like a wounded steel leviathan, and the deck pitched almost straight down ahead of Gafar, who flailed for a handhold. His hand found the railing of a ladder, and he hung on as loose bits of debris and sailors' personal effects tumbled like dice down the suddenly vertical shaft.

An active flashlight bounced out of an open hatchway above him and nearly hit him in the head as it fell past. A moment later it came to a halt—floating on the rising swell of icy seawater that was flooding into the sinking destroyer.

It took only a few seconds for the numbingly cold water to reach Gafar's feet. In less than a minute it swallowed him up to his neck. He fought to stay afloat, to ride the cresting wave to an escape, but all he found were sealed hatches and wreckage-strewn passages. Then there was nowhere left to go.

He didn't try to hold his breath.

He knew he'd freeze before he drowned.

Either way, he was as good as dead.

# ELEVEN

Every phone in the Seattle NTAC office was ringing. No one was answering them.

Tom Baldwin focused on his computer and tuned out the shrill cacophony of several dozen digital ringtones, including the one from his phone. Every extension light was flashing.

Outside his office, Diana, both Jeds, senior analyst Marco Pacella, and almost every other agent had gathered to watch the latest developments on the office's numerous televisions. From where Tom was sitting, the news anchors' overly modulated voices blended together into a steady drone of gibberish.

One channel showed live news helicopter footage of a fiery oil slick on Puget Sound—the only remaining trace of the sunken U.S. Navy destroyer *Momsen*. Another feed offered a montage of amateur home videos of the missile, which had made a supersonic pass over the city before turning back out to sea.

A third channel showcased images of panic in the streets.

*Like I needed the news to tell me about that,* Tom brooded. Helping coordinate first responders was his primary task at that moment. Most of what they were responding to was looting and traffic jams at the various military-guarded checkpoints that ringed Jordan Collier's benignly usurped city-state.

There was almost enough chaos to distract Tom from thinking about the fact that his son was inside the Collier building. Almost—but not quite.

Meghan leaned halfway through his office door. "Just got off the phone with the chief of Seattle PD," she said. "He says his people have Beacon Hill under control, so you can stand down, if you want."

"Thank God," Tom said, pulling his palms over his face to push away the fatigue. "Have you seen the footage on channel five? That was a Tomahawk."

She grimaced. "I saw it."

"I don't suppose the Navy gave us a heads-up before lobbing a cruise missile into our backyard?"

"According to SECDEF, the strike was handled on a need-to-know basis," Meghan said. "Three guesses where we fall on that list."

"Big surprise," Tom said, sharing her frustration. "What're the talking points this time?"

"I don't think they know yet."

From the main room behind Meghan, Tom heard the rising pitch of angry voices growing louder—and one of them was Diana. He bolted from his chair and moved toward the door. Meghan stepped out of his way and followed him as he hurried out to see what was going on.

Diana paced like a caged tigress, muttering vile curses under her breath while shooting fearful and angry glances at a TV screen showing images of the Tomahawk's near miss of the Collier Foundation building. She was surrounded by several other agents, including Marco and both Jeds. J.B. held up his hands and tried to halt Diana's anxious back-and-forth. "Diana, come on," he said. "It might be a mistake."

He recoiled as she snapped back, "DOD just confirmed the target! It was no *mistake!*"

"You gotta calm down," J.B. said, putting a hand on Diana's shoulder. She swatted away his attempt at consolation.

"Don't tell me to calm down!" she screamed at him, her rage boiling over into tears. "Maia was in there! The Navy just shot a *fucking missile* at my kid!"

Tom stepped between Diana and J.B. before the man could say anything else to make the situation worse. "J.B., get lost," Tom said. "And take your twin with you." The two Jeds slunk away wearing glum expressions. Tom turned back to Diana, who hid her tear-reddened eyes under one hand and crossed her other arm over her chest. Keeping his hands to himself, Tom said softly, "He doesn't have kids. He doesn't get it."

Her voice trembled with barely contained terror and rage. "They could've killed her, Tom. And Kyle, too."

"I know," Tom said, feeling his own fury rising.

Meghan approached Tom and Diana with visible caution. "Diana?" she said. "I have a call going through to Jordan's people. Do you want me to try and get Maia on the line for you?" Diana nodded, apparently too overcome with emotion to voice her response. Meghan tilted her head toward her office. "Come on. If we reach her, you can use my office." Nodding again, Diana smiled sadly at Meghan, then touched Tom's arm in a gesture of quiet gratitude. Then the two women stepped away, into the semiprivate confines of Meghan's executive office.

Turning his attention to another live image of the burning oil slick on Puget Sound, Tom felt his jaw clench and his fists curl shut. He had been dreading this day ever since Jordan Collier had challenged the U.S. government by declaring a one-square-mile chunk of Seattle as sovereign territory under his authority and renaming it "Promise City."

Marco sidled up to Tom and fixed his stare on the TV screen. "This is bad," the young Theory Room director said, adjusting his thick-rimmed, black plastic eyeglasses.

Tom glanced at the shorter, slightly built man. In his tweed jacket, linen shirt, blue jeans, and flat-soled sneakers, Marco looked more like a graduate student than the professional intelligence analyst and scientific theorist that he was.

"It's even worse than it looks," Tom said.

Cocking one eyebrow, Marco asked, "How do you figure?"

"Forget about the implications of the U.S. firing the first shot at Promise City," Tom said, fighting to stay calm and keep his temper in check. "You and I both know how powerful Jordan's people are. They could've ended this a dozen different ways. They could've self-destructed that missile, or ditched it at sea, or turned it to confetti. But they chose to use it as a weapon." Unable to hold back the tide of his wrath, Tom pounded the side of his fist on a desktop. "They killed almost four hundred men and women on that ship!"

"Not to play devil's advocate," Marco replied, "but maybe sinking the ship was an accident."

Scowling at the scene of smoking destruction on the TV, Tom shook his head. "No, that was no accident. That ship had a missile-defense system. The only way it could take a direct hit like that would be if someone compromised its defenses. Jordan and his people sank that ship on purpose." He turned and looked at Marco. "Which means that Jordan Collier thinks he's ready to go to war with the United States."

# TWELVE

"I AM *NOT* READY to go to war with the United States!"

Pointing at the moving images of destruction at sea on his office's television, Jordan continued. "There were nearly four hundred people on that ship! What the hell were you thinking?"

Kyle stood silent in front of Jordan's desk, staring into the ruddy sky outside the office's windows, where a blood-red sun dipped in slow degrees below the horizon. "I did what Cassie told me had to be done. She's never been wrong before."

Jordan massaged his temples. He was usually a calm and contemplative figure, not prone to outbursts, but the last few days had seemed to test his patience. "I don't care what Cassie said. I told you specifically not to use force without consulting me. Did you forget that conversation?"

"No, I didn't," Kyle said. "It was an emergency. We did what had to be done to keep us safe."

Recovering his Zen-like composure, Jordan reclined his chair. He kept his attention on Kyle, who avoided eye contact, choosing instead to look past Jordan and into the distance.

The leader of Promise City stood and walked past Kyle to stand in front of the television. "We always have non-violent options, even in a crisis," Jordan said. "Using them allows Promise City to retain the moral high ground. Spilling blood when we don't need to only begets more violence and tarnishes the Movement."

Between them, but seen only by Kyle, his phantom counsel Cassie said with a sneer, "Tell him what a hypocrite he is."

Goaded into the confrontation, Kyle snapped at Jordan, "You didn't seem to care about spilling blood for your Great Leap Forward. You were ready to accept *fifty percent* fatalities worldwide from promicin. That'd be, what? Three *billion* people dead? And you want me to feel guilty for taking out a few hundred military personnel who tried to *kill* us?"

"That was different," Jordan said. "At the time, I believed the potentially fatal risk of taking promicin was one of the prices we had to pay for progress as a species. I see now that I was wrong. We don't need to kill half the world in order to save the other half. What you did today was criminal."

"What we did was self-defense," Kyle said, stepping into Jordan's personal space.

Jordan held his ground, unfazed by Kyle's challenge. "Self-defense isn't the same thing as vengeance, Kyle. That's not what the Movement stands for."

"No, apparently it stands for rolling over and playing dead," Kyle replied. Cassie planted her hands on his shoulders, stoking his courage. "The Feds in Washington aren't going to take a hint, and they won't reward us for our restraint. They don't respect people who bring knives to gunfights. The only language they understand is mutually assured destruction."

"I refuse to accept that," Jordan said, stepping away from Kyle, who followed him. Jordan returned to his desk and slipped back into his chair. "There are better paths that we can take."

Planting his knuckles on Jordan's desk and leaning forward, Kyle asked, "Then why do you have people positioned all over the world, waiting to take out major cities on your order?"

"That's an insurance policy. A last resort, not a first option."

Kyle straightened and dismissed Jordan's argument with a wave of his hand. "Call it what you want, Jordan. But Cassie and I play hardball. If the U.S. Navy shoots a missile at us, they're getting a missile back. We won't strike first, but we will definitely strike last."

Jordan sighed. "Let's see if we can avoid any more strikes today at all, shall we?" He frowned as he pressed a button to activate the intercom to his assistant. "Jaime, could you come take a memo, please?"

Moments later the door opened, and Jordan's perky young assistant walked in carrying a digital recorder the size of one of her fingers. She placed herself in front of Jordan's desk beside Kyle, activated the recorder, and nodded to Jordan.

"Please issue an official statement to the media and the United States government," Jordan said. "Offer our sincere and deepest condolences to the families of those who perished in this training exercise gone tragically awry. If our people can be of any assistance in helping the Navy figure out why their Tomahawk missile malfunctioned, or to help them recover any part of the ship, we're ready to lend a hand." He waved the assistant out as he added, "Tack on the usual signatures. Thanks, Jaime."

The attractive young woman stepped out and closed the door behind her. Kyle turned back toward Jordan, who once again had fixed his countenance into the very model of beatific calm. "You want to learn how to fight a war, Kyle? Then learn this: sometimes the deadliest weapon of all is a press release."

# THIRTEEN

DENNIS RYLAND SAT in his office at Haspelcorp and shook his head in disbelief at the TV, which was tuned to live news coverage of a Promise City spokesperson reading a press release about the *Momsen* incident.

"Are you watching this?" he groused. "A malfunction? An accident? During a training exercise? Are they kidding me?"

A streaming media player on his computer monitor offered him a real-time video link to the three scientists working in the Nevada bunker laboratory. *"You have to give Collier credit,"* said Dr. Jakes, whose voice warbled from the digital processing being applied to the secure, hard-line signal. *"He's a coy one."*

"He's a goddamned liar," Dennis said, swiveling his chair to turn away from the TV and look out his window at dreary downtown Tacoma, Washington, and, far away, the majestic snow-covered peak of Mount Rainier. "Who'd believe this bullshit?"

Dr. Kuroda replied, *"It's not about what people believe,*

*Mister Ryland. It's about what they hear. So far, all they've heard is Jordan's side of the story."*

"That's because no one in D.C. knows what anybody else is doing. The president's firing missiles, but no one tells DOD or Homeland Security. Keystone Kops are running the country."

*"You should be more concerned about Collier's spin on the situation,"* said Dr. Wells. The African-American scientist continued. *"He's played the PR game admirably. By characterizing the incident as a training exercise and as an accident, he's set the narrative. And offering his help and condolences makes him seem charitable while he lets the United States off the hook for botching an attack on his headquarters."*

Dennis felt pressure building behind his eyes, like a sinus headache. He slid open his desk drawer and fished out a pack of cigarettes while the scientists kept talking at him.

*"Now the government has a serious problem,"* Dr. Jakes said. *"Because Collier got his story out to the media first, if the government wants to contradict him, they have to paint themselves as either aggressors or incompetents."*

*"Or both,"* Dr. Kuroda interjected.

Only half listening, Dennis pulled a cancer stick from the pack of Camels and stuck it between his parched, cracked lips while he tried to find his lighter.

*"In any event,"* Dr. Jakes went on, *"if the U.S. lets Collier's version of events stand, it'll still look incompetent, and he'll still come off as magnanimous. Either way, more public sympathy is likely to shift to Collier and his movement."*

Lighter in hand, Dennis ignored all of Washington

State's laws against smoking inside public buildings and places of employment. This was his office. If they wanted to come and get him for lighting up, they were welcome to try. A push of his thumb over the flint coaxed out an orange flame, which he touched to the tip of his cigarette. He inhaled and savored the oddly satisfying sting in his throat, the acrid taste, and the soft, barely audible crackle of the cigarette paper igniting. Then he exhaled two long jets of white smoke from his nostrils.

It had been decades since he'd smoked on a regular basis, but as with so many things it was like riding a bike. And with the world spiraling down the drain one day at a time, he no longer saw any reason to deny himself this long-forbidden pleasure.

Contemplating the smoldering white roll of paper and dried tobacco between his fingers, he indulged himself with a tight-lipped smile. "Everything you've said is true," he admitted. "But there is at least one glimmer of hope in all this: the simple fact that no matter how Collier spins it for the public, he and his promicin-powered freaks just sank a U.S. Navy warship with all hands—and the government knows it."

*"Very true,"* Dr. Jakes said. *"It shouldn't take much more to draw him into an all-out conflict. And when that day comes, our promicin-neutralizer will be the secret weapon that brings him and his people to their knees without a shot being fired."* Flashing a taut, malicious smile, he added, *"Push him, Mister Ryland. Push him until he breaks."*

# FOURTEEN

## JULY 23, 2008

Most places in the daily life of Marco Pacella deserved to be called lonely, but none so much as the NTAC Theory Room.

Sequestered in the basement, behind a door decorated with a sign that read WHERE THE RUBBER MEETS THE ROAD, the miniature think tank had always been sparsely staffed. At its peak, its roster had numbered three: Marco and his colleagues P.J. and Brady. Then, in the span of a few months, P.J. had gone to prison for using an ability that he had gained by illegally injecting promicin, and Brady had died after being exposed to the airborne promicin virus released by the late Danny Farrell.

P.J.'s successor in the Theory Room had been an attractive young woman named Abigail Hunnicut. Her tenure at NTAC had come to an abrupt end a few months ago, when it had been revealed that she was illegally creating clones of Danny Farrell in an effort to replicate his fifty percent lethal promicin virus. A converted "true believer," she'd hoped to use her own promicin-based ability for rearranging DNA to complete Jordan Collier's now abandoned mission to unleash airborne promicin around the globe, killing billions in the name of "progress."

Instead she'd succeeded only in getting herself killed while holding Tom and Diana hostage, and that had left Marco at a bitter crossroads. He had been deeply smitten with Abby, which had made him blind to her deceits. Now he desperately wanted to hate her for betraying him and NTAC in the name of some apocalyptic ideology, but he had a deeper need to mourn her.

*Two peers dead, one in jail*, Marco brooded. *And now there's only me.* He sipped his lukewarm Diet Coke and studied the hash of numbers projected in high definition on the room's back wall. *This would've gone a lot faster if Brady were still here.*

He heard the doorknob turning behind him, and the soft groan of the door's hinges as it swung inward. Glancing over his shoulder, he lifted his chin in greeting to Tom and Diana. "Hey, guys. Thanks for coming."

"Sure thing," Tom said. He and Diana navigated their way through the room's labyrinth of computers and other high-tech gadgets. Diana hovered over Marco's left shoulder. Tom loomed behind his right and inquired, "What've we got?"

"Bad news, and lots of it," Marco said. He pushed himself up from his chair and strolled toward the projection on the wall. "The NSA sent over a mountain of raw data yesterday. I ran a difference filter to see what they had that we didn't." He picked up a remote control off a table and clicked a button to advance the presentation. "Here's what I found."

A new screen of data snapped into focus against the wall. Marco pointed out details line by line as he continued. "Most of what got blanked from our servers had to do with transfers of high-tech components, state-of-the-art composites and materials, and—here's the fun part—a radioactive sample from CERN."

That item raised Diana's eyebrows. "CERN? As in the Large Hadron Collider?" That hint of excitement in her eyes reminded Marco of the days—not so long ago but now gone—when Diana had seemed to be excited about him. Ending their brief romantic relationship had been her choice. It was one that he had always respected but in truth had never really accepted, not even now.

"Yeah, that CERN," Marco said, keeping his personal feelings and professional duties strictly segregated. "The protocols used to move that sample had the hallmarks of a nuclear fuel shipment."

Tom wrinkled his brow in confusion. "Wait a second," he said, pointing at the screen. "Why would anyone ship nuke fuel into the U.S. from Europe when we can make our own at Livermore and Los Alamos?"

Before Marco could answer, Diana replied, "If it's from the LHC it might be antimatter, or a new transuranic element—something heavier than we can produce."

Horrified understanding shone through Tom's widened eyes. "In which case, we'd be talking about something that puts a lotta punch into a small package."

"Exactly," Marco said.

Diana stepped around Marco's chair and walked right up to the projection on the wall. Turning sideways to minimize her shadow, she traced lines with her fingers, as if it might help her to find the meaning of each detail in the puzzle of data.

"Marco," Diana said, "I've seen parts lists for homemade nuclear bombs before, but I've never seen one like this."

"That's because it's not for a nuke. You wouldn't need that many kilos of superconductive composite, or a magnetically partitioned shell. Those are the building blocks for something completely different."

Crossing his arms, Tom asked, "Care to be more specific?"

Marco hesitated to answer, because the type of device that would utilize such technologies was, as far as he had known until that morning, purely theoretical. But, since Tom had asked . . . He shrugged and said, "If I had to guess, I'd say someone's figured out how to build an antimatter bomb."

Tom looked back at the projected data and muttered, "I don't like the sound of that."

Diana turned back toward Marco and squinted into the projector beam. "Where's this stuff being shipped?"

"No idea," Marco said. "This was all the data the NSA was able to back up before its own cache got wiped. Whoever scrubbed these records zapped 'em like a pro."

"So we're talking about someone with a top-level government clearance," Diana said.

"Or a promicin ability," Marco said.

Tom sighed. "I *really* don't like the sound of that."

# FIFTEEN

"PARDON THE INTERRUPTION, Dennis. I need a moment of your time."

Dennis Ryland's lunch had just been served. He looked up from his bowl of lobster spaghetti to see his visitor. Miles Enright, Haspelcorp's executive vice president in charge of research and development, stood in a pose that was as casual as his expression was severe. The man was in his mid-fifties, gaunt and pale. He kept his perfectly round skull shaved, and he wore impenetrably opaque black sunglasses all the time, even indoors.

Gesturing with his fork at the otherwise empty, earth-and-brick-toned private dining room of the Pacific Grill, Dennis said, "I don't suppose it's a coincidence running into you here?"

"No, it's not," Enright said. He pulled out the chair opposite Dennis's and sat down. Folding his hands on the table, he continued. "I notice you've been incurring some interesting charges on the R&D budget lately."

Masking his ire with a tight-lipped smile, Dennis kept his stare level and unblinking. "Have I?"

"Yes. I admit, accounting can be a bit slow on the uptake from time to time, but even the most lethargic bean counter tends to notice when two billion dollars gets spent in less than two months with nothing to show for it."

To buy time and annoy Enright, Dennis shoveled a forkful of gourmet pasta into his mouth. Tender chunks of Maine lobster meat and jumbo shrimp mingled with the subtle richness of oven-roasted tomatoes, julienned zucchini, and crushed red pepper in a lemon-butter sauce with fresh basil. He took his time and savored as he chewed. Then he swallowed and picked up his glass for a sip of his Bonterra Viognier, a crisply acidic white wine made from organically grown grapes.

Enright sat as stoically as a golem while he watched Dennis chew, sip, and swallow.

"Order something, Miles," Dennis said. "I hear the steak salad's fantastic."

"You still haven't answered my question," Enright said.

"You haven't asked one," Dennis said.

A waitress approached the table. The slim young Asian woman moved with a light, almost soundless step through the elegantly appointed space. She set a plate and a wineglass in front of Enright, then handed him a white cloth napkin and put down a set of utensils in their correct places on either side of his plate.

"Would you like to see a menu, sir?" she asked.

Enright shook his head. "Not right now, thank you." She walked away and left the two men alone in the dining room. His face a cipher, Enright said, "Very well, Dennis." He folded his hands together. "What are you up to?"

Dennis smirked as he twirled more spaghetti into a tight coil around his fork. "Business."

"But not business as usual," Enright replied.

"What do you really think I'm going to tell you, Miles?"

Leaning forward ever so slightly, Enright projected a clear sense of menace across the table. "You're going to tell me why you're spending two billion dollars of Haspelcorp's research and development budget without consulting me first."

After another sip of wine, Dennis said, "Because I can, Miles. That's one of the beauties of being promoted to executive vice president of the entire company. I don't have to answer to people like you."

"We all answer to someone, Dennis. Even if it's only to God, or to our conscience."

"Fortunately, I don't have either of those," Dennis said. He speared a few chunks of lobster meat and pushed them down into the melted butter pooled in the bottom of his bowl.

"No, but you do answer to the president," Enright said. "And to the board of directors—on which I happen to sit." He mirrored Dennis's taunting smirk with one of his own. "I imagine the rest of the board would like to know what you did to make NTAC and the NSA go poking through our servers this morning."

Feigning nonchalance, Dennis swallowed his mouthful of buttery lobster, then patted his lips dry with the corner of his white cloth napkin. "Who says their interest had anything to do with me?"

"Their inquiries all concerned encrypted transactions conducted with your log-in credentials, Dennis. And I have to admit, their curiosity inspired a bit of my own." He reached to the chilled bucket beside the table, lifted out the bottle of Viognier, and poured a generous measure into his own wineglass. Then he returned the bottle to its chilled receptacle. Lifting the glass, he continued. "I've seen some exotic technologies in my time, Dennis, but this project of yours—it's something else." He sipped the wine, then pursed his lips and nodded. "Nice."

"Glad you like it," Dennis said.

"Let's cut through the bullshit," Enright said. "Whatever you're building, it involves some kind of high-energy nuclear fuel that you could only get from CERN. You're coloring way outside the lines on this one, and you know it."

Setting down his fork, Dennis said, "What I know, Miles, is that there are only two kinds of companies in this world: the kind that innovate, and the kind that go out of business. Our business is national security—and sometimes that means classified research."

"I know that," Enright said. "I've handled my share of top-secret projects. But I've always kept my peers and superiors informed of my efforts. You're treating this company as if it were your own private lab. Who commissioned this project of yours? If it's a DOD contract, why didn't it go through my office? If it's a spook job, why didn't you notify the board?"

Those were good questions. Up until that moment, it

hadn't occurred to Dennis to wonder how his strangely visionary rogue scientists had developed their cutting-edge technology without attracting government attention.

He leaned back and reached inside his jacket for a pack of cigarettes. He opened it, pulled one out, and put away the pack with one hand while retrieving his lighter with another.

As Dennis lifted it to ignite his cigarette, Enright said, "You can't smoke in here."

"I can smoke anywhere I damn well please," Dennis said. "As for my project, and the identity of my client, that's all being handled on a need-to-know basis—and in my opinion, it's in your best interest not to know." With a flick of his thumb, he lit his cigarette. He inhaled and then unleashed a cone of blue-gray smoke toward the ceiling. "Besides," he added, "if this works out as I hope it will, we'll all be set for life."

Enright pushed his chair back from the table and stood. "And if it goes south, you'll be *going away* for life." He picked up his fork, reached across the table, speared the biggest chunk of lobster in Dennis's bowl, and ate it. He dropped his fork on the table. "Bon appetit," he said with a malicious smile.

# SIXTEEN

TOM WAS THE last one to report to the meeting in Meghan's office. Meghan, Diana, and Marco were all waiting for him.

Though there were enough chairs for everyone to sit, they all were standing. Marco leaned against the floor-to-ceiling glass wall that separated the office from the agents' bullpen. Diana had staked out a spot right in front of Meghan's desk, and Meghan was pretending to admire the classic foreign film posters with which she had decorated her office.

"What'd I miss?" Tom asked, uncertain of whether he really wanted to know what had gone wrong.

Meghan turned to face him. "We just heard back from Homeland Security about the report we filed on those data intercepts." She stepped over to her desk and handed a file folder to Diana, who passed it to Tom. As he opened it and looked over the pages inside, Meghan continued. "They shared our data with the DOD, CIA, FBI, and NSA."

Cracking a wry smile, Tom said, "Did they do it ASAP on the QT?" His quip was met by grim, silent stares. "Tough room."

Diana replied, "Don't feel bad. My 'alphabet soup' line got the same response."

"That's 'cause the joke's on us," Meghan said. "Flip to the last page."

He did as she asked. On the last sheet of the thirty-page report, an analysis summary laid out Homeland Security's official conclusions for the President's Daily Brief.

As Tom read the intelligence community's joint findings, Marco stepped up beside him. "Nobody else has any leads on the missing parts or nuclear fuels, but DARPA agrees with our conclusion about what's being built."

Skimming quickly through the text, Tom's eyes widened as he read the last two paragraphs. "Are they serious? They think it's evidence that Jordan Collier's building a nuke?"

"Not just any nuke," Diana corrected him. "A next-generation antimatter warhead."

Marco cut in, "Never mind that the idea's insane. A regular nuclear warhead has to be triggered exactly right in order to detonate. One mistake and you end up with a dud. But an antimatter weapon would be the exact opposite. It'd be almost impossible to *keep it* from exploding. One mistake and *boom*."

"Which is why the Pentagon team is saying only Collier's people could pull it off," Meghan said. "They think he has one of his supersmart p-positives building him a doomsday weapon."

Tom shook his head in disbelief. "They gotta be

kidding me. That doesn't make any sense!" Noting his colleagues' curious glances, he continued. "I'm not saying I trust Jordan Collier, but with all the crazy powers his followers have, I don't see why he'd *need* something like this."

Diana replied, "I don't see why he'd *want* it. His entire movement has been about preventing a global catastrophe, not causing one. Whoever wrote that report hasn't got a clue as to what makes Jordan tick."

Meghan shot a prompting stare at Marco, who looked at his shoes for a moment before he said, "There's another possible explanation for the report's conclusion: someone has an agenda, and this report's been tailored to serve it."

Suspicion hardened Diana's face. "What're you saying?"

"That the government wants an excuse to launch a full-scale military strike on Promise City," Marco said.

"And we just helped them invent one," Tom said, his voice tense with rage. He closed the file folder and slapped it down onto Meghan's desktop. "That's just great . . . We gotta stop this." He threw an angry glare at Marco. "When does that briefing go to the president?"

Marco volleyed the query to Meghan with a glance.

She heaved a defeated sigh and looked at Tom. "It went to the White House an hour ago."

# SEVENTEEN

IT WAS LATE, long past sunset, and scores of private homes and squat apartment buildings were dark as Diana drove home to her condo in the Queen Anne neighborhood. Balmy summer air breezed through the open windows of her Toyota hybrid.

She wondered why she bothered going home at all. There was nothing waiting for her except some frozen dinners, a half-empty two-liter bottle of root beer that had lost its fizz, and a few white cardboard containers of leftover Chinese food that had sprouted some troubling gray-green fuzz.

*My cup runneth over*, she mused glumly, as the traffic light ahead changed from yellow to red. She tapped the brakes and stopped her car in the glow of a streetlamp. It still surprised her to hear the hybrid's engine go completely quiet when the car was stopped. After a lifetime of listening to idling engines, it made her worry each time that the engine had stalled.

All around her, Seattle felt like a ghost town. So many

people had fled since the fifty/fifty outbreak that almost every block in Queen Anne had at least one abandoned house. With the escalation of tensions between Promise City and the U.S. government during the past few months, even more people had left. Now entire streets stood deserted.

She almost expected to see a tumbleweed roll across the street as she sat at the stop light and listened to the wind.

Parks that once had bustled with playing children and hawkers selling everything from hot dogs and pretzels to bottled water or balloons now looked like sculpture parks devoted to swing sets and slides and spring-mounted fiberglass horses. Diana could count on one hand the number of times she had seen any children using the park near her home in the last month.

*It's like surviving after an apocalypse,* she brooded.

A shrill ringing made her jump. In the tomblike silence of her energy-efficient car stopped on an empty street, her cell phone sounded even more piercing than it usually did. Fumbling with both hands, she retrieved it from her jacket pocket and looked at the display screen. She didn't recognize the number, but she answered the call anyway. "Hello?"

*"Hi, Mom,"* Maia said.

Hearing her daughter's voice made Diana's eyes mist with emotion. Anger, relief, and joy clouded her thoughts. Pressing a hand to her chest to steady herself, she replied, "Hello, Maia. How are you, sweetie?"

After a telling pause, Maia said, *"I'm okay, I guess."*

Was that a hint of fear that she heard in Maia's voice?

She wondered whether the previous day's near-miss attack on the Collier Foundation had shaken the teen's resolve to remain away from home. There was no politic way to ask her that directly. For the moment, Diana would have to try to be coy.

"Do you have everything you need? Food, a place to sleep . . . ?"

"Yes," Maia said. "Jordan gave me an apartment to myself, and I can order food, like in a hotel."

"Sounds nice," Diana said. "Do they wash the dishes, too?"

"I think so. They take them away when I'm finished." She was quiet for a few seconds, but before Diana could think of a reply, Maia added, "I just wanted to let you know that I was okay. Y'know . . . because of what happened yesterday."

Under the low rustle of warm wind through the trees, Diana heard a few lonely chirps of birdsong. A single tear rolled from the corner of her eye. She palmed it from her cheek. "Thank you" was all she could say. Sniffling to clear her nose, she asked with forced aplomb, "What else is new?"

"Jordan makes me take homeschooling even though it's summer," Maia said. "It's dumb. I'm supposed to be on break."

Genuinely curious, Diana asked, "He hired you a tutor?"

"She's a volunteer," Maia said. "It's Heather Tobey, from The 4400 Center."

That bit of news gave Diana a twinge of concern.

Although Heather was a trained educator, she was also one of the original 4400; her unique ability was to nurture other people's innate talents and to help them harness and master those gifts.

Suspicion clouded Diana's thoughts. *I wonder if Jordan picked her to try to refine Maia's precognitive abilities?* Trying to be diplomatic, she said, "Well, I feel better knowing that there are grown-ups around."

Maia's tone became sharp and defensive. *"What's that supposed to mean?"*

"Nothing, sweetie," Diana said quickly, trying to think of a way to pave over her faux pas before it got out of control.

Unfortunately, Maia seemed unwilling to let it go. *"Are you saying you don't think I can handle being on my own? That I need 'grown-ups' to hold my hand?"*

"No, that's not what I . . ." Listening to herself, Diana decided she was done kowtowing. "Actually, yes. That's *exactly* what I'm saying. You *are* too young to be on your own, Maia. You're only thirteen years old, for God's sake."

*"That doesn't mean I'm a kid!"* The girl let out a growl of exasperation. *"You always do this! You act like I'm too young to use my ability, but I'm not, and you know it."*

Anger and frustration made Diana's face feel flushed with warmth, and her pulse thudded in her temples. "There's nothing wrong with using your ability, Maia, but using it to help Jordan Collier puts you in real danger."

Overenunciating each word, Maia retorted, *"So. What."*
*I love her and I want to throttle her,* Diana fumed.

"So? You're too young to get caught up in a war, Maia."

*"We're all stuck in this war, Mom—whether we like it or not. I just decided to pick a side."*

"And what makes you think you're old enough to make that decision? There's a reason children don't serve as soldiers."

Maia shouted back, *"Stop trying to protect me all the time! I'm not a baby; I can take care of myself!"*

Raising her own voice to match Maia's volume, Diana snapped, "I will *never* stop trying to protect you, Maia! You're my daughter, and worrying about you and protecting you is what I do! It's what I'll always do, because that's what being a mother is—whether *you* like it or not!"

Enraged silence reigned on both ends of the call.

Something in the car's rearview mirror caught Diana's eye. Block by block, streetlamps were going out. The few houses that still flickered with light and life went black. A forbidding darkness descended upon Queen Anne Hill.

The streetlamp above Diana's car went out, and the traffic signal—which had cycled through two changes while she had sat arguing with Maia—switched off as well.

Maia said simply, *"I have to go."*

She hung up before Diana could say "I love you."

Sitting alone in her car, which was the only light source on the street, Diana was left to wonder what had gone wrong now.

# EIGHTEEN

JORDAN COLLIER STOOD on the roof of his headquarters and watched the lights go out in Promise City.

One neighborhood after another was swallowed by the night: the residential streets of Queen Anne and Magnolia Bluff; the bohemian enclave of Capitol Hill; the skyscrapers of Belltown; the bedroom communities in Broadmoor and Madrona; the industrial sprawl of Georgetown and the blocks of Beacon Hill. Streets that sparkled with lamplight sank into shadow.

Standing a thousand feet above it all, surveying it like a lord of the night, Jordan couldn't help but smile.

The rooftop door opened with a loud squeak. He turned and clasped his hands casually behind his back as he watched his leadership council file onto the roof from the stairwell, which was lit by the dim, sickly green glow of emergency lights.

Leading the team of advisors was Kyle, whose tight-cropped blond hair still managed to be tousled by the breezes that never ceased this high aboveground. Behind him were Gary and Maia, looking like a study in opposites—a brawny young black man in a charcoal-gray designer suit and an off-white silk shirt, walking next to a petite blond teenage girl in blue jeans and a pink top.

Kyle opened his mouth to speak. Jordan trumped him. "Let me guess: the Army cut our power."

"Along with our drinking water and our sewage removal services," Kyle said without missing a beat.

It was almost enough to make Jordan laugh. "Naturally. It was only a matter of time." He smiled. "Fortunately, we've been ready for this since day one."

Folding his arms and putting on a dubious frown, Gary replied, "Ready to provide basic services, maybe. But you know that's not what this is really about."

Jordan nodded. "That's exactly what it's about. Proving that we can not only guarantee the basics of survival but do it *for free* is major public relations victory."

Kyle looked past Jordan, toward the shadowscape. "Turning out the lights isn't just some slap on the wrist," he said. "It's a setup for a military strike. And this time it won't be just one missile aimed at you. They'll come for all of us."

"I agree," Gary said. "They're probably moving troops into the city right now."

Noting the intense gaze of Maia, Jordan arched an eyebrow and inquired, "Something to add?"

"There will be shooting in the streets," she said in her ominous monotone of prophecy. "People are going to die."

There was no "unless" or "if" following her proclamation. The finality of it was sobering for Jordan. He nodded.

"Yes," he said. "I know." He turned west and breathed

in the faint scent of sea air. "The U.S. was never going to give up a city without a fight. But it's like childbirth: the moment of separation will be painful and bloody." He looked back at his three advisors. "But also completely necessary."

Visibly discomfited by Jordan's take on the situation, Gary shifted his weight and breathed a heavy sigh. "Maybe. But if so, shouldn't we be getting ready for the battle?"

This time Kyle answered for Jordan. "We already are. Sentinels are in place all over the city. When the Army makes its move, we'll make ours."

"Isn't that a bit risky?" Gary asked. "What if the Army comes at us with something we don't expect?"

Tilting his chin toward Maia, Kyle said, "That's what you're here to prevent, isn't it?"

She reacted with a steely glare at Kyle. "Even I don't see everything. The future is always changing."

"That's what I'm saying," Gary said, clearly unnerved by the detached manner in which Maia made her points. "We shouldn't get overconfident. It'll take just one mistake to bring this whole thing down on our heads." To Jordan he added, "If the U.S. government really decides to play hardball, they won't stop until they bury us. They'll wipe Promise City off the map before they let us keep it. You know that."

"Yes, I do," Jordan confessed with a smile. "As a matter of fact, I'm counting on it." He held his arms wide, as if to invite a crucifixion. "I know you might find this hard to believe, but this is all part of the plan."

# NINETEEN

NTAC's OFFICES WERE mostly empty. Only a handful of late-shift agents monitored the emergency action stations, and a single squad of uniformed security guards manned the main entrance and patrolled the ghost-town-quiet corridors. The monitors of logged-out computers filled the warren of deserted cubicles and vacant offices with a pale blue glow.

Tom Baldwin loosened the top button of his shirt and palmed sweat from his forehead. To conserve electricity, the building's air conditioners had shut off automatically at precisely 8 P.M. It was now more than an hour past that, and the atmosphere inside the facility had become warm and heavy.

The energy-saving measures had been implemented after the Army had taken the city's electrical grid offline. In compliance with Department of Homeland Security disaster protocols, NTAC had switched over to its diesel-fueled emergency generators and lithium backup batteries, which were supplemented by a hard line to an array of solar panels and a stand of six wind turbines hidden miles away on Bainbridge Island, across Elliott Bay.

Tom's footsteps echoed off the concrete steps and walls of the stairwell as he descended toward the sublevel that housed the Theory Room. The elevator would have been faster, but the need to limit power usage meant that all personnel were encouraged to use the stairs whenever possible.

As he had suspected, the Theory Room flickered with the telltale glow of video playback. He knocked once on the door, eased it open, and stepped inside. The faint aroma of pizza lingered in the air. *Pepperoni, if I know Marco*, he thought.

On the far side of the room, Marco swiveled his chair away from the full-wall projection screen. "Hey," he said, lifting his chin at Tom in salutation, then turning back to the video.

"Hey," echoed Tom, walking past rows of computer screens scrolling with data as they crunched raw intel from countless sources. "I was heading home when I saw your car in the lot. It's late. What're you still doing here?"

"Watching the world come apart at the seams," Marco said, squinting at the wall of video as Tom sidled up to him. The bespectacled theorist picked up a remote control, pressed a few buttons, and subdivided the screen into eight smaller images, each showing a different video feed. "This is footage from all over the world," he said. "Raw network feeds ripped from the satellites, pirate broadcasts. Some of it is being sent by p-positives who can transmit what they see and hear in perfect high-def. Talk about cinema verité."

Images of violence and destruction cascaded across the wall. Each subwindow switched its feed every few seconds, creating an ever-changing mosaic of chaos and unrest. It went by so quickly that Tom had difficulty taking it all in. "What am I looking at?" he asked.

"Promicin-fueled uprisings all over the planet," Marco said. He began pointing at images as they flashed by. "Monks in Tibet. Refugees in Sudan. Women in the Middle East. Settlers in Gaza. Workers in Venezuela. Rebels in Kashmir." He shook his head, then looked up at Tom. "The drug's spreading faster than we can track it. We could be looking at tens of millions of p-positives in a matter of weeks."

"Jesus Christ," Tom whispered, his voice muted in horror. "That means we'll also be looking at tens of millions of promicin deaths." He imagined distant lands littered with corpses twisted in the bloodied throes of agony. "Are they insane? Don't they know what this stuff *does*?"

Marco nodded. "They know. And they don't care." Reacting to Tom's disbelieving glare, he continued. "People in the Third World see promicin very differently than we do. They live every day with disease, starvation, genocide . . ." He shrugged. "Most of them figure they're as good as dead, anyway. They have nothing left to lose, so they roll the dice on promicin."

Tom frowned. "Makes sense. Most of the people here who took promicin were outsiders. People who'd lost hope, or felt like they'd hit bottom, or that the system had given up on them."

"Exactly," Marco said. "Now multiply that by ten million.

Most people in North America, Europe, Australia, and Japan have it pretty good, even in the worst of times. Why would they want to play Russian roulette with only a fifty/fifty chance of survival? But if you're born poor in a place like Chad or Sudan, a fifty/fifty chance at getting a superhuman ability must seem like a good risk." With a click of the remote control, he halted the rotation of the images on the wall. "And it's working. In the last four days, new p-positives have defeated genocidal warlords in Somalia, forced the Taliban out of a dozen villages in Afghanistan and Pakistan, and declared Kashmir an independent city-state." A dubious smile tugged at his mouth. "The meek are inheriting the Earth—as supermen."

Eyeing the images with both wonder and dismay, Tom had a troubling thought. "If this is spreading in the Middle East, it won't be long before groups like Al-Qaeda, Hamas, and Hezbollah get their hands on it. We could be facing militant Islamic terrorists with promicin powers. They could make 9/11 look like amateur hour."

"Possibly," Marco said, popping open a can of soda. "But that's not what I'd worry about if I were you."

"What do you mean?"

Marco sipped his soda, swallowed, then pointed at the screen. "Most of the people who are drawn to taking promicin are the have-nots: the poor, the oppressed, the enslaved. The ones who survive are hailing Jordan Collier like he's the Messiah. Even more disturbing, they're becoming the new elite of the world, and you'd better believe some of them are going to decide it's payback time. And not just on a personal level. I'm talking about an upheaval in the balance of power between nations—a global shift in the organization of human society."

Tom looked again at the chilling tableau of video feeds: an emaciated African woman psychokinetically shredding trucks and felling helicopters in Sierra Leone; a young boy melting Chinese tanks in Shingatse; an ad hoc militia of poor civilians laying siege to the capital of Myanmar. Then he looked at Marco.

"Is this as bad as I think it is?"

"Worse," Marco said. "Governments don't give up power without a fight . . . This is how world wars get started."

# Part Two

# These All Died in Faith

# TWENTY

JAKES HUNCHED HIS SHOULDERS against the frigid night air of the Nevada desert. He took a quick drag off his cigarette and craned his head back as he exhaled, the better to admire the starry dome of the sky. The stars had long been hidden in the future world that had sent him here to reshape the past. Admiring the constellations, those brilliant pinholes in the curtain of night, almost made him regret his mission.

But he had his orders. There was nowhere to go but forward.

He glanced over his shoulder at Kuroda. Her body was garbed in stained gray coveralls, her hands were covered with thick welder's gloves, and a dark welding visor masked her face. A tightly wrapped braid of her blond hair stuck out from under the back of her protective headgear.

Electric blue flashes of acetylene light made a silhou-

ette of her, and white-hot sparks from her work bounced
across the hard ground before fading away, as ephemeral as
shooting stars.

Wells emerged from the entrance to the underground
lab and shivered as he stepped into the bitter cold. Lifting one hand to shield his eyes from the blinding glare of
Kuroda's welding rod, he asked Jakes, "You sure she knows
what she's doing?"

"Better than either of us would," Jakes said. He knew
why Wells was nervous. Even a minor mistake could set
off the dead-man's switch on the antimatter warhead that
Kuroda was securing to the cargo bed of a white sport-
utility vehicle. "Leave her be," he advised his colleague.
"She's doing fine."

"If you say so," Wells replied. He walked toward the
front of the SUV and nodded for Jakes to follow him.
"Let's go over it one last time."

Jakes rolled his eyes. The plan hadn't changed in weeks,
yet Wells insisted on rehashing it ad nauseam. *Still*, Jakes
reminded himself, *best not to take anything for granted, especially when we're so close to the endgame*. He fell into step
behind Wells, who took a road map from inside his jacket
and spread it out on top of the truck's hood.

"The good news," Wells began, "is that the crisis with
Jordan Collier has the U.S. government and its military
focused on Promise City." Casting a grim look at the map,
he added, "But I'm still concerned that you'll be too exposed, for too long. Flying would be faster."

"Absolutely not," Jakes said. Icy wind threatened to steal
the map, which snapped and rustled under his and Wells's

hands. "Air traffic in this part of Nevada is much too closely monitored for us to risk that. I wouldn't make it more than two hundred kilometers before getting shot down."

Wells frowned. "Then what about a less direct driving route? Something that keeps you off the major highways?"

"You're being paranoid," Jakes said. "As long as I obey the speed limit and rules of the road, there won't be a problem."

"Don't be so sure," Wells replied. "You borrowed that body of yours months ago. Someone must have noticed by now that he's missing."

"Noticing that he's missing and actively looking for him are two very different things," Jakes said.

Cocking his head to one side, Wells replied, "Be that as it may, the less you're seen, the better." He traced Jakes's planned driving route with his fingertip. "This is more than twelve hundred kilometers of open road."

"One thousand, two hundred ninety-three, to be precise," Jakes interjected, drawing a disapproving sidelong stare from Wells. He pressed on, "At most, we're talking about fourteen hours of driving from here to the target. Under the circumstances, that's hardly a prolonged window of risk. And traffic on main roads moves with relative freedom."

"Fine," said Wells, conceding the debate. "It's just after two o'clock now. Fourteen hours on the road would make your ETA to target roughly four P.M. Pacific?"

"Yes, that sounds about right." A gust of brisk night air tossed Jakes's short brown hair into a frenzy. "You and

Kuroda need to be well away from here—preferably in the air and headed west—before I trigger the warhead."

Nodding, Wells said, "It's taken care of. We'll catch a flight to Tokyo out of McCarran at seven A.M. Once we get to Japan, we'll find new bodies and go to ground." A diabolical smile lit up his face. "When do you think Ryland will figure out that we've screwed him?"

"About an hour after the world ends," Jakes said, then chortled as he slapped his compatriot's back.

Wells folded up the map and handed it to Jakes, who nodded his thanks and tucked it inside his jacket.

The hiss and hum of activity behind the van ceased. Kuroda emerged and flipped up her visor. "All set," she said, pushing shut the SUV's hatchback with a dull thud. "Try not to hit any bumps, okay?"

"I'll do my best," Jakes said, hoping that the once-Asian woman now living in the body of a blonde was only joking. He opened the driver's door and started to get in, but paused as Wells offered him his hand. He reached over and shook it.

"Thank you," Wells said. "I don't know that I could go through with it, if I were in your place."

"Sure you could," Jakes said, certain that it was true. "It's just my turn, that's all."

Kuroda stripped off her work gloves and shook Jakes's hand, as well. "If you're having second thoughts, we could trade—"

"No, I wouldn't dream of it," he cut in. "Besides, only you can use your airline tickets. The decision's made. Time to go."

He let go of her hand and eased himself into the vehicle's driver's seat. His two colleagues stepped back as he shut the door and keyed the ignition.

The engine turned over with a low purr of combustion. In the truck's rearview mirror, he saw a cloud of gray vapor rise from its exhaust pipe and dissipate into the night.

For a moment, he felt a twinge of hesitation. Then he recalled that this was exactly what he had volunteered for. It was for a mission such as this that he had agreed to have his consciousness downloaded into nanites and exiled forever to the past. This was the moment for which he had come.

"Clock's ticking," he said with a smile to his comrades. "Don't miss your flight." Then he shifted the vehicle into gear and drove away to keep his appointment with Armageddon.

# TWENTY-ONE

## 7:04 A.M.

A SHRILL RINGING stirred Jordan Collier from a deep sleep.

He rolled over, still groggy, and flailed for the phone. His limbs felt heavy and clumsy, as if he were drunk. It took him a few slaps of his hand on the end table before he planted it on the phone's receiver and plucked it from its cradle.

*And to think*, he mused ruefully, *I used to be a morning person.* Rubbing the sleep from his eyes, he pressed the receiver to his ear and mumbled, "Hello?"

Jaime, his personal assistant, replied, *"Sorry to wake you, Mister Collier. Please hold for the secretary of state."*

There was a click on the line, followed by a man's voice. *"Mister Collier, this is Secretary Greisman."* His voice sounded distant and was backed by the weak echo of someone conversing via speakerphone. *"I don't have time to play games with you, sir, so I'll come right to the point: Did you and your people cause this disaster?"*

At the risk of sounding like an idiot or like someone mouthing a pathetic denial, Collier asked with genuine, sincere confusion, "What disaster, Mister Secretary?"

*"Are you serious? Turn on your goddamn television."*

Jordan groaned softly as he sat up and reached for the remote control to his bedroom's wall-mounted flat-screen TV. "What channel?"

*"All of them,"* Greisman said. *"Make it fast."*

He aimed the remote at the TV and thumbed the power-on button. As the screen cycled up from its standby state, there was a knock on his bedroom door. He pressed the mute on his phone and said in a hoarse morning voice, "Come in."

The door opened. Jaime stepped in holding its knob, and Kyle walked past her and stopped at the foot of the bed, just out of Jordan's line of sight to the television.

An image of widespread destruction faded up on the screen. Behind the news ticker headline MASSIVE EARTHQUAKE DEVASTATES SOUTHERN CALIFORNIA was a shattered metropolis, its skyscrapers reduced to smears of debris on the ground and replaced by countless towers of smoke rising from the rubble and mushrooming into the sky. "Good God," Jordan muttered as he unmuted the phone.

*"It was a magnitude nine-point-four quake,"* Greisman said, obviously intuiting what Jordan was seeing on the news. *"It hit about thirty minutes ago. Leveled Frisco, L.A., and San Diego."*

Flipping to another channel, Jordan's eyes went wide at the sight of the collapsed Golden Gate Bridge. All that remained of the iconic structure were its two colossal red arches; the span between them was all but gone, broken and vanished into the bay.

*"There are tsunamis heading for Chile, Hawaii, and Japan,"* Greisman continued. *"We haven't even started calculating the death toll in California, so there's no telling what those waves'll do. But the projections aren't good."*

"We'll take care of the tsunami before it makes landfall," Jordan said. He covered the mouthpiece and told Kyle, "Wake up Raj." Resuming his conversation with the secretary, he said, "If there's anything we can do to help with rescue and recovery—"

Greisman let out a short, bitter chortle. *"Like you 'helped' in Seattle? No, thanks."* Hardening his tone, he went on, *"I'll ask you again, Collier: Did your people do this?"*

Turning his baleful stare toward Kyle, Jordan told the secretary, "No, sir. I did not order such an attack, I did not sanction it, and my people did not cause it." Kyle returned Jordan's gaze with his own unyielding glare, betraying nothing. Finishing his thought, Jordan added, "As horrible a tragedy as this is, I'm afraid it's an act of God."

*"For your sake, it'd better be. Good-bye, Mister Collier."* A sharp click led to silence as the secretary hung up.

Jordan returned the phone to its cradle at his bedside. Then he picked it back up and pressed a button to call his assistant's internal line. She picked up on the first ring.

*"Yes, sir?"*

"Jaime, wake up Hal and Lucas. I need them to help Raj neutralize the tsunami caused by the California earthquake."

Jaime acknowledged his instructions, then hung up to carry them out. Setting the phone down once again, Jordan sighed and threw a weary look in Kyle's direction. "I didn't just lie to the secretary of state, did I, Kyle?"

"I don't know," Kyle replied. "Did you?"

"Don't play dumb with me. Did we or didn't we have anything to do with causing this morning's earthquake in California?" Sensing the young man's reluctance to answer, Jordan pressed him. "Kyle, we're standing on the brink of war, and this could be what pushes us over the edge. I need to know: Did we do this? Have you and Cassie pushed us into a war?"

Kyle turned away from Jordan, but his face was still visible in the mirror above Jordan's dresser. The youth seemed to be struggling for an answer, but Jordan suspected that Kyle was getting his talking points from Cassie.

At first a guilty pall washed over Kyle's features. Within seconds it was pushed aside by a mask of fear. Then his mien turned blank; his eyes went dead and his expression took on the slack neutrality of a sociopath. He turned back to face Jordan.

"It's impossible to say for certain," Kyle declared. "There are a lot of rogue p-positives out there. A lot of them have grudges against the government. It would only take one going off the reservation to cause something like this."

It was an artless evasion, in Jordan's opinion. Kyle was good at many things, but lying persuasively was not one of them.

"That's not what I asked, Kyle, and you know it. But

since you seem committed to misinterpreting me, allow me to rephrase my question: Did you—or did Cassie, acting through you—plan, order, or sanction, personally or through a proxy, the initiation or exacerbation of this morning's earthquake by any promicin-positive group or individual?"

The ghost of a smirk haunted Kyle's face. "Good question," he said, walking toward the open bedroom door. As he left, he said over his shoulder, "I'll look into it and get back to you."

Kyle closed the door behind him. It shut with a heavy, wooden thud. Jordan stood and stared dumbly at it, unsure what troubled him more: the fact that Kyle was obviously lying to him, or that the youth and his dark muse had just given the United States the perfect excuse to declare war on Promise City.

# TWENTY-TWO

## 8:05 A.M.

TOM HAD JUST settled in at his desk across from Diana when a muffled roar of frustration from outside their office called them back to their feet. They nearly collided in the doorway as they gazed past the NTAC bullpen, where a dozen agents were prairie-dogging over the walls of their cubicles, all of them looking at the source of the commotion: the director's office.

Meghan Doyle was going berserk.

She slammed the handset of her phone up and down against its base on her desk. With one yank she tore the phone's cord from its floor jack, picked up the whole unit, and let out a scream of rage as she hurled it at the wall. The phone shattered into a storm of plastic debris, loose wires, and orphaned computer chips that scattered across her office's floor. Then Meghan slumped back into her chair, planted her elbows on her desk, and buried her face in her hands.

All the agents in the bullpen stared for several seconds at their silently exasperated director. Then, like a flock of birds turning in unison, they swiveled their heads toward Tom, who recoiled slightly from their unspoken collective plea.

He looked at Diana. She was staring at him, too.

Holding out his upturned palms in desperate supplication, he implored his partner, "Oh, c'mon. Why me?"

"She's *your* girlfriend," Diana said, arching her eyebrows.

*Goddammit, I really hate it when she's right,* Tom fumed.

He felt the weight of the room's attention as he emerged from his office, crossed the bullpen with his hands tucked sheepishly into his pants pockets, and ambled toward the door of Meghan's office. J.R. lifted his coffee mug as a salute to Tom as he passed by his desk. On the other side of the bullpen, J.B. used tactical hand signals to sarcastically warn Tom, *Keep your eyes open and your head down.*

As Tom drew closer to his destination, he wondered why things like this always seemed to happen before he got a chance to drink his first cup of coffee. *One cup of java before the world falls apart,* he brooded. *Is that really so much to ask?*

When he reached Meghan's office, he looked back at Diana for encouragement. She motioned him forward with a backhanded flicking gesture that made her look as if she were shooing a fly. He grimaced, lifted his hand, and with the knuckle of his middle finger knocked so softly that he barely felt his hand make contact. Then he listened with his ear to the door.

"What?" Meghan demanded from behind the closed portal.

Figuring that was as close to an invitation as he was likely to receive under the circumstances, Tom opened the door and slipped inside. Easing the door shut behind him with one hand, he reached with the other for the rod that adjusted the angle of the Venetian blinds on her office's window-wall, which faced the bullpen. He turned it to fold the slats of the blinds closed for privacy. "Rough morning?" he asked.

Her face was still in her hands. "What gave you that idea?"

"Nothing in particular," he said, hoping to ease into the conversation with some mild ironic humor. "Just a feeling."

She sat up, reclined her chair, and stared at the ceiling. "I just got off the phone with the secretary of Homeland Security," she said. "It was a short conversation. He did most of the talking." She sighed. "The good news is that I'm being transferred to a warmer climate—the Atlanta office."

Swallowing to suppress his rising sensation of dread, Tom asked, "And the bad news is . . . ?"

"I'm being demoted," Meghan said, flashing a thin smile taut with rage. "He's making me a field agent, despite the fact that I have no law enforcement experience or tactical training." She shook her head. "I get the impression this is payback for his being strong-armed into giving me this job in the first place."

Bits of broken plastic crunched under Tom's shoes as he

circled around the desk to be closer to Meghan. He sat on the edge of her desk and took her left hand in both of his. "Did he even give you a reason why?"

"Oh, yeah, he gave me a reason, all right," she said, rolling her eyes in disgust. "He said someone filed a complaint about the fact that I've been sleeping with you. 'Inappropriate fraternization with a subordinate,' he called it. Like I'm single-handedly corrupting the integrity of the republic."

Tom clenched his jaw to keep from spouting profanities. "Dammit, Meghan, I'm sorry. I never meant for—"

"Stop," she cut in. "You have nothing to be sorry for." She huffed with contempt. "They're just using the dating thing as an excuse. I know what this is *really* about: they blame me for losing Seattle to Collier, and they think the earthquake in California is the direct result of that. Face it: I'm a scapegoat." She shut her eyes and bared her teeth in furious denial. "I can't believe I have to move to Georgia."

"You could resign," Tom said.

That almost made her laugh. "Yeah, right. That's exactly what that sonofabitch in D.C. wants me to do. Forget it."

"All right, then," Tom said. "I'll request a transfer to Atlanta and go with you."

She went quiet for a moment, telegraphing more bad news. "Actually," she said, "you're being transferred to Milwaukee."

He waited for a punch line that never came.

"Hang on," he said. "They're sending me to *Wisconsin*?"

"Yup."

"But . . ." he began, then his voice trailed off. "Wait a minute! If you're in Atlanta and I'm in Milwaukee, who's gonna be in charge here?"

"No one," Meghan said wearily. She looked into his eyes. "They're shutting us down."

Standing beside Meghan's desk with his fists clenched white-knuckle tight, Tom suddenly wished that Meghan had another phone—so that he could throw it against the wall.

Diana thought she had heard her partner wrong. "Shut down? What the hell are they thinking?" Glancing around the Theory Room at Marco and the two Jeds, she asked, "What does that mean for us?"

"It means pack our desks and get ready to bug out," Tom said to the group, which stood in a small circle near the projection screen. "Meghan's upstairs breaking the news to the rest of the unit. DHS just gave us a priority-one evac order. They want us all on a transport out of Boeing Field in less than an hour. She and I already have our new assignments. The rest of you will get your orders when we touch down in D.C."

Anxious looks were volleyed from agent to agent. "Easy for them to say," Marco replied. "It's not like I came to work this morning with a bag packed."

J.B. added, "I don't even have my passport."

"Or my toothbrush," J.R. quipped.

"Too bad," Tom said. "Cars, property, pets, and anything else you can't carry on the plane stays here. Only immediate family will be allowed on the evac flight."

J.R. looked at his twin and said, "Fine by me. I never liked cousin Ted, anyway." J.B. nodded in agreement.

"Guys," Diana snapped at the Jeds, "this isn't funny." Reining in her temper, she asked Tom, "What about Maia? She's holed up in Collier's headquarters."

Frowning with regret, Tom said, "If she isn't on the plane with you at nine A.M., she gets left behind."

"Well that's just great," Diana said, seething with anger. "How am I supposed to convince her to leave Promise City when she won't even talk to me?"

"Tell her the truth," Marco said. "If Homeland Security's rushing us outta here, it probably means the military's about to make a major attack on the city."

"Do *not* tell Maia that," Tom interjected. "If it's true, tipping off Collier's people would be treason. And if it's not, we might incite a panic that could get people killed."

"I don't give a damn about that," Diana said. Unable to remain still, she stepped away from the circle and began pacing in front of the blank screen. "But you're right not to tell Maia what's coming. It'll only make her dig in deeper with Collier."

"Maybe you could trick her," Tom said. "Tell her whatever she wants to hear."

"Right," J.B. chimed in. "The key is to get her outta that building. Say you're ready to give her everything she wants, if she'll just come meet you to talk over breakfast."

Rolling her eyes, Diana replied, "Maia won't fall for that. She knows I'd never give up that easily."

Marco folded his arms. "Whatever we're gonna do, we

better do it fast. The buses leave here in twenty minutes, and our plane goes wheels-up in forty."

Rubbing his chin pensively, J.B. said, "We could play it head-on. Walk in the front door of Collier's headquarters, find Maia, and walk her back out."

J.R. added, "Risky move, but it might have the element of surprise on its side."

"Don't even think about it," Tom said. "Jordan's people won't let you get within a hundred feet of that building. He's got sentries who can melt your brain, paralyze you on sight, or make you walk away and think it was your idea."

Undaunted, J.R. looked at Marco and asked, "What about your teleporting ability? You could pop in, grab Maia, and pop back out before his people know you're there."

Shaking his head, Marco replied, "First, I can't jump in blind. I'd need a photo reference or a video image of my destination. Second, I haven't had much luck bringing other people with me when I teleport. So far the biggest passenger I've been able to move has been my cat. Plus, Collier's been installing all kinds of exotic defenses in that building for months. Trying to 'pop in' might get me killed."

"There's always the roof," J.B. said.

"What about it?" asked Marco.

"Well, we've got tons of photo references on that. You could jump to there, blow the lock on the access door with a C-4 charge, and enter through the main stairwell."

Tom narrowed his eyes in cynical disapproval. "J.B., think for a second. Collier lives on the top floor of that building. Do you really think he hasn't secured the roof access? Besides, we don't even know which floor Maia's on. If we go in there guns blazing, on some kind of commando mission to take Maia by force, we're gonna get our asses handed to us." Adopting an apologetic tone, he said to Diana, "If you think you can talk her out of there, you should do it now."

"She won't leave," Diana said, imagining how Maia would react to the coming crisis. "Not like this."

"Then we'd better get ready to go," Tom said.

"I'm not leaving," Diana replied. "If Maia stays, so do I."

Concern hardened Tom's countenance. "The evacuation's not optional, Diana. We're under orders. All NTAC personnel have to be on that plane."

"Then I'll resign," Diana said, proudly defiant.

Marco and the Jeds traded worried looks. J.B. said to Diana, "You don't really think it'll be *that* easy, do you?"

"He's right," Marco said. "The law says that in times of national emergency, we're all in for the duration. We can't just quit." With a crooked smile he added, "On the bright side, at least it means we have job security."

Diana looked to Tom for some sliver of hope. "Meghan won't enforce that, will she?"

"It's not up to her," Tom said with a shrug. "Meghan just got demoted, remember? She doesn't have the authority to let you stay even if she wants to. The tactical unit's in charge of the evacuation, and Major Falkner has his orders directly from the secretary. One way or another, Falkner *will* put you on that plane—as a prisoner if he has to."

"Fine," Diana said, already formulating a plan. "Since there's no way we can avoid getting on the plane, we'll just have to think of a way off."

# TWENTY-THREE

## 8:55 A.M.

MEGHAN DOYLE STOOD beside an open door that led out of the King County International Airport terminal to the tarmac, where a 737NG passenger jet was warming up for takeoff. A line of NTAC agents filed past her, empty-handed as they marched to their forced evacuation from Seattle, escorted by tactical personnel garbed in black uniforms and loaded with gear and weapons.

A balmy breeze tainted with the odor of jet fuel mussed her blond hair. The whine of the jet's turbines pitched upward and grew louder. She squinted against the early-morning sunlight reflecting off the plane's tail, then looked away and checked her watch. In less than five minutes, the transport would taxi away from the terminal, escorted by a pair of F-14 fighters from the adjacent Washington Air National Guard base.

She had been keeping a mental tally of who had passed her and who had yet to board the plane. Searching the art deco interior of the terminal, she spotted one of her two AWOL agents. Tom was standing next to the door of the men's room, checking his own watch. As the end of the line of agents walked past her, she called out to him, "Tom! Let's go!"

"I'm waiting for Marco," he yelled back. Pushing open the door, he shouted into the restroom, "C'mon, Marco! Pinch it off! Our ride's leaving!"

"All right, all right," Marco hollered back, his voice echoing from inside the bathroom. He stepped out a moment later, paused to look back, raised his compact digital camera, and snapped a photo before following Tom to the boarding gate.

Ushering both men out ahead of her, Meghan asked Marco, "Do you always photograph bathrooms after you use them?"

"I'm photographing everything," he said, snapping another shot of the terminal over his shoulder as they climbed the steps to the plane. At the top of the stairs, he looked back and added wistfully, "All of this might be gone tomorrow."

"Well, we need to be gone in sixty seconds, so get in the plane," Meghan said, nudging him inside. She followed him in and said to the flight attendant, "We're all aboard. Close it up."

The young military officer nodded and sealed the hatch, which closed with a leaden *thunk*. All at once, the shriek of engines fell away to a dull drone that reverberated through the aircraft's aluminum hull and was partly muffled by the white noise of the ventilation system, which recirculated overprocessed air inside the passenger cabin.

Meghan followed Tom and Marco aft to their seats, which were in the last row of the business class section. There was no barrier between business class and coach; the only difference between them was that the seats in business class were wider and had more forward legroom than those of coach.

As Meghan fumbled to find and connect the two halves of her seat belt, a man's southern-accented voice drawled over the cabin's PA speaker, *"Mornin', folks. This is Captain Dan Harper, and I'll be your pilot today. At this time, I need to ask y'all to buckle up and set your seats to their upright positions as we wait for our turn on the runway. We'll be servin' breakfast once we reach cruisin' altitude, so just sit tight, and enjoy the ride. Flight crew, prepare for takeoff."*

Everyone settled in except for Marco, whose face contorted with what looked like the first sign of nausea. He got up from his seat and moved aft, toward the lavatory, where he talked his way past a flight attendant who tried to intercept him.

Leaning across the aisle, Diana asked Tom in a confidential hush, "What's wrong with Marco?"

"Dunno," Tom said with a shrug and a shake of his head. "He's been feeling queasy ever since we left NTAC."

Diana frowned, then unfastened her seat belt and stood up. "I'd better go check on him," she said, heading aft.

Meghan watched Diana make her way to the back of the aircraft. Diana knocked on the lavatory door, then stepped clear as it opened, blocking her from view.

Perplexed, Meghan shot Tom a questioning look.

"They used to date," he said.

She nodded as if that explained everything, but something still seemed off-kilter. To pass the time, she looked out the window at the distant peak of Mount Rainier, or at the lines slowly passing under the wing of the plane as they taxied to the end of the runway, or at her own faint reflection on the window.

Then Tom unfastened his seat belt and got up. "I'm gonna go see what's taking them so long," he said. "Be right back." Before Meghan could tell him to stay put, he was hurrying aft. She leaned across his seat and looked back in time to see him knock on the lavatory door and, like Diana, step back to let it open. The door remained open for several seconds.

Her curiosity was turning to suspicion. She muttered, "What the hell is going on?"

The two Jeds poked their heads up over their seat backs from the row ahead of her. J.B. smiled and said, "Maybe they're trying to join the Mile-High Club."

"You have to be in the air before you can do that," Meghan said. "And I doubt that's what they're doing."

J.R. asked, "Want us to go round 'em up?"

"Would you mind?"

"Not at all," J.R. said. The two Jeds undid their safety belts, got up, and marched aft.

A minute later, none of the agents who had gone aft had come back. Meghan decided it was time to see for herself what the hell was going on back there. She liberated herself from her own seat belt and quick-stepped down the aisle to the lavatory, where J.R. stood holding the door open.

Meghan asked, "What's going on, Garrity?"

"Nothing," he said with a poker face. "Everything's fine."

"Let go of the door and step back," she said. "Right now, Agent. That's an *order*."

Reluctantly, he let go of the door and backed up against the aft bulkhead. Meghan closed the door and stepped past it, then pulled it back open to see what the hell was going on inside the closet-sized lavatory.

As she feared, it was empty.

"Is he breathing?" Tom asked.

"Barely," Diana said, holding the wrist of the unconscious Marco. The dark-haired young analyst sat slumped in the backseat of the fugitive agents' commandeered car, which was hurtling north on I-5 at breakneck speed. "His pulse is weak."

J.B. was at the wheel, weaving through traffic as if their car were thread and the highway a needle. He threw a nervous look over his shoulder at Marco, then asked Tom, "How messed up is he? Should I head for the VA hospital? It's the closest."

Tom volleyed the question to Diana. "Your call."

"I don't know," she said. "I'm not a doctor."

She was still amazed that Marco had been able to teleport off the plane and back into the terminal's men's room with her along for the ride. They had blinked from one place to the next without any visible sense of transition.

For Diana, it had been almost magical. But judging from the pallid hue of Marco's face, she realized it must have been far more arduous for him.

To manage such a feat even once would have represented a major step forward in the maturation of his promicin ability; the fact that he had then used a digital photo taken inside the aircraft's lavatory to teleport back to the plane, which had still been visible taxiing down the runway, and then repeated the round-trip journey twice more—first to smuggle Tom back to the terminal and then, on his last trip, J.B.—had been nothing short of miraculous.

But then, before he could make one last jaunt to extricate J.R. from the plane, Marco had collapsed to the floor, where he'd lain racked with spasms for several seconds before losing consciousness. Out of time, and with no way back to the plane, they'd stuck to their plan, which had called for getting out of the terminal as quickly as possible. J.B. had gone to the parking lot, commandeered a car, and pulled around to the side entrance, where he'd picked up Diana and Tom, who had carried Marco.

What would happen next was anyone's guess, unfortunately.

Trusting her instincts, Diana said, "I think he's just exhausted, not dying. Let's stay clear of the hospitals."

"Okay," Tom said. "Keep an eye on him though. If anything changes before we get back to the office, we can divert to Harborview or First Hill."

"Copy that," J.B. said, swerving through another cluster of vehicles traveling at less than a hundred miles per hour. "So we're definitely heading back to NTAC?"

"Unless you can think of someplace else to make our stand," Tom said. No one had any better suggestions.

The skyscrapers of downtown gleamed in the morning sun and loomed closer as the car continued heading north. After a few minutes, Diana was relieved to feel an increase in the strength and tempo of Marco's pulse. His breathing returned to normal, and then his eyes fluttered weakly open.

Lolling his head to one side to take in his surroundings, Marco mumbled, "Guess we made it."

"So far," Diana said, favoring him with a grateful smile. "But we'd be nowhere without you. That was really something."

He grinned. "Just a little trick I've been working on."

Looking over his shoulder, Tom asked, "How do you feel?"

"I've been better," Marco said, wincing as he sat up. "Which one of you used my head for batting practice?"

J.B. smiled at Marco in the rearview mirror. "We were afraid you might've busted something."

"Nothing a year in the tropics won't fix," Marco said, before mustering a weak smile. "But I'd settle for some aspirin, an ice pack, and a nap."

Leaning forward and searching the skies for who-knew-what, Tom replied, "Your nap might have to wait. Something is definitely going on."

Looking out the windows, Diana said, "What're you talking about? I don't see anything."

"Exactly," Tom said. "When was the last time you saw the sky this empty above Seattle? Where's the usual air traffic? I mean, we should at least be seeing high-altitude flyovers."

Marco pressed the side of his face against one of the car's rear windows and stared at the slivers of blue between the high-rises that lined the interstate. "You think they're clearing the airspace," he said. "Preparing the battlefield."

Tom's expression turned grim. "I think we need to get to cover, on the double."

Facing a wall of television screens in the Collier Foundation's executive conference room, Jordan saw the moment taking shape in all of its terrible glory.

All around him, his advisors and assistants chattered frantically as new intelligence came in. The air in the room was heavy with the funk of unwashed bodies and morning halitosis.

In the two and a half hours since the secretary of state had woken him up, Jordan had not had time to eat or even bathe. He'd barely had time to scramble into a suit without a tie and summon his inner circle. Now that they were gathered, Jordan felt like the ringleader of a circus run amok.

"We have reports of soldiers entering Magnolia Bluff from the Fort Lawton Reserve," Gary Navarro said, from Jordan's left.

From his right, Kyle added, "Tanks are crossing the Evergreen Point and Lake Washington bridges."

"It could be more posturing," interjected Lucas, the gestalt telepath, who was standing by with several of his most frequent psychic collaborators. "Another empty show of force."

"Not likely," said Jordan's assistant, Jaime, who shouldered her way into the trio of men. "All NTAC personnel just left Seattle on a government jet from Boeing Field."

The room went quiet as Jordan digested this latest news. He looked at the faces that surrounded him: at Gary and Kyle, at Jaime and Maia, at Hal and Renata and dozens of others. "I don't need a shaman or the power of precognition to predict what's about to happen," he said, addressing the room. "Tell everyone this is it: the battle for Promise City has begun."

# TWENTY-FOUR

Tom stood beside Diana and watched her enter her security code into the keypad next to the front door. Drop-down titanium bars blocked the door, which itself was made of double-thick steel.

"Nice to see they remembered to lock up on their way out," Tom joked. His three companions responded with unamused frowns.

Diana tapped in the last digit of her code and pressed ENTER on the pad. With a barely audible hum and vibration, the bars lowered and withdrew into the command center's foundation of reinforced concrete.

J.B., who had been waiting with his keycard in hand, stepped forward and unlocked the door, then pulled it open for the rest of the team. Tom entered first, followed by Diana, Marco, and then J.B., who relocked the door behind him.

It felt strange to Tom to see the security checkpoints

unmanned, the metal detectors and chemical-sniffing arches offline, and the overhead lights switched off. The only lighting was residual illumination. Most of it came from a row of juice and soda machines; the rest was the product of permanently lit exit signs set at regular intervals along the ceiling.

The four agents raced out of the lobby and sprinted through the corridors to the crisis center. Their running footsteps resounded in the empty hallways. The echoes were so sharp and loud that it made Tom self-conscious, despite the fact that there was no one else in the building to hear them.

Like the rest of the facility, the crisis center was dark. Almost as if by instinct, Tom started issuing orders. "Marco," he said. "Get us data feeds from the outside, on the double. I'll help Diana boot up the command system. J.B., get to the armory and scare us up some Kevlar and some firepower, in case somebody tries to take a shot at us."

Marco and J.B. hurried away in different directions, leaving Tom and Diana to go from one station to another, bringing the crisis center online one terminal at a time.

Keying her log-on credentials into the system, Diana said with unconcealed anxiety, "If Meghan's reported us as AWOL to the people in D.C.—"

"I know," Tom said, not needing to be reminded that their access privileges to the nation's unified security database, as well as to most of NTAC's local intelligence-gathering sources, could be terminated remotely by their superiors at the Pentagon. "Let's just hope Marco has a way to keep us in the game." He heard Diana tapping keys. Then followed silence.

She stood at a terminal, hands pressed together in front of her face as if she were praying.

"Anything?" Tom asked, watching the screen in front of him spin a circle while chewing on the codes he'd entered.

"Still processing," she said from behind her hands. All at once she relaxed and dropped her hands. "We're in! Our passwords are still active."

Half a second later, the terminal in front of Tom became active, scrolling with priority alerts from the Pentagon. "Okay," he said. "Let's finish booting up."

They moved from one station to the next, entering their codes. Within minutes they were surrounded by more incoming data than they could possibly monitor at once with only four agents. As they powered up the last two adjacent workstations, Diana wondered aloud, "What are we supposed to do once we get everything working? Make popcorn and watch the city burn?"

"That depends," Tom said. "Is there any popcorn left in the kitchen?" Rebuked by Diana's scathing glare, he showed her his palms and continued: "Look, the whole reason for coming back was to save Maia. And to be honest, right now, I have no idea how to do that. But this is the safest base of operations we have. All we can do now is watch and wait. And I promise you, come hell or high water, we are *not* leaving the city without her."

"Ditto that," added J.B., who lumbered back into the center with an armload of full-torso bulletproof vests, two assault rifles strapped diagonally across his back, and two more rifles slung at his sides. "Your little girl's comin' home, Skouris."

"Damn straight," Marco said as he returned. He settled in at one of the supervisors' terminals and began typing furiously. "Give me ten minutes and I should be able to keep them from locking us out. At the very least, I'll be able to set up a back door so we can stay connected to the database."

"Good work," Tom said. "I'll start pulling up the latest orders from SECDEF, see what's going on out there."

J.B. handed a rifle and a vest to Tom, then delivered matching gear to Diana and Marco. Walking past Tom, he stopped and said, "I need to make a few more trips. We need spare clips for the rifles, plus a Glock and some reloads for Marco."

"Thanks, J.B.," Tom said, giving his fellow agent a reassuring slap on the shoulder.

"There's just one of me here, Tom. You can call me 'Jed' again."

Tom nodded. "You got it."

As Marco typed, Jed started walking, and Tom focused on the scads of raw data flooding into NTAC, Diana cleared her throat in a dramatic manner that was clearly meant to draw their attention. "Guys . . . ," she said.

All three men halted and looked at Diana. She stood, arms folded, looking a little misty-eyed. "There's something I meant to say earlier, but I . . . the moment never seemed . . ." She paused for a moment, then tried again. "I just want to say . . . thank you. First for helping me get off the jet, and even more for coming with me. Once you got me off the plane, you could have left me to do this on my own. Instead, you're all standing with me in the middle of a war zone." She brushed a single tear from her cheek and shook her head. "Maia's my daughter, I have to be here. But you guys—"

"I have to be here, too," Tom said. "And not just 'cause of my son. Because I'm your partner."

Marco told her with a crooked, bittersweet smile, "If you're here, I'm here."

"NTAC tellin' you to leave your kid? That wasn't right," Jed said. "The moment they did that, I was all-in for you. Whatever happens, I've got your back—and Maia's."

Diana grinned with what Tom took to be embarrassed joy, then sleeved fresh tears from her face. "Thanks, guys," she said, forcing herself back into a semblance of composure. She lifted her Kevlar vest over her head, lowered it into place, and fastened its Velcro straps around her ribs.

"Now let's get ready to kick some ass," she said.

# TWENTY-FIVE

## 10:14 A.M.

No matter how far back Jordan stood from the details of the battle unfolding all around him, he felt as if he couldn't see the bigger picture. Too many pieces were moving too quickly. For the first time since his return from the future, he wondered if he'd taken on more than he could master.

"Hal, Lucas, Renata," he said to the core members of his telepathic gestalt, "we need an update on incoming aircraft."

"Three combat wings spotted so far," said Hal, the legally blind remote-viewer. "A dozen A-10 bombers inbound low and slow over Puget Sound. Ten F-22s on high-altitude approach from the northeast. From the southeast, sixteen Black Hawk helicopters loaded with troops. Plus, two AWACS support aircraft."

Turning his attention to a bank of video monitors, Jordan noted the lines of tanks advancing over the bridges leading into Promise City from the east. He knew that a hard decision was at hand. "Gary? What's going on down there?"

The athletic young telepath shook his head and frowned. "We're taking casualties and losing ground," he said.

Kyle stepped forward, invading Jordan's personal space. "We're losing ground because our hands are tied," he said, his voice sharp with anger. "You've got our people using nonlethal, passive defenses. The Army has snipers picking our people off from a distance. If we don't start fighting back—"

"Destroy the bridges," Jordan said, cutting off Kyle's rant. "Pull our people back to cover, then have Dieter and Stefka knock those tanks into the river."

"Done," Kyle said, stepping away to relay the order.

Even though the ventilation system inside the conference room was pumping out cool, conditioned air at full blast, Jordan's face felt warm. He palmed a sheen of perspiration from his brow, then took a deep breath.

Emil, one of Jordan's personal bodyguards, nodded while listening to someone over a phone, then looked up and reported, "The enhanced beacons are holding. There are roughly three hundred Marines stuck west of Thirty-sixth Avenue and north of West Emerson Street."

"What about the north-side bridges?" Jordan asked.

"No contacts at Ballard, Aurora, or Fremont," Emil replied.

Gary grumbled with naked sarcasm, "Well, that's a relief. I guess we've got nothing left to worry about—except for naval bombardment, biological warfare, and a possible nuclear attack."

"Speak o' the devil," Hal said. "I see multiple warships at the far western end of Puget Sound gearing up their missile batteries. I think there's a whole lotta metal comin' our way."

"All right," Jordan said, doing his best to project calm and confidence to the room full of people looking to him for leadership. "We've prepared for this. Alert everyone on the air-defense team to stand ready."

Telepathic senders and assistants with cell phones issued warnings to a legion of sentries posted on rooftops and in hidden positions throughout Promise City. Many of the sentries were electrokineticists, with talents ranging from force fields to signal scrambling to magnetic disruption.

Jordan hoped that with the help of other gestalt telepaths and the guidance of various clairvoyants, the electrokinetic guardians of Promise City would be strong enough and quick enough to deflect any missile attack, but he remembered a frequent bit of advice from his currently self-exiled friend Richard Tyler: *Hope for the best, but plan for the worst.*

He sighed and regretted not having the benefit of Richard's military experience at such a crucial moment for the Movement. To his chagrin, he knew that he had no one to blame for Richard's absence but himself. To stop the Marked, Jordan had pressured Richard into becoming something that he wasn't: an assassin. It hadn't taken long for Richard to sour on the assignment—and, by extension, on his association with Jordan.

But that was the past. Jordan had to focus on the present. *Maybe I should order a preemptive strike against the guided-missile cruisers,* he thought. *Not to destroy them, but to disarm them. It might be easier than intercepting missiles in flight . . .* He was about to give the order when he heard Maia gasp.

"Stop!" she screamed, cutting through the heavy chatter in the conference room. "It's all a decoy!"

Motioning for everyone else to stay quiet, Jordan asked Maia, "What's a decoy, Maia?"

"All of it!" she cried. "The ships, the planes, the soldiers. That's not the attack!" She pointed at the ceiling. "The real attack's coming from up there!"

Everyone looked up except Kyle, who turned away, apparently listening intently to his invisible oracle. Then he, too, turned his gaze upward, revealing the look of terror on his face. "A satellite!" he shouted. "Cassie says it's a strike from orbit, and we're the target!"

"Evacuate the building!" Jordan bellowed. "Hal, Lucas, Renata! I need you with me." He turned to Gary. "Go with Kyle, and get Maia to safety."

Gary nodded and followed Kyle to the door, where he waited for Maia to catch up to him. Then he took her hand and led her out into the corridor packed with people running for the stairs.

Jordan faced his trio of gestalt specialists. "Is there any chance you three could stop the satellite?" he asked.

"If you can point me at it," Renata said, "I can try to fry it before it shoots."

"Finding it'll be the trick," Hal said, adjusting his opaque black glasses.

Gripping their shoulders, Jordan said, "Try. Quickly."

Lucas reached out and joined hands with Hal and Renata. All three of them bowed their heads and concentrated.

"I'm looking for it," Hal said, his frustration evident. "But I don't know where to start. Space is so vast . . . so *empty*."

"Keep trying," Jordan urged him.

Shaking his head, Hal replied, "I'm sorry, it all looks the same. I have no point of reference, no place to start from."

Kyle leaned back in through the conference room door and barked at Jordan, "Ninety seconds!"

Even though Jordan harbored serious fears about Cassie's bloodthirsty tendencies, she had never been wrong before, and he wasn't going to test her now. "That's it," he said, pushing the gestalt trio ahead of him toward the door. "Run!"

### 10:22 A.M.

Captain Arthur Desmond, commanding officer of the nuclear aircraft carrier U.S.S. *Abraham Lincoln*, stood in the center of the warship's dim but bustling Combat Direction Center. The compartment was bathed in a deep blue glow that was pierced at regular intervals by the tactical monitors' brilliant displays, which ranged in hue from bright green to bloodred to amber.

Radio chatter filled the air. It was matched by the low buzz of personnel speaking softly into their headsets.

Desmond stood silently, awaiting final confirmation of the ship's orders. On a bulkhead packed with flat-screen video monitors, the center screen displayed a satellite

image of downtown Seattle, over which had been super-
imposed a computer-generated three-dimensional wire-
frame and targeting sight.

Commander Serena Hess, the ship's executive officer,
hovered above the communications officer. She nodded
once as the young ensign finished delivering his report,
then crossed the cramped compartment to Desmond's
side. "The tac officer confirms all units are in position,
and the firing solution is clear. U.S. Space Command has
verified the satellite is ready, and that we have control,"
she said.

"Thank you," Desmond said. From the console in front
of him, he picked up the handset of a phone that was on a
ready line to the Pentagon. "Admiral Kazansky?"

*"Go ahead, Captain,"* replied the chief of the Navy.

"The Air Force confirms ready on the HEL, sir. Holding for final confirmation of the order."

*"Stand by,"* Kazansky said. It took only a matter of
seconds for the admiral to relay the request to the White
House.

The next voice on the line was one Desmond had hoped
never to hear: *"Captain, this is the president. Fire the weapon."*

"Yes, Mister President. *Abraham Lincoln* out." Desmond hung up the phone, turned to his XO, and said,
"Do it."

Hess nodded to the tactical action officer, who spoke
to the weapons officer, who pressed a single button on
his console, releasing a ten-second burst from a high-
energy laser mounted on a classified satellite in orbit,
high above the planet.

One word spoken . . . one button pushed . . . one flash of light.

And a building vanished.

An executive express elevator delivered Jordan and his senior advisors to the ground floor of the Collier building less than thirty seconds after they had evacuated the conference room. As the tiny group sprinted out of the building and down the steps onto Cherry Street, the cloudless blue sky above boomed with thunder.

A sword of fire from the heavens lanced down, brighter than the sun, and hammered through the core of the sky-scraper behind them. Fire erupted from every window and filled the ground floor. The ground shook, and the concrete plaza that surrounded the building fractured. Parts of it heaved upward; others sank.

"Run!" Jordan ordered, leading his people across the street, through the open-air plaza of Seattle City Hall.

The sidewalks were choked with pedestrians and the streets were packed with cars whose drivers all stared upward, agape at the towering spectacle of destruction above them, too shocked to realize they ought to take cover, until it was too late do so. Burning debris fell amid a storm of shattered glass, some of it in huge plates and shards that impaled the trapped bystanders.

A deafening blast knocked Jordan and his entourage flat on the glass-dusted concrete and peppered them with shrapnel. Fighting with bloodied palms to push himself back to his feet, he heard behind him the first rumbling death throes of the doomed skyscraper, which began to implode from the top down.

"Go!" Jordan barked at his people, waving them past him.

Gary picked up Maia and carried the stunned teen with him as he continued running southeast across the plaza, amid hundreds of fleeing civilians, toward James Street. Emil led the sightless Hal, Lucas carried the wounded and bleeding Renata, and Kyle flanked Jordan.

The collapse of the Collier Foundation tower accelerated. As the building vanished into itself, a mountain of dark gray ash and smoke bloomed around it and rushed outward.

*We're not going to make it,* Jordan realized as he looked back and saw the black blizzard descend upon him.

Then something unseen held him fast, and he saw his friends pulled toward him by an invisible force. It took him a moment to process that it was the handiwork of his bodyguard Emil, who had used his telekinetic ability to pull everyone to himself.

The diminutive young man raised his arms and touched his fingers together high over his head, forming an inverted V.

As the crushing torrent of pulverized concrete, broken metal, shattered glass, and choking dust fell, it struck Emil's psychokinetic barrier high overhead and broke wide to the left and right of the plaza's James Street staircase, leaving Jordan and the others huddled on a narrow wedge of safe ground.

All that Jordan could smell was smoke and gasoline. Dust and superfine glass powder stung his eyes, and the whole world sounded muffled, as if it were underwater. His eyes cascaded with tears to cleanse themselves, then he blinked through the pain and looked back.

A smoldering mountain of gray rubble loomed above him. There was no sign of the skyscraper he had claimed as his headquarters just a few months earlier, nor of Seattle City Hall. Where moments earlier he had seen streets jammed with cars, he saw only heaps of jagged concrete and twisted steel.

Emil extended his hand to Jordan and helped him stand. Peering through the grimy haze, Jordan saw that Kyle, Gary, Maia, Hal, Lucas, and Renata were still with him. Like himself, they all were painted gray with dust and hacking and coughing.

Shaking Emil's hand, Jordan said, "Good work." Though the young man had not yet demonstrated the same kind of precision control over his psychokinesis that Richard Tyler had, Emil had just proved that he was certainly Richard's equal in raw power.

Jordan turned to the others. "Is everyone all right?"

Lucas, who was kneeling beside the bloodied and gasping Renata, looked up and answered in a voice shaken by grief, "No."

Gary, Kyle, and Maia gathered in front of Jordan.

"I'm not sensing many minds nearby," Gary said. "Aside from us, I'd say only a couple hundred people made it out alive."

Kyle's face was a portrait of rage. "There were thousands of people in there," he said. "And who knows how many more in City Hall, and on the street, and the other buildings?" He seized Jordan's arm. "We warned them not to attack us. Now it's time to make them pay. One word from you and we can wipe out any city you want: New York, D.C., Boston. Just name it."

Jordan pulled free of Kyle's grasp. "I have a better idea. Follow me." Walking toward Lucas, Hal, and Renata, he continued. "The U.S. military's greatest strength is its global information network. But a strength can become a dependency, and a dependency is a weakness." He kneeled and took Renata's hand. "Forgive me, but I need to ask you to do one last thing."

The dying woman replied through a mouth stained with blood and caked with dust, "Anything."

He looked at Kyle. "Can Cassie tell us what the control point was for the satellite that just hit us?"

"Um . . ." Kyle said, recoiling a little at being put on the spot. He frowned as he averted his eyes and half turned away from Jordan. Then his confidence returned, and he pivoted back to face the group. "An aircraft carrier on the Pacific coast, twenty-five nautical miles west of the Strait of Juan de Fuca."

"Tell her I said thank you," Jordan said. To his gestalt trio, he continued. "I want you three to find that carrier. Renata, the ship's computers might still have a link to the satellite that hit us, and through that, to America's entire network of military satellites. Do your best to tap into it."

She nodded. "I'll try."

Lucas, Hal, and Renata joined hands, bowed their heads, and closed their eyes. Jordan, Kyle, Gary, and Maia gathered around them as they communed.

"I see the ship," Hal said. His black glasses were broken, revealing his unseeing eyes looking in different directions. "I've found its captain. He's in its command center."

Renata coughed up a mouthful of blood, then said, "This is the place. I'm moving through its computers." She wheezed as she fought for breath, and her exhalations sounded wet. "They still have a link to the satellite."

"Is it the one that attacked us?" Jordan asked.

"Yes," she said, her voice fading. "I can still see the order in its activity log. The weapon is recharging."

Crouching beside her, Jordan whispered into her ear, "Is it connected to any other satellites?"

Renata's voice became faint and monotonal. "It's linked to something. I can follow it . . ." The color drained from her face. "It's the U.S. Space Command center at the Pentagon."

"This is what we talked about," Jordan said. "From here, you can knock out all the satellites at once." The woman began to slump, and Jordan saw her hands slipping from those of Hal and Lucas. He caught her in his arms and held her in place. "Renata, please hang on. We need you to do this. Just one time."

"Too many," she protested, as if she were sleep-talking. "Too big. I can't."

"We're here, Renata," Lucas said in a soothing timbre. "Hal and I can help you. Use our strength to clear your mind. Take what you need from us."

Inhaling slowly and deeply, Renata seemed to recover some of her focus, and she nodded once. "All right," she said. "One more time . . ." The intensity of her exertion put deep furrows in her brow. "I'm inside the command system . . . All the satellites are linked now . . . And I'm sending them priority self-destruct orders." She flashed an amused smile. "Bye-bye birdies."

"It's done," Hal said. "I can see all the satellites in orbit. Their cores are overloading and slagging their internal components." He nodded with grim satisfaction. "They're fried."

Lucas released Hal and Renata's hands. "I've ended the link," he said.

Jordan embraced Renata, whose life he could feel slipping away. "You did it," he said. "You've just crippled the greatest military in the world."

"That'll show 'em," she said through a bloodstained grin.

Then she let go of one last, quiet breath, and lay still in Jordan's arms. He gently laid her body on the ash-covered concrete steps, then stood and faced the others. "Find as many survivors as you can, and quickly," he said. "We don't have much time. We need to get to shelter before the soldiers come."

# TWENTY-SIX

## 10:25 A.M.

"Goddamn," Jed said. "It's a free-for-all out there."

Tom stared at the mayhem depicted on the various wall screens and computer monitors in NTAC's crisis center, and he had to admit that Jed was right. Seattle had become a madhouse. Rioters roamed the streets, destroying cars and setting fires. Looters smashed in store windows and pillaged private homes—whether or not their owners were there to offer resistance.

"How many of those lunatics do you think are p-positive?" asked Jed, arms crossed over his Kevlar-lined black tactical vest. "There are people in those crowds levitating things, disintegrating things, and doing God knows what else."

Marco adjusted his glasses, apparently considering the question. "Given the exodus of p-negatives after the fifty/fifty epidemic last year, I'd estimate up to three-quarters of our troublemakers are sporting some kind of superpower."

"No wonder Seattle PD's nowhere in sight," Tom said, imagining how nightmarish the current scenario must look from the perspective of a beat cop without promicin powers. He loosened a side strap on his tactical vest to scratch at an itch that was working its way across his ribs and lower back. "Even Jordan's 'peace officers' look like they're getting clobbered," he noted, watching what appeared to be an altercation between a psychokinetic officer and a rioter who could induce seizures with a simple touch.

Shaking his head, Jed remarked, "Is the fire department even trying to answer calls? I'm looking at three buildings going up in—"

He was cut off by a blinding flash of white light from a monitor showing a long-distance image of the downtown Seattle skyline. For a moment, Tom felt a twist of raw terror in his gut as he imagined it might be a nuclear warhead detonating. Then the aperture self-adjusted on whatever camera was providing the feed, and all four NTAC agents saw clearly the beam of energy slicing straight down from the sky into the Collier building.

Watching the tower shatter into fire and fragments, all that Tom could think about was Kyle. From the back of the room, he heard Diana whisper in abject horror, "Maia . . ."

The skyscraper imploded from the top down, sinking into itself even as its base erupted and buried several blocks of the city in rubble and a thick gray cloud. Watching the collapse, Tom relived all his worst memories of September 11, 2001. Despite his best efforts not to show his emotions, his eyes burned and misted with tears.

Jed staggered a bit and lowered himself into a chair, all the while unable to take his eyes off the screen. "Jesus," he mumbled, sounding like someone in shock.

Tom swallowed hard and bit back on his fear. He walked over to Marco and gripped the younger man's shoulder. "Can you get me a line out? Cell, landline, anything? I have to call Kyle, and Diana needs to reach Maia, now."

"I'll try," Marco said, tapping madly at a communications station keyboard. The monitor attached to it gave him nothing but flashing-red negative responses. "Nothing," he said. "The Army cut the landlines, and they're jamming all nonmilitary frequencies." He kicked the wall under his workstation. "We're completely cut off."

"That does it," Diana said. She drew her sidearm, removed and checked the clip, then reloaded the weapon, released the safety, and holstered it. "The cops are MIA, Jordan's peace officers are useless, and the military's part of the damn problem." She slung her assault rifle across her back in the same manner that Jed wore his and picked up her extra ammunition clips as she walked with a purpose toward the door.

Stepping into her path and holding out one hand, Tom said, "Whoa! You're not going out there."

"The hell I'm not," Diana said, her gaze fierce and unyielding. "I've had enough, Tom. If Maia's alive—if, by some miracle, whether it was made by God or by promicin, she got out of that building in one piece—I'm gonna find her, and I'm gonna get her out of the city once and for all."

"Diana," Tom said, trying to talk sense to her. "It's literally a *war zone* out there. We don't have any backup. For all we know, we've been classified as targets. And if Maia's alive, then she's surrounded by some of the most powerful people on the planet."

"That's easy for you to say," Diana replied. "Your son's a grown man. He can handle himself in a crisis. Maia's only thirteen years old, Tom! She's still a child, for God's sake."

"I know she's thirteen, but I'd hardly call her a child, Diana. You didn't see her in that meeting with Jordan. She handles herself better than some so-called adults I've known."

Looking not the least bit persuaded by his argument, Diana said, "You have three choices, Tom. You can come with me. You can stay here." She regarded him with an unblinking stare.

After several seconds of tense silence, he asked warily, "What's choice number three?"

She drew her pistol and aimed it at his face.

He backed up one full stride, then stepped out of her path and let her pass. She marched past him, girded for battle, and walked away without a backward glance.

Tom watched her go, then turned back toward Marco and Jed. "You know she's crazy, right?" The other two men nodded. "I mean, I'm not wrong about this, am I?" His friends shook their heads. "Tactically speaking, staying here is the safest choice." More nods from his comrades.

He looked toward the video screens and saw the spreading blot of ash, dust, and smoke blanketing downtown Seattle. The fleeing crowds of civilians, the raging fires, the mayhem in the streets, the Black Hawk helicopters entering the city's airspace unopposed by Jordan's people.

For a very long minute, he couldn't decide if the gnawing sensation in his gut was his sense of duty, a pang of guilt, or a brand-new peptic ulcer.

Then he drew his sidearm, checked the clip, reloaded it, and holstered his weapon. He stuffed two magazines for his rifle into pockets on his tactical vest, walked to the door, and looked back at Jed and Marco.

"You know I have to go with her, right?"

The two men nodded in understanding.

"Hold the fort," Tom said. "We'll be back."

### 10:56 A.M.

"Can anyone explain to me exactly why the hell our satellites even *have* self-destruct systems?"

Keith Bain, the secretary of defense, stared down the table at the Joint Chiefs and several high-ranking members of the U.S. intelligence community who were gathered in the Pentagon's situation room, and waited for an answer to his question. No one seemed in a hurry to speak up.

Then, in a gruff, matter-of-fact voice, General Wheeler of the Air Force said, "We use it to prevent reverse engineering. If an enemy captures one of our birds, we slag it."

"Has that ever been necessary?" Bain asked the lean and wiry man, who at fifty-one was the youngest of the chiefs.

Wheeler looked up with a tired, put-upon countenance. "Not yet, Mister Secretary."

Bain nodded. "That's quite confidence-inspiring, General. It would be even more impressive if our entire satellite network hadn't just been reduced to an orbital junkyard." Looking to the others, Bain said, "Someone spell this out for me: How bad a hit did we just take?"

Admiral Kazansky replied, "Those satellites were the basis of our Global Positioning System." All eyes turned to the trim, white-haired officer. "Without them, our ships, aircraft, and ground units will be forced to rely on less precise means of navigation. We also can't guarantee the accuracy of any guided-weapon systems, such as cruise missiles."

"We can compensate for that," added the heavy-jowled, gray-haired General Hirsch, chief of the Army. "Laser-guided munitions won't be affected."

"But they will be dependent on personnel deployed against forward positions," Kazansky said. "Which in turn limits our target-selection options and operational range."

The secretary of defense sipped his tepid black coffee and grimaced at its bitter aftertaste. "What about SIGINT?"

"The NSA's still up on anything that passes through a landline or a switching center," replied General Braddock, the square-jawed commandant of the U.S. Marine Corps. "But our ability to pick calls out of the air is offline. And whatever took down our birds also scrambled the Carnivore mainframes." He nodded across the table at deputy directors from the CIA and FBI. "Which leaves you boys shit out of luck, too."

A tall and gangly civilian with a silver crew cut and a

mustache like a wire brush interjected, "The NRO's also down, which means most of our global tracking of foreign ships, submarines, and aircraft is offline." Casting an almost apologetic glance at General Wheeler, he added, "And unless I'm mistaken, General, NORAD's lost its missile-warning system."

The room's collective focus landed on the Air Force chief, who shifted uncomfortably in his seat.

Secretary Bain fixed the man with a steely glare. "Is that true, General? Are we currently without an adequate defense against a possible nuclear missile attack?"

After a pause that only served to ratchet up the tension in the room, Wheeler said, "Yes, sir. For now, I'm afraid it is."

"Holy shit," Bain said, arching his eyebrows in disbelief. He massaged the fatigue from his forehead, then asked Kazansky, "Admiral, do we have a working landline to NS Everett?"

"Yes, Mister Secretary." He placed his hand on the phone receiver directly in front of them. "They're standing by on this line for new orders."

"Good," Bain said. "Tell them to pass the word to General Maddow: Operation Stormfront is authorized. Deploy all enhanced soldiers into Seattle immediately. We're taking back the city."

# TWENTY-SEVEN

## 11:08 A.M.

ALL THAT KYLE could taste was dust. He had followed Jordan and his small but growing band of survivors as they'd started their long walk away from the fallen Collier building, but the toppled skyscraper's cloud of ash was spreading faster than they were walking. Now the gray-brown haze lay over the city like a filthy shroud and filled Kyle's mouth with sticky grit.

Hacking and struggling for air, he almost hadn't heard Cassie calling his name. Squinting through the wind-driven dust, he saw her beckon him off the road. "Follow me," she said.

He left Jordan's group and staggered toward Cassie.

Her appearance was immaculate. *One of the advantages of existing only in my mind*, Kyle thought with a twinge of envy.

"This way," she said, pulling him through the earthen fog. He still didn't understand how it was possible for him to "feel" her when she wasn't really there, but some reading he had done in recent months—coupled with repeated viewings of *The Matrix*—had led him to think that it had something to do with his mind fooling itself into believing that she was real.

She led him to a soot-covered door that swung open as he put his weight against it. He stumbled into a small stairway enclosed on three sides by glass walls that had been rendered opaque by the ongoing deluge of pulverized human remains.

Looking up, he blinked his eyes clear and realized the staircase serviced a multistory parking garage. Voices echoed from somewhere high overhead, probably from other survivors using the garage for shelter.

He turned and glowered at Cassie, who leaned against the wall and regarded him with a smug expression. "Well, well," Kyle said. "If it isn't my very own personal demon."

"Oh, I'm sorry," Cassie replied with mock contrition. "You'd rather be coughing your guts out back in the street? Don't let me keep you. *Vaya con Dios.*"

"Fine," Kyle said, waving one hand at her while planting the other on his knee to support himself while he doubled over and coughed a few more times. "Thanks for the break." He spit a bad taste from his mouth, then stood up. "What do you want?"

Feigning indignation, Cassie replied, "Who says I want something?"

"When do you not?"

She prowled toward him with a salacious smile. "Maybe I just want to keep you safe," she said with a teasing lilt. "After all, I'd be nothing without you." Caressing his dirty face with her pale fingertips, she added, "And vice versa."

Kyle froze as Cassie's fingers traced the line of his jaw, traveled down his neck, and then slid down the front of his shirt. He knew from past experience that he found it all too easy to surrender to Cassie's charms. When she wanted to manipulate him, she had a knack for making herself irresistible. The gleam in her powder-blue eyes, the shine of light off her coppery red hair, and the seductive purr of her voice all worked together to make him her helpless puppet.

*Not this time,* he decided.

"Enough," he said, sidestepping her to free himself momentarily from her wiles. "Get to the point."

"I was trying to," she said with a come-hither smirk.

"You didn't pull me in here for a quickie," he shot back.

She unfastened the top button of her jeans. "You sure?"

"Let me know when you're ready to be serious." He opened the door, letting in a gust of filth.

"Fine," she said, slapping her hand on the door and pushing it shut. "I thought we could mix business with pleasure, but you're clearly not in the mood."

Holding his arms from his sides, he cast an appalled look at his grime-caked clothes and grumbled, "Gee, I wonder why?"

"It's time to start making some changes," she said.

Sensing the gravity of her message, he eyed her warily. "Changes to what?"

"To the Movement," Cassie said. "It's falling apart, Kyle. You can see that, can't you?"

He paced beside the stairs and frowned. "Exaggerate much?"

"You know what I'm talking about," said his red-haired

hallucination. "The Navy shoots a missile at Jordan, and he sends back a press release. They blow his headquarters to bits, he knocks out some of their satellites." She stepped into Kyle's path and leaned her face toward his, as if they were rams locking horns. "He's not playing to win, Kyle. And in a war, if you don't play to win, you're guaranteed to lose."

Pivoting away from her, Kyle replied, "I tried telling him that. You were there. He doesn't want to hear it."

As Kyle walked to the gray-filmed window, Cassie retorted, "Jordan doesn't want to listen to anyone but himself. Do you know how many of our people died in that building collapse?" He heard her walk toward him, then her voice was behind his shoulder. "Jordan's not the leader the Movement needs, Kyle. In a time of war, we need someone in charge who isn't afraid to use force. Someone who's ready to get their hands dirty."

Her fingers closed with firm but gentle intimacy on his shoulder and turned him to face her. "This is your moment, Kyle. It's time for you to step up and lead the Movement."

He recoiled from the mere suggestion. "What? No! I don't want to be in charge!"

"Don't be so selfish, Kyle. It's not about what you want, it's about what the Movement *needs*."

His mind reeled with horror at the notion. "No way, that's crazy," he said. "The last thing the Movement needs is a power struggle at the top. Besides, even if I did challenge Jordan, who the hell would follow me?"

Pinching his chin between her thumb and forefinger, Cassie smiled and said, "Silly! I'm not saying we should hold an election. This is wartime. Bad things happen. If

Jordan were to wind up on the receiving end of a sniper's bullet . . ." She let go of his chin and gave the tip of his nose a gingerly tap. "Guess who'd be next in line to lead the Movement to victory?"

They regarded each other with wide-eyed stares—hers one of mad ambition, his one of mute horror.

"No," he said, shaking his head. "There's no way I could—"

"Liar," Cassie said, her words a warm hush across his lips. "You did it once before . . ." She sank to a low crouch in front of him as she added, "You can do it again."

Frozen in place, all he could muster was a feeble denial. "But that wasn't really me that shot Jordan . . . it was the Marked. I was just a puppet."

"I know," Cassie said, lowering the zipper of his jeans. He closed his eyes and tried to pretend he didn't feel the velvet stroke of her fingers or the sultry kiss of her breath as she whispered, "But I'm sure you remember how to do the deed . . ."

Diana watched flames dance inside the charred husks of cars that had been abandoned on nearly every street in downtown Seattle.

A golden-brown haze made it impossible to see more than ten yards ahead, forcing her to drive at a creeping pace through the dazed, wandering packs of survivors. The kaleidoscopic effect of tears in her eyes only made it that much harder for her to see. An acrid stench of burnt hair and scorched steel snaked through the car's vents and made her cough, then hold her breath.

Beside her, Tom sat leaning forward, his forehead almost touching the windshield. He peered through the narrow arc cut by the wiper blade through the car's thickening layer of grime, searching for any sign of anyone who looked like Maia. Both of his hands were under the glove compartment, wrapped around his semiautomatic pistol, ready to react to any threat.

On either side of the car, looters—some in bandannas and ski goggles, others sporting military surplus gas masks—emerged from storefronts with their arms filled with everything they could carry. Diana gazed at them with contempt.

"Middle of a war zone, and all these morons can think about is swiping a new TV," she said, swerving through a slalom of jaywalking thieves portering massive cardboard boxes.

Tom chortled grimly. "If you want to run a few of 'em over, it's fine by me."

"Don't tempt me," Diana said, feeling genuinely homicidal.

They turned a corner a few blocks from the former site of the Collier Foundation. The fog was heavier here. Grit crackled under the car's tires as Diana steered slowly around massive blocks of shattered concrete sporting twisted lengths of iron rebar. She heard a high-pitched scrape as one of the metal protrusions left its mark on the side of her sedan.

Another turn led to another street blanketed in ashen fallout, but the haze in the air was brighter, backlit by the afternoon sun.

Diana stepped on the brakes.

Shadows took shape in the wall of dust. Silhouetted in the pale smoke, human figures of all shapes and sizes walked toward Diana and Tom's car.

For Diana, it was a moment of déjà vu. Her mind flashed back to the day of the 4400's arrival, nearly four years earlier on the shores of Highland Beach. From a thick white fog rolling off the crystal-clear waters of a mountain lake, forty-four hundred people—some of whom had been missing for years, others for decades—had appeared from a ball of light, with no memories of their abductions and no explanations for their return.

She opened her door and got out of the car.

"Diana!" Tom shouted, but she ignored him and stepped around her door to stand in front of her vehicle.

From behind her, she heard Tom's door open. A moment later he was standing beside her, wincing and wrinkling his face against the onslaught of foul-smelling fog.

Together they watched human beings appear from the penumbra of dust, which had painted its victims a uniform ghostly gray. Even robbed of color, familiar faces appeared.

At the forefront of the crowd was Jordan Collier.

Behind him followed Gary Navarro.

And sheltered under Gary's brotherly arm was Maia.

Diana rushed forward. Maia bolted away from Gary and leaped into her mother's arms. Wrapping her daughter in a fierce hug, Diana wept with relief. "Thank God, Maia!"

Between desperate sobs, Maia said, "They said you left! This morning, on the plane!"

"No, sweetie," Diana said, stroking Maia's dust-caked hair. "They tried to make me go. But I'd never leave you. Never."

She lingered, grateful to be holding her daughter even as the world went to pieces all around them. Then she realized that Jordan and his legion of followers had halted in the street and were watching her and Maia.

Jordan regarded them darkly.

"Maia," he said. "We need to keep moving."

"I know," Maia said, extricating herself from Diana's embrace.

Gary walked away, heading northeast, leading the crowd past Diana, Tom, Maia, and Jordan.

"Wait, no!" Diana protested. "Maia, you need to come with me, honey. We need to get back to NTAC until this is over."

Maia shook her head. "No, Mom. My place is with my people."

"We need her, Diana," Jordan said. "She predicted the attack on our headquarters, and she knows where the enhanced soldiers are going to strike. The entire city's a target now, and NTAC's no exception."

As shade-pale survivors shambled around her, Diana directed her fury at Jordan. "At least NTAC has some defenses! Bring your people there; we can help you."

"Thicker walls won't save us this time," Jordan said. "All my people who have abilities they can use in combat have been sent to meet the enhanced soldiers. Everyone else is coming with me to find shelter."

As Diana struggled to tame her anger and find the words to change Maia's mind, Tom stepped between her and Jordan. "Have you seen Kyle?" Tom asked. "Did he survive the attack?"

"Kyle's fine," Jordan said. Nodding at the passing crowd,

he added, "If you want to wait, I'm sure he'll be along sooner or later." With a featherlight touch, he nudged Maia into motion beside him as he resumed walking. "Let's go."

Tom stayed behind as Diana hurried along beside Maia. "Honey, please," Diana said. "Don't do this. You need to come with me. It's not safe out here."

"It's not safe anywhere," Maia said. "But I'm safer with my people than with yours." She reached out and took Diana's hand as they walked side by side. "Come with us. We'll protect you."

She desperately wished she could make Maia understand. "I can't do that, sweetie. I have a duty, to NTAC . . ." She glanced over her shoulder as her voice tapered off. The ensuing silence smothered her unexpressed thought, *And a duty to Tom.*

"I understand," Maia said. "You have your duty, and I have mine." She looked up at Diana with a surprisingly mature mien. "Don't worry," she continued. "We'll see each other again before this is over. I promise."

Maia let go of Diana's hand.

Diana stopped walking and let her go. Within seconds, her daughter had vanished into the amber afterglow of destruction, trailed by Jordan's newborn army of gray ghosts.

Minutes passed without a word being spoken. Tom stepped up beside her, and they stared into the bright veil of dust.

"We raise our kids so that someday we can let them live their own lives," Diana said. "But how do I make myself let go?"

Tom frowned. "If I ever figure it out, I'll let you know."

# TWENTY-EIGHT

## 11:39 A.M.

COMMANDER ERIC FROST marked targets with a red grease pencil on a laminated map, which was spread flat on the concrete floor of the Elliott West CSO Control Facility. He and the other twenty-nine enhanced soldiers who surrounded him were garbed in black-and-gray urban combat uniforms whose pockets were stuffed with everything from bottled water to smoke grenades.

"Alpha Team, we'll be tracking Jordan Collier and the senior members of his leadership council," the Navy SEAL said to his fellow enhanced soldiers. "Our latest intel says they made it out of their headquarters before it went down, so we need to assess where they're most likely to go next."

Brian Gerhart, a Marine Corps lieutenant with a face that reminded Frost of a knuckle with eyes, lifted his hand. Frost nodded to the man, who closed his eyes and said, "I have an image of them moving on foot. Looks like they're heading northeast on Madison. Near Pike Street."

"Not toward NTAC, then," noted Sergeant Knight, an Army Ranger whose pale complexion, blue eyes, and sharp features gave him the affect of a man made of ice and steel. Pointing at the map, he continued: "I'd say there's an eighty-seven-percent chance they'll turn north on Nineteenth Avenue."

"In which case we'll be playing catch-up," Frost said. "That means we'll need cover, and lots of it." He circled the city block labeled Seattle Center. "Bravo Team, we need you to draw Collier's people out of our way while we head east. Start with the Space Needle and improvise from there."

Bravo's leader, Captain Hayes, who stood out because of his Sioux ancestry and the fact that he had biceps larger than most men's thighs, nodded once. "Got it," he said.

Frost looked to the next team commander, a gaunt and dead-eyed Green Beret lieutenant named John Conway. "Charlie Team, you guys have a change of plan. The GPS satellites are down, so the Navy's switching to laser-guided munitions. You'll have to paint Collier's high-value targets with UV and wait while the *Shoup* takes 'em out one at a time. Start with bridges, elevated freeways, and hardened sites."

"Roger that," Conway said without taking his eyes from the map. Frost grasped the nature of Conway's focused concentration: he was memorizing the map of central Seattle.

Hayes raised one huge, thick-fingered hand. "Question."

With a half nod, Frost said, "Go ahead."

"What are the rules of engagement out there, sir?"

"Check your targets," Frost said. "There are four companies of regular Army on the move in there, plus at least one company of Marines, all in urban camo. That said, anybody on the street who's not one of ours is a valid target unless confirmed otherwise," Frost said. "Don't target city police unless they engage you first. Any civvie who shows signs of a promicin ability gets lit up. Everybody clear?"

Heads nodded in confirmation all around him.

"Okay," Frost said, rolling up the map. "That's it. This is a daylight op, so watch your asses out there. Maintain radio silence unless you're totally FUBAR. Check your gear, lock-'n'-load, move out. Hooyah!"

The other SEALs in the company shouted back "Hooyah!" while the Marines bellowed "Oorah!" and the Army boys roared "Hooah!"—all part of a shared military tradition, each subtly unique.

Bravo Team was the first to deploy. Hayes led his men out of the CSO facility through a door to the building's north parking lot. From there, Frost knew, the mission plan called for them to make a rapid crossing of Elliott Avenue West, followed by a fast scramble up a grassy slope to West Mercer Street. From there, Bravo Team would double-quicktime three-fifths of a mile to Seattle Center, set munitions at the base of the Space Needle (which was strategically worthless but ideal for creating a distraction), and unleash hell at precisely noon.

Conway's unit had a more difficult mission profile. He and each member of his team—ten men in all—would have their own list of prioritized targets, located throughout the city. After Charlie Team deployed from the CSO facility, each of its members would have to act independently for the rest of the engagement. None of them would have the luxury of calling for backup or extraction. To get out of the combat zone, each man would have to direct the demolition of all targets on his list and then reach the designated exfiltration point at the southernmost point of Lake Union at precisely midnight.

While the men of Charlie Team made a final review of their targets and their timetables, Frost led Alpha Team through a six-foot-wide open valve hatchway, back into the Combined Sewer Overflow pipeline. This had been his platoon's means of ingress into Promise City. He and his men had SCUBA-dived to the outfall pipes, which lay submerged in sixty feet of water 340 feet offshore from Myrtle Edwards Park in Elliott Bay. The pipes varied in diameter from six to eight feet from there to the Elliott West CSO Control Facility. It had been a narrow passage for men laden with combat gear, but they had made it.

The portion of the tunnel that ran east from the control facility was fourteen feet wide; it extended underneath Mercer Street to Dexter Avenue, where it angled northeast parallel to Broad Street. At Eighth Avenue and Roy Street, there would be another valve hatch that would lead to a manhole cover. From there, Frost and his men would deploy to street level in northern Seattle and continue on to their target.

He splashed down into ankle-deep stagnant water and forced himself to ignore the putrid, sulfur-and-methane-heavy stench of sewage and rotting vegetation. Thumbing the switch on his flashlight, he made a quick head count and confirmed that all nine of his men were with him.

"Okay, gents," he barked. "We've got fifteen minutes to hump our butts a mile and a quarter. Move out!"

Frost's men fell in behind him, running single-file through the tunnel with only his lone flashlight beam to light the way. The roar of feet slapping through the water echoed inside the circular concrete passageway and bled into a wall of noise.

The SEAL focused on the sensations of his footfalls breaking the water's surface, the comforting weight of his rifle on his back and his Beretta at his side, and the seconds ticking by on his digital watch.

In fourteen minutes and ten seconds, they would exit the tunnel via the manhole at Roy Street.

If everything went according to plan, in less than twenty-four hours Promise City would once again become Seattle—and Jordan Collier and his movement would be on their way to history's dustbin, where they belonged.

# TWENTY-NINE

## 11:45 A.M.

IT WAS THE MOMENT that Dennis Ryland had been waiting for.

Every cable-TV channel he flipped to brought him images of chaos and unrest in Seattle. A gaping hole in the city's downtown skyline belched black smoke into the sky. Panicked residents, opportunistic thieves, and violent malcontents mixed in the dust-shrouded streets to wreak mayhem.

He sipped his coffee and smiled.

*That's more like it*, he gloated.

It pained him to know that his old office in the former Haspelcorp Building was gone, reduced to slag and ashes by one blazing ray from space, but such were the fortunes of war. *A small price to pay if it convinces the president to let me rid the world of this menace once and for all*, he told himself.

Outside his window, Tacoma was the very portrait of

drab serenity. Except for the television spewing news of an erupting civil war less than a twenty-minute drive away, it was a perfect summer's day in Seattle's often-overlooked neighboring city. Dennis considered waiting until after lunch to capitalize on the crisis in Promise City, then thought better of it.

*No time like the present,* he decided. He walked to his desk, set down his coffee, and relaxed into his chair. His fingers keyed in his security code for Haspelcorp's encrypted hard-line link to its Nevada research laboratory. Moments later, the system confirmed his codes. He used the graphic interface to initiate a real-time video channel to the lab.

An animated wheel replaced the cursor on his monitor. As it spun, the word BUFFERING appeared beneath it.

Dennis sighed and imagined the slack-jawed look of stunned surprise that his boss Miles would be wearing when he learned the truth about how Dennis had invested the company's research budget during the past three months. Then he let himself daydream for a moment about the smorgasbord of high-level government jobs that would once again be within his grasp after the White House learned that he personally had spearheaded the solution to the world's promicin problem, while simultaneously sparing the country and the world a bloody, protracted war.

*I could be in line for a cabinet post*, he assured himself. *Maybe a diplomatic posting.* It almost made him laugh to think of himself as an ambassador, or to imagine people addressing him as "Your Excellency." He made up his mind: he wanted to be the U.S. ambassador to the Bahamas.

The little wheel on his screen was still spinning.

*What's taking so long?* he wondered. He pulled a cigarette from the pack in his desk drawer, lit it, inhaled, and breathed an off-white plume of sharp-odored smoke across his monitor.

The channel stopped buffering. The spinning wheel vanished and gave him back his cursor. A moving image filled his screen.

At first the picture was too dark for Dennis to pick out any details. He thought that perhaps the lab was in night mode, shut down while the scientists rested.

Then he saw the flames. Small licks of orange fire poked into the bottom of the frame, silhouetting the shapes of broken machinery in the foreground.

Dennis turned up the brightness on his screen and fiddled with the contrast to coax more of the scene into view.

The lab had been destroyed. It looked as if someone had detonated a bomb inside it. All the computers were smashed. The priceless, ultrahigh-tech devices that he had acquired at great risk and expense had been reduced to smoldering junk.

He switched between the lab's many internal secure video feeds and was only marginally thankful that the surveillance system had been hardened against a calamity such as this.

*What the hell happened?* His mind raced with idle speculations. Had the lab been attacked by Collier's people?

Could it have been corporate espionage? Might the U.S. government have traced the movement of sensitive materials to the lab and raided it in the name of national security?

As these questions circled each other in ever-more-paranoid flights of hysterical panic, he tabbed quickly through the lab's multiple video feeds, struggling to form a mental picture of what might have transpired out there in the desert.

When he finished, he realized that what he found most troubling were the things that he *hadn't* seen.

He hadn't seen any of the scientists' bodies.

He hadn't seen the corpses of any attackers.

And he hadn't seen any sign of the device that his trio of mysterious researchers had been assembling.

He abandoned his wilder theories and applied Occam's razor, fixing his mind upon the simplest explanation that fit the available evidence: the scientists and their invention were gone, and the lab had been demolished by means of arson.

Feeling his blood pressure rising with each puff of his cigarette, Dennis closed his left hand into a fist and felt his jaw clench with rage as he faced the truth.

*Those assholes ripped me off.*

Then a nagging feeling of dread made him wonder why. Were the scientists just looking to steal his thunder by unveiling the promicin neutralizer themselves? That seemed unlikely. If they had planned to give the device to the government, why go to the trouble of persuading Dennis to subsidize it at Haspelcorp and shelter the project in a hidden lab?

*Maybe they plan to sell it,* Dennis thought. *But who the hell would buy it? A foreign government? Another corporation?*

Nothing about this mess made any sense to him. All that he knew for certain was that if he didn't recover that device soon, it was going to cost him his job—and possibly much more—when Miles found out the desert lab had been totaled.

Too distracted to smoke or savor his java, he extinguished his cigarette in his coffee mug. The butt plunged into the brown dregs with a low hiss.

*I can't ask the company's security division to help me get the device back,* he reasoned. *They'd have to file a report with the board, and that'd be my ass. That rules out the cops and the Feds, too. But nobody else has the resources to find something like this in a pinch . . .*

His eyes drifted across the knickknacks on his office shelves, then landed once more on the wall-mounted TV screen. The cable news channel was running (for the millionth time that morning) its loop of overtaxed first responders in Seattle.

That was when Dennis realized what he had to do, and whom he had to ask for help, while he still had time to save his neck.

Disgusted but duly impressed by the dark irony of his situation, he silently cursed God while laughing out loud.

He had to go back to Promise City.

# THIRTY

## 11:55 A.M.

THE AIR OUTSIDE The 4400 Center stank of sweat, smoke, and blood, and it was filled with cries of pain.

Shawn Farrell was beyond tired, but the wounded continued to appear in droves. They had come from every part of the city: from the points where soldiers had breached its defenses; from the aftermath of the Collier building's collapse in Belltown; from the riot-torn streets of Beacon Hill.

"Please help us," they'd said. Some asked for shelter. Most begged for his healing touch. A few offered money.

Heather Tobey, bless her, had forced some sense of order onto the desperate throng. Even as Shawn had reeled from the overwhelming demand for his aid, she had put the staff of the Center to work triaging the wounded. Those with the most grievous injuries were brought to Shawn first. The rest were organized according to their needs.

One soot-stained, bloody face followed another.

Shawn's hands were sticky with the half-dried, reddish-brown blood of others. Every body he repaired took its toll on his own, but he couldn't bring himself to turn anyone away. So he went on.

Tears streamed from his eyes as he despaired at all the ways people found to hurt each other. He wept for the woman stabbed by a stranger, the young boy beaten by a gang of p-negative teens merely because he could turn playground sand into glass sculptures with his promicin ability, the man felled in front of his four-year-old daughter by a sniper's bullet.

One horror after another was placed into his hands.

His strength was leaving him, but he couldn't stop.

A family of four, their bodies and faces burned red and black because a renegade fifty/fifty had set their home ablaze in a misguided act of vengeance, joined hands as Shawn laid hands on the children's foreheads. He felt the flames that had tried to devour them, the agony of two parents stumbling through a wall of fire while trying to shield their sons beneath their bathrobes, the fear and the suffering of the children.

Shawn stumbled backward, and the family looked up at him, their faces healed and their bodies whole, their blackened garments the only evidence of their brush with tragedy. They shed tears of joy and reached out to embrace him, but he was already being pulled toward another victim in need of succor.

He mended broken bones, regenerated ruined eyes, reattached severed digits, repaired ruptured organs, and erased the scars of fire.

When he paused to breathe, he scanned the crowd and saw that the number of those in need had only multiplied. There was no rest in sight, no sign of a respite from his labors. All he wanted to do was surrender to fatigue and sleep for a day, a week, a year. Pressure pounded in his temples and behind his eyes. It hurt so badly that it made him sick to his stomach and left him feeling dizzy and overheated, as if he had a fever.

Going on was too much to contemplate. He felt ancient, run-down, utterly exhausted in the most literal definition of the word.

He bent over, hands planted on his knees, and made himself breathe slowly in an effort to clear his head.

Within moments, Heather was at his side, one arm resting gently across his shoulders, the other supporting his chest. "You need to stop for a while," she said, her voice soft but freighted with concern. "This is taking too much out of you."

"I'm okay," Shawn lied. "I just need a moment, that's all."

Apparently unconvinced by his performance, Heather frowned at him, then waved to one of the Center employees nearby. "Bring me water, some sports drinks, and a breakfast bar," she said to the man. Then she added with urgency, "Quickly."

While the young man sprinted inside the Center to fetch fluids and nourishment, Heather stayed by Shawn's side and kept him standing when all he wanted to do was lie down and pass out.

He wondered whether anyone would notice how she doted on him and deduce that they were, in fact, lovers.

Straightening his back, he let his head loll back until he was looking at blue sky. The sun was almost directly overhead, and it beat down on him with a tangible fury. He became aware of the sweat that coated his forehead and soaked his blood-and-grime-sullied white dress shirt.

Drawing an especially deep breath brought Shawn not relief or reinvigoration but a sharp stab of pain between the upper ribs on his left side. He winced and doubled over.

Heather caught him as she cried out, "Shawn!"

He bit down on the pain and forced it into retreat. "I'm all right," he said to her. "This'll sound weird, but I don't think it was my pain I was feeling."

Her face twisted in confusion. "You felt someone else's pain? Are you sure?"

"Positive," Shawn said, nodding. "It felt just like it does when I lay hands." He turned slowly, searching the faces in the crowd. "Someone near me is having chest pains, bad ones."

Sitting on the ground beside the Center's driveway was a semiconscious, middle-aged man clutching his chest; he was balding, heavyset, and flanked by a frightened-looking woman of a similar age who Shawn guessed was his wife. The man's eyes had the distant, glassy quality of someone whose life was slipping out of his grasp. Behind the gaze was a silent plea for help.

Shawn met the man's gaze and held it.

Opening his senses and his mind, Shawn felt the dull aches and irregular jabs of the man's failing heart. He lifted one bloodstained hand in the man's direction and closed his eyes. In his imagination, he saw damaged cardiac muscle, clogged and hardened arteries, and potentially fatal clots waiting to break free into the man's bloodstream.

One by one, Shawn unmade each ailment. With each effort, the pain in his own chest grew deeper, until it felt as if a vise were crushing his ribs and squeezing out his last breaths.

Then it was done, and he gasped, suddenly free of the pain. He fell backward into Heather's arms. The employee she'd sent inside had returned, and he handed Heather a bottle of orange-flavored Gatorade with its cap off and a straw poking from it. She held it in front of Shawn's mouth.

"Drink," she insisted.

He sipped from the straw, slowly at first. Each mouthful of the sweet and vaguely salty beverage renewed a tiny fraction of his depleted strength. Before he knew it, he'd emptied the bottle. He blinked, recovered his bearings, and said to the male employee, "I'll take that breakfast bar now."

It took Shawn less than thirty seconds to devour the chocolate-covered granola snack. As he washed it down with the bottle of water the man had brought him, he saw through the surrounding woods that more people were walking down the long, tree-lined, curving driveway of The 4400 Center.

*How many this time?* he wondered. *Twenty-five? Fifty? A hundred more souls in need of a healer?*

The approaching crowd swelled in numbers, and Shawn noticed that most of them were without any sign of serious injury. As they rounded the last bend in the driveway, the person at the front of the procession stepped into view.

It was Jordan Collier.

Shawn discarded his empty bottle and walked forward, away from the sick and wounded, to meet Jordan's people. Heather and several employees of the Center stepped out of the crowd to stand close at Shawn's back.

Nearly four years earlier, Jordan had converted the Center from its previous use as an art museum into a safe haven for the 4400. It had been his first headquarters as the de facto leader of the Promicin-Positive Movement, his sanctum sanctorum. It also was where Jordan was seemingly assassinated by a sniper—an event that had put the responsibility for running the Center on Shawn's young and, at the time, utterly unprepared shoulders.

The months that followed had brought many bitter ordeals for Shawn, but the cruelest test had come after Jordan's nigh miraculous return from the grave. Shawn had opposed Jordan's plan to distribute promicin to the public, because while Jordan could accept that 50 percent of all who took the drug would die agonizing deaths as a result, Shawn couldn't. They'd parted ways with more than a little mutual hostility.

Despite the fact that Shawn had helped cure Jordan of his possession by one of the Marked and had brokered negotiations between Jordan and the agents at NTAC, the two men remained separated by the kind of bitterness that existed only between those who once were friends.

Jordan came to a halt in front of Shawn, and the crowd that followed him stopped a few rows at a time, creating a ripple effect that worked its way backward though the snaking mass of bodies. Both Jordan and his entourage of hundreds—which Shawn noted included Gary Navarro, Maia Skouris, and his own cousin, Kyle—were caked in dark gray dust.

"Hello, Shawn," Jordan said.

Taking care to keep his conscious mind blank just in case Gary was telepathically eavesdropping, Shawn dipped his chin and replied with guarded suspicion, "Jordan."

"I can see you're busy," Jordan said, nodding at the supplicants who were massed in front of the Center's entrance. "And we're a bit pressed for time ourselves, so I'll get to the point: we're here to ask for sanctuary."

"Sanctuary?" Shawn narrowed his eyes. "Are you kidding?"

"No, Shawn, I'm not." Gesturing at the people behind him, he continued: "I know that not all of my people are 4400s. Some took promicin by choice; some were exposed during the epidemic. But the soldiers who've come to kill us don't care how any of us got promicin. To them, we're all just targets."

Jordan cast a nostalgic look at the curving white façade of the Center. "When I opened this place, it was for the original returnees, because that's who I thought I was meant to serve." He paused, then looked Shawn in the eye. "When you and I parted ways, it was because I thought my purpose was to spread promicin. I believed that convincing everyone to take it would solve the world's problems, and that the costs, however tragic, would be worth the gains."

His face slackened with remorse. "But I was wrong. And you were right, Shawn. We can't save humanity by condemning half of it to death. That's not a future worth fighting for."

Everyone around them was quiet, huddled in a hush of tense anticipation. The history of animosity between Shawn and Jordan was well-known, and it seemed as if everyone sensed that the future of the Movement, and of Promise City, hinged on Shawn's reply.

He offered his hand to Jordan, who accepted it.

As they shook hands, Shawn declared for all to hear, "Let's get everyone inside."

# THIRTY-ONE

## 12:01 P.M.

DIANA CURSED UNDER her breath as another barricade of burning cars and stacked debris forced her to make her sixth unplanned detour down a side street in as many minutes.

"Told you we shoulda taken I-Five," Tom said.

She snapped back, "You want to drive?" Gesturing with one hand at the smoke-filled disaster zone outside their vehicle, she went on, "Say the word, Tom! If you can predict which street the nutjobs'll block next, be my guest and take the wheel!"

Tom seemed to be concocting a reply, but he placed his right hand over his mouth and looked out the window instead. Diana chalked up his silence to a tiny victory of discretion.

She made a right turn onto Beacon Avenue South and hoped that this time she might make it to South Spokane Street, and from there to the Seattle Freeway.

They got as far as the three-way intersection at South Forest Street and Seventeenth Avenue South before the shooting started.

Large-caliber bullets ripped across their car's hood with a chattering roar. Steam geysered from the engine and obscured the windshield with a spray of atomized grease.

Diana stomped on the brakes. She and Tom ducked as another barrage blasted out their windows and showered them with glass.

Then came a crackling noise, like that of an electrical transformer dancing with lightning.

Peeking over the dash, Tom and Diana saw two civilians, a man and a woman, emerge from behind a parked car on their left and extend their hands toward an auto repair garage on their right—which, Diana realized, had been the origin of the gunfire.

The man hurled wild bolts of forked lightning from his fingers into the garage, illuminating the soldiers hiding inside and igniting fires around them at the same time. The woman next to him threw fireballs under the cars and trucks parked in the garage's lot, detonating their gas tanks like bombs.

Red-hot shrapnel peppered Tom and Diana's car. Then came a flurry of burning gasoline that set their vehicle ablaze, along with half the street in front of and behind them.

Tom unlocked his door. "Stay low, move fast, and head for the green building behind us. We should be out of the crossfire once we get past its corner."

"Ready," Diana said, unlocking her own door.

A metallic creaking from outside coaxed Diana to peek over the dash again. Cars that moments earlier had been parked along the street ahead of them hurtled through the air at the one being used for cover by the two civilians.

The man and woman scrambled in panicked retreat as several tons of metal rained down. The automotive projectiles tumbled over them, like giant steel dice.

Tom and Diana's car wobbled and started to rise.

They gave each other the same wide-eyed stare.

"Time to go," Tom said.

They opened their doors and rolled out of the car onto the street, which was littered with broken glass, jagged steel, and burning fuel. Diana landed hard and narrowly missed a fiery smear of oil.

She hoped the wall of jet-black smoke rising from the exploded vehicles would impair the soldiers' vision enough to let her and Tom scramble to cover behind the corner of what she now saw was the Beacon Hill Library.

Behind her, their car soared away and smashed through the front of a nearby house.

Tom reached the corner of the library less than a second before she did. As she slipped behind him and put her back to the wall, she asked, "Okay, now what?"

"Don't look at me," he said over his shoulder. "I got us out of the car. Next bright idea's up to you."

"Great," she muttered. She was about to suggest they go back the way they'd come, until she saw the angry mob moving toward them from that direction. "I think we have a problem."

Following her worried stare, Tom let out a groan of dismay. "You gotta be kidding me," he said. "A mob that'll kill us for being with NTAC, jarheads that'll kill us just for being here. We can't win today." He cast a quick series of glances at the library. "Stay close," he said, jogging to the building's rear entrance as he drew his Glock.

He stopped a few feet from the glass door and fired three shots, shattering the portal into shards. Then he reached in, unlocked the door, and pulled it open. "C'mon," he said. "We'll go out the other side, into the parking lot."

She followed him into the library, an elegant, modern space with a lofty arched ceiling whose shape and jutting, riblike exposed beams made Diana think of the inside of a cartoon whale. They raced past the long, curving shelves and freestanding stacks to the far side of the building. Tom opened the door to the parking lot, and they hurried back outside.

They were two steps out the door before they saw they'd stumbled past four riflemen in black-and-gray urban camouflage lying in ambush behind some foliage near the door. The soldiers spun and raised their weapons.

The NTAC agents raised their hands by reflex.

"Whoa!" Tom said! "Friendlies!"

"Identify yourselves," said the closest of the soldiers, all of whom Diana saw wore no rank insignia or identification.

"Agent Tom Baldwin, NTAC," Tom said, "and this is my partner, Agent Diana Skouris. We have ID in our pockets."

"Slowly," said the soldier.

Moving with deliberate caution, Diana and Tom each kept one hand raised while using the other to pull their flip-folds with their NTAC credentials from their pants pockets. They handed them to the soldier, who studied them, then nodded.

"Okay," he said, handing back the credentials. "The whole city's a free-fire zone, so you two better take cover on the double." With a dismissive upward nod, he added, "Get going."

"Thanks," Tom said, tucking his ID back into his pocket. Diana did the same, and stayed close at Tom's side as they started moving toward the street.

A flash of motion on Diana's right turned her head. Five people were running on a narrow strip of grass between the library and a redbrick apartment building: a man shepherding two young girls and a woman carrying an infant.

The older girl had blond hair exactly like Maia's.

The younger one had radiant halos of jade-colored light around her head and her hands.

Both girls shrieked and twitched as the soldiers raked them with a spray of bullets. Their father screamed in anger, their mother wailed with grief, and the infant cried in pure terror as they fell beside the girls, ripped apart by a storm of metal.

Diana stopped and stared, mesmerized and aghast.

The blond girl lay dying, racked by spasms and choking on the blood in her mouth. Then her eyes dimmed, and she lay still. Her family's blood speckled her face and her hair.

Tears of rage burned in Diana's eyes.

The girl's hair looked *exactly* like Maia's.

The soldiers broke from cover to verify their kills.

Diana drew her Glock and opened fire.

Her first shot slammed through the lead soldier's head, and he fell backward, through a plate-glass window into the library.

Her second shot ripped through another soldier's throat. He dropped and hit the ground like a sack of wet cement.

The next soldier turned and raised his rifle halfway into position before Diana's third shot struck him in the face.

The last soldier had her in his sights, and she prepared to die.

Then came another crack of pistol fire, and the soldier fell backward with a bullet hole in his forehead.

She looked over her shoulder and saw a gray wisp of smoke rise from the muzzle of Tom's pistol. He lowered his weapon.

Diana did the same as she threw a guilty look at Tom. "I guess I just picked a side."

"So did I," he said with no hint of regret. "Yours." He holstered his Glock. "Let's get the hell outta here."

# THIRTY-TWO

## 12:27 P.M.

THERE HADN'T BEEN time for Jordan to shower, but he had stolen a few moments inside an executive washroom on the top floor of The 4400 Center to rinse the tacky gray filth from his hands and face. His clothes and shoes remained irreparably soiled, and his long hair was matted to his head by the sticky dust, which had taken on the consistency of paste when it became wet.

He picked up a bottle of water and guzzled two mouthfuls, grateful to have his mouth cleansed of the taste of ashes.

Jordan didn't think of himself as jaded. The faces of those who perished for the Movement haunted him; and yet, staring at his dirty, haggard reflection in the bathroom mirror, he felt oddly sanguine about the horrors he'd lived through less than two hours earlier.

*I must be in shock,* he thought. *This is my mind coping with trauma. When the danger is past, I'm going to feel this.*

He sighed and regarded himself with a grimace. *I can hardly wait.*

He took a hand towel from a stack next to the sink, patted his face dry, and rubbed the moisture from his hands. He dropped the towel in a laundry basket on his way out of the bathroom.

His bodyguards Emil and Tristine were standing outside the bathroom door, exactly where he'd left them. The duo fell into step behind Jordan as he walked quickly down the hallway to the executive meeting room.

The double doors of the main entrance were propped open. Inside, assembled around the long, dark conference table, was a war council that consisted of Jordan's and Shawn's top people. Their attention was focused on a handful of large maps.

"Bring me up to speed," Jordan said, edging into the group beside Kyle, who was standing next to his cousin, Shawn.

Pointing at makeshift markers—including a matchbook, an eraser, someone's car keys, and a silver dollar—placed on a map of the greater Seattle area, Kyle said, "Our remote-viewers have seen three groups of enhanced soldiers inside Promise City, in addition to multiple units of regular military personnel."

"The enhanced soldiers," Jordan said, studying the map. "What do we know about their capabilities?"

Shawn replied, "They have at least one telekinetic, possibly two. The squad that attacked the Space Needle a few minutes ago had an electrokinetic, a pyrokinetic, and a guy who can paralyze by touch."

"Most of the others have abilities geared toward information gathering," Gary added. "Lucas and Hal helped me scout most of them a few minutes ago. They've got the expected assortment of trackers, remote-viewers, limited precognitives, psychic transmitters, healers, and so on. The only guy I'm really worried about seems to be the one in charge."

Jordan cast a worried glance at the young telepath. "Why? What's his story?"

"That's the problem," Gary said. "I have no idea. All I know about him is what little I've been able to read from the minds of his men, but most of them don't know much besides his name, rank, and specialty: Commander Eric Frost, Navy SEAL."

From the corner of his eye, Jordan saw a young man whisper to Shawn and hand him a sheet of paper. While Shawn read the report, Heather crossed her arms and asked Gary, "Do we know *anything* else? Even small details might make a difference."

Gary said, "Including Frost, there are thirty enhanced soldiers working as a single unit inside Promise City. From his troops' memories, I found out they entered the city through some underwater sewage tunnels in Elliott Bay. Once they got into the city, they split into three groups of ten men."

Shawn interrupted, "His troops are wreaking havoc all over Belltown. They're knocking out sections of the freeways and starting fires faster than we can put them out."

Nodding, Gary continued. "I think their job is to keep us busy and off-balance while Frost and his team head east and look for us. The last time his men saw him and his command team, they were crawling back into the Mercer Street flood control tunnel, on their way to a manhole at Eighth and Roy."

"Which means they're probably coming here," Jordan said. "Where are they now?"

"No idea," Gary said. "Frost is able to hide himself and the men with him. We haven't been able to find him with telepathy, remote-viewing, or anything else."

Looking hopefully at his brooding shaman, Jordan asked, "What about you, Kyle? Any suggestions on how or where we might head off Commander Frost and his team?"

Kyle stared at his shoes, then shook his head in defeat. "Sorry," he said. "Cassie and I are drawing a blank. But we know their mission is to cap us, so we ought to start digging in. Cover the windows and doors, post sentries, the works. Maybe even—oh, I don't know—get our hands on some guns?"

Gary added with an apprehensive sidelong look, "Guns might not be a bad idea, Jordan."

"I don't think we need them," Jordan said. "But if they'll make any of you feel better, be my guests." He pointed at the assorted objects dotting the map. "While we're getting ready for a showdown with Frost, let's not forget to deal with the regular troops." Looking at Gary, he asked, "Is Marisol still holding the line in Georgetown?"

"Last I heard," Gary said.

"Good. Tell her to go on the attack; start taking back some lost ground. Send Raul and Qi Xian to help her."

Turning to Shawn and Kyle, he asked, "Have either of you heard any news about the troops that breached our line out at Fort Lawton?"

Kyle pointed at the barren strip of land between Magnolia Bluff and Queen Anne. "Orson's holding them at the fallback line west of the railroad tracks."

"He'll need reinforcements," Jordan said. "Send over Sandra, Aasif, and Oliver. Make sure they know I want those soldiers back on their base by sundown."

"Done," Kyle said, stepping away to relay the order to one of the telepathic senders, who served as the Movement's primary means of clandestine communication.

Jordan clapped his hands together. "Okay. Everyone else, let's get to work securing the Center. Go." The war council dispersed, and people moved quickly, taking their specific instructions from Shawn, Kyle, Gary, and the few of Jordan's bodyguards who had professional close protection experience. Watching them all swing into action, it took Jordan a moment to notice that Maia was standing just behind him, staring at him.

"It won't be enough," she said.

"It never is," Jordan replied, steeling himself for the worst, which he knew was yet to come. "It never is."

# THIRTY-THREE

## 12:42 P.M.

MARCO TAPPED AND dragged icons, windows, and widgets across his computer's touchscreen with such force that he nearly knocked it off the desk. He was struggling to keep up with the accelerating cascade failures of the city's traffic monitoring cameras, which he had been using in a desperate effort to find Tom and Diana, who had gone missing after an altercation with a squad of enhanced soldiers nearly half an hour earlier.

Jed watched over Marco's shoulder and cautioned him, "Easy, buddy. You'll find 'em."

"Not at this rate, I won't," Marco said, frustrated beyond all reason by the collapsing municipal data network. "The Army's fragging all our public surveillance systems. By this time tomorrow, I won't even be able to tell if it's raining without looking out the window."

"Sure you will," Jed said. With a wry smile, he added, "This is Seattle. It's almost *always* raining."

Behind them, a man said in a gruff voice, "Ever the optimist, eh, Jed?"

They spun about. Jed started to raise his rifle—and froze.

Dennis Ryland stood in the doorway of the crisis center, his pistol raised and pointed at Jed and Marco. "Don't get up," he said. "I'm glad to see Homeland Security left somebody running the show here at NTAC, but I was kind of hoping it'd be more than just the two of you." After a brief pause, he added, "No offense, of course."

"None taken," Jed said. "Mind telling us how you got in?"

Dennis shrugged. "I still have a few backdoor codes in the system," he said. He smiled at Marco. "No thanks to you." Pointing at Marco's vest, he added, "Got enough gear, son? I've never seen anybody stuff the pockets of a tac vest like that."

"I like to be prepared," Marco said.

"Obviously. You must've been a Boy Scout." Lifting his chin at Jed, Dennis said, "Would you mind putting down your rifle? It makes me a little nervous."

Jed flashed an insincere smile. "And we wouldn't want that, now would we?"

A pistol's muzzle edged into view from the dark corridor and pressed against the back of Dennis's neck as Tom Baldwin answered, "No, we sure as hell wouldn't. Put your weapon on the floor, Dennis. Right now."

The former director of NTAC did as he was told. He lowered his pistol, bent down slowly, and set it at his feet.

Tom said, "Kick it over to Jed."

With a tap of his foot, Dennis sent his sidearm skittering across the tiled floor to Jed, who caught it under his shoe while lifting his rifle and aiming it at Dennis.

"Step inside and take a seat," Tom said, nudging Dennis forward. Tom followed Dennis into the crisis center. Half a step behind him was Diana, who entered with her own pistol leveled at Dennis's head.

The middle-aged man settled into a chair and responded to the agents' intense glares with an infuriatingly nonplussed smile. "Guys, don't you think you're overreacting here?"

Diana said, "I haven't shot you yet, have I?"

"You might want to hear what I have to say before you blow my brains out."

Tom holstered his weapon and nodded for Diana to do the same. She hesitated until Jed said, "It's okay, Skouris. I've got him covered." Reassured, Diana holstered her pistol.

"Okay," Tom said to Dennis. "You want to talk? Talk."

The smile faded from Dennis's careworn features. "I'm in trouble," he began.

Diana quipped, "And we give a shit because . . . ?"

He ignored her and pressed on. "I authorized an off-the-books research project at Haspelcorp. Three scientists told me they could make a device to mass-neutralize promicin. Before long it turned into a multibillion-dollar investment."

"Wait, I've heard this story before," Tom said with a cynical frown. "'And then, something went horribly wrong . . .'"

Dennis's furrowed brow betrayed his growing irritation. "At some point in the last twenty-four hours, those three scientists carried that device out the front door of a top-secret lab. By now it could be just about anywhere. Including here."

"I don't mean to sound callous," Tom said, "but so what? A device that can neutralize promicin might be able to put an end to this little civil war."

Lifting his eyebrows, Dennis said, "Exactly! That's why I backed their project in the first place. It was the solution I'd been looking for—a way to end Collier's insane movement without risking any more innocent lives."

Diana wore a quizzical expression. "But why would they steal it? Corporate espionage? Personal agenda?"

"I honestly don't know," Dennis said. "I've been trying to figure that out for the last hour, but no answer I can think of makes any sense."

Tom paced behind Dennis, on the other side of a row of computers. "Before we can figure out the *why*, we need to take a closer look at the *who*. These three scientists— you said they approached you with the project. Did they work for Haspelcorp?"

"No, they were independent contractors. I'd never heard of them, but a background check verified their credentials, so I listened to their pitch."

Marco's curiosity was fully engaged. "If these guys are major players in promicin research, I might know who they are," he said. "What're their names?"

"Peter Jakes, Robert Wells, and Helen Kuroda."

Marco shook his head, stumped. "Never heard of 'em."

Tom cast a horrified glare at Dennis. "Did you say their

last names were Jakes, Wells, and Kuroda?" Dennis confirmed it with a curt nod, and Tom recoiled in shock. He said to Diana, "Those were the real names of three of the Marked agents."

"Whoa!" Marco said. "Are you saying Haspelcorp backed a research project by the Marked?" He stared at Dennis. "Are you one-hundred-percent sure you know what they were building?"

"Of course," Dennis said. "I saw it with my own eyes."

Doubtful looks passed between the agents.

Marco said, "No offense, Dennis, but you can't even use a computer."

He replied defensively, "I'm learning."

"Can you tell a hodoscope from a cavity magnetron?"

"Sure."

Staring him down, Marco asked, "How?"

Dennis hemmed and hawed for a few seconds before mumbling, "Um . . . one has a cavity?"

"Nice try," Marco said. "Tell me everything you procured for the Marked: parts, raw materials, fuels—the works."

Rolling his eyes, Dennis said, "For God's sake, Marco! There was so much, I can't remember it all off the top of my head. But the one they really broke my balls about a couple days ago was the shipment from CERN—"

"Antimatter and a new transuranic element?" Marco cut in.

"Yes," Dennis said, apparently caught off guard. "How . . . ?"

Marco felt the blood rush from his face. He looked at

Tom and Diana, who also had paled at Dennis's unwitting revelation.

"Oh, shit," Tom said. He stared, dumbstruck, at Dennis. "Do you have any idea what you've done? Who those people were? Or what you just put into their hands?"

Dennis studied their reactions, frowned, then replied, "Apparently not."

Diana ran a hand through her hair. "Okay, let's think this through: Whatever it is the Marked had Dennis bring in from CERN, that's what gave the U.S. government an excuse to attack Seattle. Now the Marked have an antimatter bomb. So the question we need to be asking is: What's their target?"

"There might be evidence at the lab," Dennis said. "They set it on fire before they left. They must've been trying to hide something."

"Makes sense," Tom said. "Do you have any pictures of the lab, either inside or out?"

"On my phone," Dennis said. "I downloaded thirty seconds of video from the secure feed, in case we had to analyze it."

"Good," Tom said. "Give it to Marco."

Pulling open his suit jacket, he said, "I'm going to reach in very slowly." Tom nodded for him to continue.

Dennis produced his phone and handed it to Marco, who quickly accessed its most recent saved video file and hit PLAY.

The image on the phone's screen was so dark and murky that Marco could barely discern any details. "Not sure I can use this," he said to Tom. "I need to see a bit more of where I'm—hang on . . ." The image changed to an exterior shot of the lab. He saw smoke belching up from a half-imploded ramshackle building in a barren desert. He looked at Dennis. "Nevada?"

"Yes. Good guess."

"Thanks," Marco said. "Okay, this I can work with." He made sure that he had his own phone secure inside a closed pocket of his tactical vest, then stood up and nodded to Tom and Diana.

"Back in a few," he said.

Then he stared deeply into the grainy video on the phone's LCD screen. His eyes saw through the moving image, and the edges of his vision blurred, until all that he could see was the baked-white sand and sun-bleached sky of the desert . . .

Marco blinked and squinted against the desert sun.

It felt as if there was as much heat radiating up from the runway tarmac at his feet as there was beating down on him from above. The combination of direct and reflected sunlight was blinding, and painful pricklings needled his exposed skin.

*This is what it feels like to get cooked alive,* he mused.

The sand-scoured wooden shack that hid the entrance to the secret Haspelcorp lab was dozens of yards away. As in the recorded video on Dennis's phone, it continued to spew smoke through rents in its roof of rusted, corrugated metal.

Eager to get out of the sun, Marco walk-jogged toward the dilapidated building. His footsteps slapped against the paved runway surface, making a tiny sound that was all but lost in the vast, lonely spaces of the deep desert. It was difficult for Marco to move so quickly in such dry, brutal heat, but he feared that if he slowed his pace or stopped to rest, the soles of his sneakers would melt under his feet.

He reached the shack. Littering the ground by the entrance were a few small bits of metallic debris. Some of the pieces' edges were straight and clean; others were scorched and melted. Though he didn't know what to make of them offhand, he suspected they might be worth analyzing later. He gathered the pieces, stuffed them into his pants pockets, then moved on to the shack.

He tried to open the door and tore it from its corroded and heat-warped hinges. Part of the wall fell away with it, reduced to a smoldering slab of charcoal. It broke into dusty black cinders at his feet.

"Construction by the lowest bidder," he mumbled, even though the joke was solely for his own ears. Something about the profound emptiness of the landscape that surrounded him made Marco want to talk to himself.

Edging through the door, he paused to let his eyes adjust to the shadows inside the shack. Ahead of him, the fire had exposed and destroyed what looked like some high-tech security devices mounted inside the wall. Next to them was another half-disintegrated door, beyond which was a short hallway.

Everything inside the shack stank of burnt wood.

Marco pushed the sliding door open. It caught on something in its glide track. The grinding noise it produced made Marco suspect that it was ashes or other debris deposited by the fire. With effort he shoved it through the obstruction, opening the portal fully. He was rewarded with a faceful of smoke that stung his eyes until they watered.

Waving away the acrid cloud, Marco walked with caution down the corridor, testing each floorboard's integrity before trusting it with his full weight. A few boards answered his steps with ominous creaks, but the path felt solid.

Another open doorway at the end of the hall led to an elevator shaft, but there was no elevator. Perched at the edge, Marco stole a look down the shaft, which fell away into total darkness. To either side of him were motor housings that had likely controlled the elevator car, but they appeared to be warped and blackened, and their cables were missing.

Looking around, Marco muttered, "I guess some stairs would be a bit too much to ask for." He cast another stare into the seemingly bottomless abyss. "No, let's just have an elevator be the only way to the lab. What could possibly go wrong?"

He unsnapped the flap on one of his tactical vest's many pockets. "Let's see who's laughing now, Dennis," he said as he dug out four glow sticks that were tied together with a spare shoelace. With simple bending motions, he activated the flexible plastic rods. As the chemicals inside them mixed, they gave off a ghostly but intense white light. "That'll do," he said, then dropped them down the elevator shaft.

They fell almost directly straight down, with what

seemed to Marco like surreal slowness, but he timed their fall with his watch at just over four seconds. Doing the math in his head, he concluded that the sticks had fallen roughly three hundred feet.

"Let's have a look at what's down there," he said to himself while retrieving a pair of compact but powerful binoculars from another bulging pouch on the front of his vest. He wrapped the field glasses' strap around his wrist to keep from dropping them, then laid down beside the shaft's edge.

Aiming the binoculars toward the distant glow sticks, he adjusted the focus until he had a sharp image of the bottom of the shaft. It was filled with the wreckage of the elevator car. Checking the sides, he saw a gap in one wall that he suspected would lead into the hidden laboratory.

He pictured himself prone atop a level portion of the wrecked elevator car . . .

. . . and then he was there.

*God, I love teleporting,* he thought with a broad grin as he clambered down off the mangled elevator car. Grabbing the glow sticks, he took a few careful steps into the lab. He coughed as he inhaled more toxic-smelling smoke. Somewhat belatedly, he hoped that the fumes in the lab weren't laced with deadly chemicals or radioactive particles. *Too late now,* he figured.

Moving through the lab, he felt suffocated both by the heat and the odor of gasoline. The smell was strongest in the areas that seemed to be the flashpoints of the fire.

Multiple ignition points and the presence of accelerant: those two factors alone would have been enough to suggest arson even if the scientists hadn't already absconded with the warhead they had built. Adding to Marco's certainty that the lab had been deliberately destroyed was the rather uniform manner in which all of its computers had been smashed and piled together in the center of one workroom.

"Subtle, guys," Marco said sotto voce. "Real subtle."

He wandered from one room to the next, searching for more clues, no matter how trivial they might appear.

The blaze had scoured the lab of almost every scrap of paper. Glass beakers and vials had melted. Even most of the metal had been deformed by the extreme heat.

In a room that he guessed had served as one of the scientists' temporary quarters, he saw the corner of a book on a table partly covered by a toppled locker. He climbed awkwardly over the locker to examine the book. Its front cover was seared black and its pages had been half consumed by fire, but its back cover was only slightly browned. Delicately, he opened it just enough to see what kind of tome it was.

It was a world atlas.

Marco pulled the book free from under the fallen locker cabinet and saw something else on the desk: a small rock. He reached over and picked it up. It was feather-light. Turning it in his fingers, he saw that it was oddly shaped and pitted with small cavities. *Must be volcanic,* he concluded. *Interesting.*

He stuffed the rock in a pocket apart from the metal he'd found outside the shack and tucked the burnt book under his arm. It wasn't much, but he suspected there wasn't anything else in the lab that was worth finding.

"Homeward bound," he said, taking out his wallet and flipping it open to a photo of the NTAC Theory Room.

Staring at the image of his home-away-from-home, he knew he would momentarily be there.

"I don't know how I could've doubted you, Marco," Dennis said, in a tone so neutral that Tom knew it had to be sarcasm. "You've really blown this thing wide open."

Marco sat, arms folded, eyebrows knitting together with sullen indignation, at his desk in the Theory Room. Tom, Jed, Diana, and Dennis had come downstairs at his request after he had returned from the Haspelcorp lab several minutes earlier.

Dennis poked at the volcanic rock on Marco's desk. "I mean, these are the clues we were waiting for: a pebble, some scrap metal, and an atlas that's been used for kindling. Nice work."

"Fifteen minutes ago we didn't have anything," Diana said to him. "All we knew was that you got duped into helping three fanatics from the future build a doomsday weapon. And in case you forgot, you came here looking for help from us. So why don't you do yourself a favor and shut up?"

Jed added, "Couldn't have said it better myself."

Tom directed his remarks to Marco. "What kind of analysis can we do on this stuff?"

"Nothing more than basic tests, for now," Marco said. "The rock and the metal I can put under a microscope, maybe confirm what they're made of. One thing I will say about the rock is that it wasn't from the desert near the lab. But without access to a full forensic suite, I can't tell you much more than that."

Diana asked, "What about the book?"

"A common atlas," Marco said. "Published two years ago. I checked all the pages for markings, notes, or pieces torn out. Except for the parts that burned, it's all there and unmarked."

Picking up a piece of the metal, Jed asked, "Did this get slagged in the fire?"

"I don't think so," Marco said. "The heat damage is only on one side of each piece, and there's no carbon residue. Plus, if my guess is right, those pieces are probably either aluminum or an aluminum alloy, in which case they would've shown a lot more deformation had they been in the lab when it got torched."

"Let me see that," Tom said to Jed, who handed him the piece of lightweight metal. "This heat damage on the side . . . could that have been caused by welding?"

That got Marco's attention. "Now that you mention it, yeah. That's exactly what that looks like."

Tom turned and saw that Dennis was nodding, but Jed and Diana were waiting for an explanation. "The scientists didn't carry that warhead out of the desert on their backs. They had a vehicle—maybe a plane or a helicopter or a car."

Confusion narrowed Diana's eyes. "And they welded it to the vehicle? What for?"

Dennis replied, "Because the vehicle's the delivery method."

"Exactly," Tom said. "They're either flying it or driving

it to their target. The only good news is that their lab was pretty far from anything worth attacking."

"Whoa, hang on," Jed said. "It's less than ninety nautical miles from Las Vegas. That's pretty high-value."

"Not if your goal is to wipe out Jordan's promicin movement," Tom said. His thoughts were a whirlwind as he struggled to see the big picture. He asked Dennis, "How much of that new superelement did you have shipped in from CERN?"

"Just a few ounces," Dennis said. "Plus some antimatter."

"Okay," Tom said. "Marco, what would be the yield on that?"

Marco rolled his eyes. "Ballpark figure? Assuming what Dennis told us about it is true and accurate, a few ounces would be enough to take out a major city. The effective blast radius would be somewhere between eight and ten miles."

"Which means they'd only need to get close to their target," Diana said. "They wouldn't even have to show themselves."

"You know what they say," Marco replied. "'*Almost* only counts in horseshoes, hand grenades, and thermonuclear devices.'"

Dennis said, "Can we cut the gallows humor and stay focused here? Wherever that warhead *is*, we need to find it before it gets where it's *going*."

"He's right," Tom said. "Let's pull up the last twenty-four hours of satellite imagery for—"

"Forget it," Marco interrupted. "Satellites are all fragged. No GPS, no communications, no spy satellites. Any data they had was wiped."

Diana shot back, "What about the archives at the NSA?"

"If we could get a line out, I'd be doing it already," Marco said. "The Army cut our landlines, and they're blocking all cellular and radio signals in the Seattle area. Right now we're completely cut off from the Internet, cable television, and the national communications grid."

Jed sighed in frustration. "If we can't analyze this stuff, and we can't move any data in or out, what the hell are we supposed to do? Sit here with our thumbs up our asses?"

Tom was certain that he knew what Marco was going to say next. He hoped that he was wrong . . . but he wasn't.

"I hate to say it," Marco confessed, "but I think we need to ask either Shawn or Jordan for help."

# THIRTY-FOUR

## 1:21 P.M.

AFTER ELEVEN HOURS in the driver's seat, Jakes could barely feel his ass. It had gone numb hours earlier, somewhere between Salt Lake City and Ogden, Utah. He didn't mind, though, since itching had been all he'd felt from his hind quarters since crossing the Nevada-Utah border at Wendover.

*It's my own fault,* he chided himself. *I should've made sure the air-conditioning in this heap worked before I left.*

He glanced at his left arm, perched on his door, elbow jutting out the open window. The sun had baked a rich brown hue into his skin; his left arm was now two or three shades darker than his right. A gas station attendant in Steptoe, Nevada, had called it a "driver's tan."

Gray clouds had begun to crowd the sky shortly after Jakes had passed Salt Lake City, giving him some relief from the relentless barrage of ultraviolet solar radiation. Cruising north on the divided I-15 freeway into Idaho, he looked up and around. The sky was the color of dirty dishwater, and the humid air smelled of rain.

As usual, there was nothing but crap on the radio.

The road cut a mostly straight line across the Idaho landscape. It had two lanes heading north and two more heading south. Between the two sides of the road was a wide, gully-shaped median packed with hardy desert bushes and loose rocks.

Flanking the highway were broad plains patched with tall weeds and browned soil and dotted occasionally with lonely, small trees. Beyond the plains rose low hills covered with scrub brush, lined up one after another, packed together into long walls of earth. No matter how much of it rolled by, it all looked the same to Jakes.

By some minor miracle, the radio's seek function landed on a station whose music Jakes didn't actually hate, and he locked it in. Though his sojourn in the past had been relatively brief, he had come to appreciate much of America's early-twenty-first-century culture, including its food and cinema, but especially its music, most of which had been lost by his own time. He drummed his hands on the steering wheel in time with the beat.

It seemed a shame to consign so many of mankind's creations to oblivion, but his mission didn't allow him the luxury of sentimentalism. He could no more permit himself to become attached to this enviously privileged era of human civilization than a livestock farmer could allow himself to feel sympathy for animals led by necessity to the slaughter. For Jakes's future to live, this sybaritic epoch had to die.

The whoop of a siren cut through the music.

Jakes looked in his rearview mirror. Red and blue flashing lights raced up from behind him. He recognized the white V-stripe markings on the Idaho State Police car chasing him, and he cursed himself for getting careless. Between the music, the hum of his engine, and the drone of the road passing under his wheels, he had lost focus on where he was and what he was doing.

He slapped the turn signal to the right, slowed, pulled over to the shoulder, and stopped his SUV. The police cruiser rolled to a stop a few car lengths behind him. Jakes turned off his engine and radio, then waited with his hands on his steering wheel and his safety belt still secured.

The sound of a car door opening followed by the snap of booted feet stepping across asphalt drew his eyes to his side-view mirror. The driver of the police car had emerged from his vehicle and was walking toward Jakes's door. Another officer was still inside the car, on the passenger side.

*Where were they hiding?* Jakes wondered. *No billboards out here. Must've been behind a cluster of brush off the shoulder.*

Standing a few feet from his door was the imposing figure of an Idaho State Police trooper. Attired in dark gray pants, a black shirt, mirror-shaded sunglasses, and a black "Smoky the Bear" hat, the trooper stood in a loose but attentive pose, with one hand resting on the grip of his sidearm.

"Sir, do you know why I stopped you?"

"Yes, Officer," Jakes replied. "I was driving too fast."

"You were doing ninety-two in a posted seventy-five zone."

Keeping his voice as level and calm as possible, Jakes said, "Yes, sir. I got caught up in the music I was listening to, and I lost track of my speed. I have no excuse. I'm sorry."

Jakes's statement of contrition didn't seem to do much to satisfy the trooper, who regarded him with a stern mask of disdain. "Can I see your license and registration, please?"

"Of course," Jakes said. "They're right here." He opened the glove compartment and retrieved his driver's license and vehicle registration, both of which were completely legitimate for the body he was inhabiting. As he leaned back to hand his papers to the trooper, he stole a look down at the semiautomatic pistol tucked between his seat and the gear shift.

The trooper took the papers and eyed them with one raised eyebrow. "California? Long way from home."

"Yes, sir." The first rule of talking to law enforcement personnel, Jakes had learned, was to keep one's answers short.

"And what brings you to Idaho?"

"Vacation," Jakes said.

"Uh-huh," the trooper said, still perusing the license and registration. He turned his head and looked through the SUV's rear windows at the tarp-covered warhead in the cargo area. "Whatcha got back there?"

"Camping equipment," Jakes said. The second rule of talking to law enforcement officers was never to volunteer a single bit more information than was absolutely necessary.

Stepping closer to the vehicle and shading his eyes with one hand as he looked through the rear driver's-side window, the trooper said, "Doesn't look like you brought much gear."

"I travel light."

"I can see that." Deeper notes of suspicion crept into his voice. "Mind showing me what's under that tarp, sir?"

"Not at all," Jakes said. "I can release the rear hatch from here, if you like."

The cop walked to the rear of the SUV. "Open it up."

Jakes undid his seat belt, bent forward, and reached down with his left hand to pull the release lever for the hatchback. He set his right hand on the grip of the pistol next to his seat. With a tug, he unlocked the rear hatch, which raised slightly.

The trooper lifted the hatch fully open. Then he leaned in and supported his weight with one hand while he pulled aside the tarpaulin with the other. His jaw went slack when he saw the warhead inside its protective aluminum frame. "What the . . ."

Without a word, Jakes drew his pistol, twisted around, and fired one shot through the trooper's forehead, painting the road behind him with a reddish-gray spray of brain matter.

As the dead man's body slumped to the ground, Jakes fired three more shots at the parked police cruiser. Its windshield became veined with cracks as one slug after another pierced it and slammed into the head and chest of the second state trooper.

After the thunder of four consecutive gunshots within

the confines of his vehicle, the silence that followed felt almost surreal. The air inside the SUV was sharp with the sulfurous fumes of expended gunpowder.

That was Jakes's third rule of talking to law enforcement officers: knowing when to end the conversation.

*What a goddamn inconvenience,* Jakes fumed as he holstered his weapon and got out of his SUV.

He walked behind his vehicle, draped the tarp back over the warhead, and shut the hatch. Then he grabbed the dead trooper by his collar and dragged him back to the police cruiser.

There were no other cars anywhere in sight, and for that small mercy Jakes was grateful to the universe at large. He opened the driver's door of the cruiser and pushed the dead sergeant back inside beside his slain partner.

*Now to mop up,* he told himself. He pulled the memory stick and the DVD from the vehicle's standard-issue dashboard camera system, then used the car's onboard computer to see whether they had already made a query based on his car's license plate; the cop who had remained in the car had been in the process of entering the data when Jakes had shot him. So far, there was no official record of this traffic stop. Jakes canceled the entry.

He shifted the police cruiser into neutral and pushed it off the road into a small stand of thick bushes. To drivers approaching it from behind, it would look like the world's worst-hidden speed trap. Drivers on the other side of the divided highway would see it only from a distance, and the scrub brush would obscure the damage to the windshield.

It would likely be several hours before anyone realized that these two men had gone missing. By then, Jakes would be long gone. Even if they found his fingerprints or DNA inside the car, it wouldn't matter. His new identity had no criminal record. There would be no matching records on file.

Walking back to his vehicle, he squinted up at the bruised-black underbelly of a leaden sky. It looked as if a storm was coming. He climbed back inside his SUV, tossed the memory stick and recordable DVD on the floor in front of the passenger seat, restarted the engine, and shifted into gear.

A catchy song came on the radio.

He turned it off. *Eyes on the road*, he admonished himself. There was still a long way to go—and no more room for error.

# THIRTY-FIVE

## 1:53 P.M.

THE LAST THING Tom had wanted to do was go back out and brave the crossfire hurricane that had descended on Seattle. But there were no working phone lines or e-mail, and cell phones spat out nothing but static. He might have tried sending smoke signals if half the city hadn't already been on fire.

Since no one else had been willing to drive, Tom had ended up behind the wheel of one of NTAC's armored SUVs. Now he was dodging fireballs, bullets, and dozens of random, telepathically hurled projectiles on every block, as he navigated the narrow residential streets of Madrona.

*Yeah, this is exactly what I wanted to be doing today,* he brooded while swerving through a slalom of overturned cars and trucks set ablaze.

Diana was riding shotgun, and Dennis was sandwiched in an awkward pose between Jed and Marco in the backseat.

"If I'd known we were taking the scenic route, I'd have

brought my camera," Dennis said, making no effort to mask his sour mood.

Tom bashed aside the stripped husk of an old Trans Am that was blocking the road, then replied, "Don't thank me, Dennis, thank the Army. They're the ones who turned the interstate into Swiss cheese."

"We'll have more room once we make the turn onto Madison," Diana said, and she was right. Half a minute later, Tom pulled their vehicle through a tight, wheels-squealing, high-speed turn onto East Madison Street that pinned Tom and Jed against the SUV's driver's-side doors, and squashed Dennis even more firmly between Jed and Marco.

The latest in a series of random gunshots ricocheted off their back window, leaving a dull gray scuff. "Good thing this ride's got bullet-resistant glass," Jed said, "or else this would've been a damn short trip."

"It'll be short enough as it is," Tom said. "We'd better figure out what we plan to say to Shawn before we get there."

Diana seemed surprised. "I thought you and Shawn were on good terms."

"We were, but . . ." He didn't know how to finish the sentence. "You know how things get with family. And the way he did Maia's dirty work at that meeting with Jordan didn't help, either."

Dennis leaned forward. "I have a suggestion."

Seeing his former boss's head thrust between the two front seats filled Tom with the urge to whack Dennis's noggin with a mallet.

*Like a human Whac-A-Mole*, Tom mused with a smile.

"Let's hear it," Tom said, momentarily suppressing his mischievous impulse.

"I know this'll sound like a radical idea coming from me, but maybe we should tell your nephew the truth."

Diana directed a dubious look at Dennis. "Before I make any assumptions, exactly what do you define as 'the truth' in this situation, Dennis?"

"We tell him that the Marked have an antimatter bomb and are on their way to nuke Seattle unless his people help us find them and stop them."

Tom shook his head. "And when he asks how the Marked managed to build an antimatter bomb?"

"Well, I don't think we need to go into that," Dennis said.

Marco covered his mouth with his fist and fake-coughed as he muttered, *"Bullshit."*

"Use your head," Jed said. "Some of these people are freakin' mind readers, okay? The second you walk in there, they're gonna know what you did and why you did it, so if I were you, I'd get ready to come clean."

Dennis let out an angry sigh and sat back. "Fine."

Jed wondered aloud, "What if Jordan's people went to the Center?" Diana turned and looked back at him as he added, "I mean, what if we have to deal with not just Shawn, but Jordan, too? That'd make things, well . . . tense."

"The city's getting blown to bits as we speak," Diana said. "And you're worried things might *become* tense?"

Looking around for some kind of support but finding none, Jed replied like a scolded schoolboy, "You know what I mean."

It was Marco and Diana's turn to get pinned to their doors as Tom steered the SUV through a hard, fast, uphill left turn onto Twenty-third Avenue East. Barring attacks and detours, the rest of their trip would be a straight shot north until they reached Crescent and made the turn toward The 4400 Center.

"The big question," Diana said, in her thinking-out-loud way of speaking to no one in particular, "is what are we going to ask Shawn or Jordan's people to do about the bomb if they find it? Do we want them to destroy it?"

Dennis said, "I'd rather they didn't."

"Yeah," Marco interjected sarcastically. "You might lose your job if that happened."

"There's also the fact that it represents a major scientific achievement," Dennis said. "I'd think you and Diana could at least appreciate its value on that level. Simply destroying it would be a waste."

Jed grimaced with doubt. "Maybe, but the last thing you want is for Collier's people to get their hands on a future-tech bomb that won't even set off a radiation detector."

Marco replied, "What would Jordan Collier want with a bomb? He's already got people who can wipe out cities with their promicin abilities."

"Maybe," Jed said, "but it never hurts to have an ace in the hole." He leaned forward. "What do you think, Tom? Could you sleep at night knowing Collier had a nuke?"

"I don't sleep at night as it is," Tom said. "But I can't imagine that would make it any better."

Diana held out her open palms. "All right, then. We want their help finding the bomb, but we don't want them to be the ones who get it back. So we'll do that. We ask them to give us the intel and let us handle the rest."

"Sounds like a great plan," Dennis said. "And what do you think they'll ask for in return?" Mild looks of surprise were volleyed between Diana, Jed, and Marco. Dennis continued: "Do you really think they're going to drop everything while fighting off an invasion of their shiny new city-state just to help you find one little rogue nuke?"

Tom said, "They might if we convince them it's on its way here."

Dennis considered that with a pensive tilt of his head. "Maybe. Maybe not." He raised his eyebrows. "But you're missing my point, Tom. If they decide to go looking for *quid pro quo* in this little scheme, you're in a world of shit. Because they might be able to give you quid, but you're fresh out of quo."

"He's right, Tom," Diana said, putting on her most serious face. "We'd better stop and get them a Starbucks gift card."

Tom replied, "Okay, but don't go cheap like you did for Secret Santa. Get an Applebee's card while you're at it."

"Right," Diana said with mock gravity.

"And a fruit basket," Marco added. "Everybody likes those."

"Wait, are we chipping in on this?" asked Jed. "'Cause all I've got is a twenty."

Frowning at the casual ease with which the NTAC agents riffed on one another's sarcastic quips, Dennis deadpanned, "This is why I miss working with all of you: your professionalism."

Hurtling down a narrow street in a potential urban war zone at ninety miles per hour was probably the worst possible place to lose one's focus for even a second, but for half a minute all that Tom, Diana, Jed, and Marco could do was laugh.

"All right," Tom said at last. "Put a cork in it. We're almost there." He made the left turn onto Crescent, then slowed as he navigated the Center's snaking downhill driveway. "I know we don't have jack or squat to offer. I guess we'll just have to hope that there's enough goodwill left between me and Shawn to get him to help us."

"And if worse comes to worst," Jed said, "we'll offer them Dennis as a human sacrifice."

"That won't work," Diana said. "A human sacrifice is supposed to be someone of value."

As they rounded the next-to-last curve in the driveway, Tom saw Dennis in the rearview mirror, opening his mouth to reply.

Then the SUV slammed to a halt with an earsplitting bang, as if Tom had driven it into a brick wall at twice the speed.

The next thing Tom saw was the steering-column airbag as it hit him in the face. After that, his entire world turned red and purple for what seemed like several seconds.

Gradually, the airbag ceased its oppressive pushing against his face and chest, and then it deflated across the steering wheel. Around him, all of the vehicle's other airbags shrank and went limp, releasing his stunned passengers. Tom wondered if any of them had headaches that hurt as badly as his own.

The SUV's front end had buckled into an accordion shape, and all its windows were fractured from the brutal impact.

"Is everybody hurt?" Tom asked. "Is anybody okay?"

"Yes, and no," Diana said.

Nobody asked what had happened. In a world where telekinesis was an increasingly common fact of life, the cause of their calamitous instant deceleration was easy to guess.

In between the throbbing pains in his skull that kept tempo with his pulse, Tom heard an unfamiliar masculine voice inside his head: **Don't move.**

He looked at Diana, then at Marco. "Anyone else hear that?"

"I think we all just heard that," Marco said. Everyone else in the car nodded to confirm his hypothesis.

**Stay inside your vehicle,** the voice commanded them. **And keep your hands where we can see them. We have you surrounded.**

Diana pressed the cold-gel pack to her cheek and tried not to think about the bruise that was probably going to cover the right side of her face by tomorrow morning—assuming she and the rest of Promise City lived that long.

The group from the SUV sat on one side of the long table in the conference room where, only two days earlier, they had met with Jordan and his inner circle. Diana was flanked by Tom on her left and Marco on her right; Jed occupied the seat past Tom, and Dennis was at the opposite end, next to Marco.

All four men held cold-gel packs against various parts of their anatomies. Tom pressed his to his nose. Jed was icing his neck. Marco had draped his gel pack over the top of his head, and Dennis had used his to cover his eyes.

For the first time since intercepting him at the NTAC crisis center, Diana noted that Dennis looked like the odd man out, as he was the only one in their group not outfitted with a bullet-resistant tactical vest.

A door opened. Shawn entered the room. He looked haggard. His clothes were stained and wrinkled, and his hands bore a patina of dried blood. Grime and sweat had matted his hair, and his normally bright eyes were rimmed with dark circles born of fatigue. He was followed closely by Heather Tobey, who was only marginally less frazzled-looking than Shawn.

Walking in behind her was Jordan Collier. His clothes remained a spectral shade of gray, and his hair was caked with pale dust, but his face and hands had been rinsed enough to once again reveal flesh.

The entourage that followed him—Gary, Kyle, Maia, and a trio of others whose names Diana never managed to remember—had apparently been too busy to clean themselves. They all were still painted the same ashen hue from head to toe, and carried with them the acrid pall of death wrought by fire.

All of them, from first to last, remained standing on their side of the table. "Forgive us if we don't sit down," Jordan said. "We're a bit busy right now."

"Gee," Tom said, "thanks for penciling us in, then."

Jordan responded with a thin, humorless smile. "The only reason you're not all dead right now is because Gary assured me that your intentions are peaceful."

Speaking directly to Gary, Diana asked, "What else have you plucked from our heads? Do we even need to say why we're here?"

"All I know is that you were coming to bring us a warning. Once the airbags hit you, your thoughts got hard to read."

Marco chortled. "Probably 'cause we were all thinking the same thing: *Ouch*."

"For Christ's sake, we're wasting time," Dennis snapped. He looked at Tom and Diana. "Tell them."

Kyle pointed menacingly at Dennis. "If I were you, I'd shut up for the rest of this meeting." He gestured at the four NTAC agents. "They've earned some slack. *You haven't.*"

Jordan lifted a hand and signaled Kyle to back off. As the young man took a half step backward, Jordan said to the NTAC team, "Someone give me the high points—quickly, please."

Tom leaned forward and folded his hands on the table. "Three agents of the Marked tricked Dennis into helping them build some kind of undetectable, miniature anti-matter warhead. Sometime in the last twenty-four hours, they stole it and went rogue. We think they're looking to deploy the weapon."

Shawn asked, "Against Promise City?"

Diana shrugged. "We're not sure. That's why we're here. We've lost access to most of the tools that would help us track the bomb. We need your help to find it before it goes off."

Concern creased Jordan's brow. "You described the weapon as a 'miniature' warhead. How big a threat is this bomb?"

"It'll vaporize everything in an eight-mile radius," Marco said, "and the shock wave and thermal effects will wipe out everything for twenty miles beyond that."

"Sounds big enough to me," Jed said.

Heather asked, "What about fallout?"

"That's probably the only good news in all of this," Marco said. "An antimatter weapon has a near-total conversion of matter to energy, so there'd be almost no residual radiation."

Jordan looked at Gary, who gave a single, grave nod of confirmation. "All truthful," said the telepath.

That provoked a small chortle from Jordan, whose eyes widened as he shook his head. "I guess it's true what they say. There's no situation so bad that it can't be made worse."

"What bothers me," Tom said, "is that this doesn't fit the Marked's MO."

"How so?" Jordan asked.

"They tend to think bigger than this," Tom said. "Maybe they're counting on you being too distracted fighting the military to see them coming, but they'd have to know that's a long shot. I mean, even if they took you down, there'd still be p-positive people all over the world who'd continue the fight."

Nodding, Jordan said, "True. But if we each have our part to play in shaping the future, maybe getting rid of one person at the right time is all they need to do to win." He sighed. "Unfortunately, my people have their hands full fighting this invasion. Until we've secured the city, there's nothing we can do to help you. I'm sorry."

As Jordan turned to leave, Tom said to his nephew, "What about you, Shawn? Are you letting Jordan talk for you? Is he back in charge here?"

"That's a low blow, Uncle Tommy," Shawn said. "And no, I'm still in charge of the Center. But right now he and I are working together to protect the city and our people."

Marco lifted his rucksack and opened the top flap. "Please," the analyst begged. "All we need is someone to help us study the clues we already found. We're not asking you to fight the battle for us, just to point us in the right direction."

"Sorry," Shawn said. "Maybe when the city's safe we can do something then." He began ushering everyone else out of the conference room. "If you want to go back to NTAC, we—"

"We have to help them," Maia said, halting the exiting group and silencing the room. All eyes turned toward the young teen, whose intense mien was made all the more unnerving by its deathly gray patina of chalky dust. She faced Jordan. "If we don't help them, the Movement ends today."

The NTAC agents and Dennis got out of their chairs and joined everyone else in a cluster around Maia.

Jordan dropped to one knee in front of her and placed his hands on her shoulders. "What do you see, Maia? How does the Movement end?"

With the icy finality of words spoken from beyond the grave, Maia said, "The world turns gray and dies."

# THIRTY-SIX

THERE WAS A knock on the conference room's door. Shawn opened it, revealing the shy young Asian man standing on the other side. "Come in," Shawn said, motioning the newcomer forward.

Moving in small, timid steps, the bookish man-boy edged into the conference room. Noting the large number of people standing there waiting for him, he swallowed nervously and adjusted his cheap bifocals, which were held together at the bridge by a thick wrapping of cloth-backed tape.

"Everyone," Shawn said, "this is Chongrak Panyarachun, the one I told you about." He led Chongrak to the chair at the head of the table. On the tabletop had been arranged the book, rock, and bits of metal that Marco Pacella had brought with him.

Pulling out the chair, Shawn said to Chongrak, "It's okay. Have a seat." The American-born son of Thai immigrants hesitated in front of the chair for a moment, then shrank into it, as if he hoped to disappear simply by sitting down.

Shawn stepped back as he nodded to Heather, who moved forward and squatted beside Chongrak. She placed her hand atop his with subtle tenderness and smiled. "Thank you for coming."

All at once, Chongrak's face brightened. He smiled back at Heather in a manner that conveyed his trust for her.

Watching the way that Heather brought out people's innate talents and nurtured their best aspects moved Shawn as deeply now as it had the first time he had seen her in action. At best, Shawn could restore someone to what they were before they met him; Heather's gift helped people improve themselves. He did not envy her ability, but he deeply admired and respected it.

"We need you to examine these objects," Heather said to Chongrak, while waving her hand over Marco's evidence. "Can you do that for us, and tell us what you see?"

Chongrak nodded. With his left hand he reached forward and tentatively took hold of one of the pieces of half-melted aluminum. As soon as he had hold of it, his fingers seized it like the talons of an eagle around its prey, and his entire demeanor changed. He closed his eyes. Sat up straight. Held his head high. Before everyone's eyes, he transformed from a wallflower into the person whose presence owned the room.

"It's scrap from a welding process," Chongrak declared in a confident, rich baritone that seemed too large for his body. "Aluminum. It was chosen for its light weight and its strength."

Modulating her voice to a soothing volume and pitch, Heather asked, "Chosen by whom? Can you see the welding now?"

The young man's face tensed with effortful concentration.

"I see her," Chongrak said. "She's young. Blond." Though his eyes were still closed, he reached forward with his right hand and picked up another piece of metal. "It's nighttime. She's creating a frame for something. Inside a truck."

Meaningful looks traveled from person to person around the room. Taking the cue, Heather asked Chongrak, "What kind of truck? Tell me about it."

"It's white," Chongrak said. "A sport-utility vehicle. With a hatchback." He winced profoundly enough to bare his teeth for a moment. "Can't see what model . . . That's all there is." The two pieces of metal fell from his hands and clanged brightly as they bounced across the tabletop.

From across the room, Marco waved for Heather's attention and pointed at the burned book. She reached over and nudged it into Chongrak's grasp.

He picked it up with both hands, hugged it to his chest, and let out a pained gasp. "Fire!" he cried. "Pages burning!"

"Go back further," Heather urged softly, placing a consoling hand on his arm. "Before the fire. Has anyone ever read this book?"

Chongrak calmed and took a breath. "Yes," he said. His fingers traveled slowly along the book's charred edges. "They all did. They read it together."

"Who are they?" asked Heather. "What do they look like?"

"Two men and the blond woman. One man is white, the other is black." He paused and cocked his head at an angle. "They're flipping pages. Looking for something. A map."

Shawn grew anxious as he felt time slipping past, and he made a circling motion with his hand to ask Heather to pick up the pace. She nodded and turned back to the psychometric man.

"Chongrak," Heather said. "What map are they looking at?"

"The United States."

Confused glances circuited the room. No one seemed to know what to make of that. Shawn threw a questioning look at Heather, who shrugged in frustration. She asked Chongrak, "Is there any part of the map that they seem most interested in?"

"Not sure," he said. "They're looking at the whole western half . . . The white man is pointing at something; I don't know what. Could be Idaho, or Montana, or Wyoming . . . They're closing the book. That's all." He dropped the book back on the table with a resounding slam.

All that was left was the rock. Heather picked it up and placed it gently into Chongrak's hand. "Take your time," she said.

He breathed in deeply and tilted his head back, as if he were staring at the sky. "It's the white man who was reading the book. He's picking up the rock. From barren ground covered with water. Skinny trees in the distance." Chongrak smiled. "Steam. There's a pillar of steam rising from the ground. A geyser."

Marco blurted out, "A geyser?" Despite Heather's glare,

he continued. "Is the rock from Yellowstone National Park?"

"Yes," Chongrak said. "The man is in Yellowstone Park."

Reeling with shocked understanding, Marco collapsed into a chair and exclaimed, "Oh, my God."

Shawn sensed that a breakthrough had been made, so he nodded to Heather, who tapped Chongrak's shoulder. The young Thai man opened his eyes, and his reticent disposition returned.

Heather relieved him of the rock in his hand. "Thank you, Chongrak," she said. "You've been a great help. You can go now."

He smiled without looking her in the eye, then crept from his seat and walked in tiny steps to the door. Shawn opened it ahead of the boyish man, who slipped out of the room without another word or even a single look back.

As the door closed, Jordan said to Marco, "Explain."

"It makes sense now," Marco said. "The Marked are looking for a game-changer. Something that'll neutralize your movement in one shot. They're taking the bomb to Yellowstone."

Everyone except Marco looked utterly mystified. It was Jordan who asked, "So? So what?"

"So," Marco said with naked scorn, "the park sits right on top of the Yellowstone Caldera."

Shawn and most of the other people in the room still had no idea what Marco was talking about, but one person did: Diana.

She fell into a chair and covered her open mouth with her hands. "Oh, Jesus."

Tom looked perplexed as he said to Diana, "Seeing as Marco can't explain his way out of a wet paper bag on this, you want to take a shot?"

Diana nodded, lowered her hands, and took a breath. "The Yellowstone Caldera is the remnant of the last eruption of the Yellowstone supervolcano," she said.

Kyle asked, "There's a volcano under Yellowstone Park?"

Marco replied, "Not just any volcano—*the* volcano. The largest active volcanic system on Earth—an extinction-level event waiting to happen."

"And the Marked are looking to make it happen today," Diana said. "That antimatter bomb they built is powerful enough to blow the bedrock cap right off the top of the caldera."

Jordan said, "And when it does . . . ?"

"It'll be like shaking up a bottle of seltzer on a hot summer day, then shooting off the cap," Marco replied. "Imagine a pool of superhot molten rock three times larger than Los Angeles. And trapped inside it is gas under pressure. Rip off the cap, and all that trapped gas goes *boom*, straight up. It'll be the biggest volcanic eruption in human history."

Jed held up his hands. "Okay, but it's in the middle of Nowhere, Wyoming. So, what?"

"With an eruption that big," Diana said, "it won't matter where it happens. If that caldera goes up, it's game over. Kiss the human race good-bye."

Genuinely petrified, Shawn asked, "Are you sure you're not exaggerating a bit? Can one volcanic eruption really be that big a disaster?"

Standing up, Marco said, "Let me put this in perspective for all of you. The last eruption that was even *close* to what this would be happened seventy-four thousand years ago, at Lake Toba in Sumatra. That one blast nearly ended the human species."

He circled the table as he continued his impromptu lecture. "It blotted out the sun all over the globe, wiped out animal populations, killed plants, and dropped temperatures to near freezing everywhere except the equator.

"Genetic research into mitochondrial DNA has identified that moment as a 'choke point' in the history of the human genome. It whittled our population down to a few thousand breeding pairs worldwide. The fact that it didn't render us extinct might've just been a lucky break."

Stopping at the head of the table, Marco added, "This eruption will be much, much worse. It'll bury North America from coast to coast with more than two feet of toxic ash. It'll blot out the sun for years, maybe a decade, triggering a nuclear winter and then a new Ice Age that'll last thousands of years. This is the world ending with both a bang and a whimper."

Horrified silence followed.

Then all eyes turned to Maia, who stepped from the room's periphery and planted herself in front of Jordan. "Like I said: the world turns gray and dies."

# THIRTY-SEVEN

## 2:45 P.M.

TOM STOOD IN Shawn's office near the closed door, not yet ready to accept Jordan's invitation to take part in some crazy psychic communion. "Will this be like that time with the pie?"

"No, Tom," Jordan said. "The phenomenon you experienced in Evanston simply allowed people to share memories. This is about creating a blended perception in real time."

Three people stood behind Jordan, all of them waiting for Tom. Gary was the only one whom Tom knew. Jordan had introduced the other two as Lucas, whose ability was to create telepathic gestalts, and Hal, a remote-viewer whose specialty was finding people or things even when they were in motion or very far away.

"I don't want anybody reading my thoughts," Tom said.

Lucas replied, "It's not like that. When we link, we'll see and hear the same things, but our thoughts will stay private unless we choose to share them."

With a wry, mischievous smile, Gary added, "As private as they can be with a telepath in the room."

"You're not helping," Tom said to Gary.

Gary held up one hand and bowed his head in a gesture of apology. "Relax, Tom. I have more control than I used to. These days I can search people's minds for specific information, like whether they're a friend or an enemy, or if they're hiding something important. Now that I know you're on our side—"

"I wouldn't say I'm *on your side*, exactly," Tom protested. "I'd say we have a common interest in stopping Armageddon."

The telepath's jaw clenched for half a second, as if he were resisting the urge to speak in anger. "Call it what you will. The point is, I won't be poking around inside your head."

"Tom, I invited you to join us for two reasons," Jordan said. "The first is so that you can have unfiltered access to the same information we have. That way you'll know we're not keeping any secrets from you. The second reason is that once we find this bomb, you and your team will have to come up with a plan for stopping it. All my people who have abilities suited for combat are busy fighting the troops in the city or defending this Center from an impending attack. I can't spare anyone until the battle for the city is over."

Tom nodded and stepped forward to stand with the group. "All right," he said. "I understand. Let's get on with it."

The five men joined hands and shut their eyes.

At first, the summons of the gestalt was like a whisper, barely detectable amid the noise of random thoughts in Tom's consciousness. Then it washed over him like a warm, gentle wave.

He felt his breathing and his pulse synchronize with those of the others. Though his eyes were still closed, he saw himself and the others in the circle from above, and he instinctively knew that this was Hal's remote-viewing ability being shared.

Jordan asked, "Where should we start, Tom?"

"I'm guessing our vehicle's been on the road for a while," Tom said. "Marco said the fire at the lab was mostly out by the time he got there, so it must've been set in the early hours of the morning. By now, the truck could be almost to Yellowstone."

The remote-viewing perspective raced up and away, through the Center's roof as if it were vapor, and beyond the clouds, to where the horizon began to show the first hint of a curve. Then they sped southeast, Earth beneath them a blur. Arrowing through mountains of cloud, they flew past Mount Rainier, arced over the Rockies, and soared over the western plains.

"We'll start at the park and work our way backward along the most likely route," Hal said.

The others murmured their agreement.

As they spiraled down to ground level, Tom felt a queasy churning in his gut and a sick dizziness in his head. All he saw was a blur of landscape. "How do you know where you are?"

"I just sense it," Hal said. "I imagine where I want to look, and then I feel my way there."

Seconds later they were racing parallel to the ground, tracing the path of the road, the dotted traffic lines bleeding into a nonstop yellow stripe.

Over the course of several minutes, cars of every kind whipped past, some alone, others in tight clusters.

At the first sign of any white vehicle, Hal slowed their flight and lingered for a better look. The first was a compact car; the second was a sports car.

On the highway, some distance from Yellowstone, they spotted a third white vehicle, a van.

"Let's check it out," Tom said.

Jordan said, "I thought we were looking for an SUV."

"Close enough. We can't risk missing this thing."

Hal guided their floating point of view toward the van, then they pierced its side and were inside. Its cargo area was packed with hanging drapes of fabric, bundled metal rods, and boxes of tools and small parts—but nothing that looked like a bomb. "Not our guy," Gary said. "He works for a department store, installing window treatments."

"Okay," Tom said. "Move on."

Their disembodied view of the world reversed direction, slipping like a ghost from the van. Miles zipped by, the flat expanse of highway all but unchanging as it twisted like a ribbon toward the horizon beneath an overcast dome of sky.

Something in the distance caught Tom's eye. "There," he said. "White SUV, coming our way."

"Got it," Hal said, accelerating toward the vehicle.

In a blink they were through the windshield and in the passenger seat beside the driver. He was a Caucasian man in his early forties, with brown hair and a slim build. There was dried blood along the edges of his fingernails. Tucked between his seat and the gearshift was a Glock semiautomatic pistol.

In the cargo area was an ominously warhead-shaped lump under a dark green canvas tarp.

"Bingo," Tom said.

"This is definitely our guy," Gary said. "It's Jakes. The whole plan's clear in his head. He's heading for the western shore of Yellowstone Lake. When he gets there, he'll arm the bomb and roll his truck into the lake, to keep anyone from tampering with the warhead before it detonates."

"What about his conspirators?" asked Jordan. "The other members of the Marked?"

"Wells and Kuroda are on a flight out of Vegas. They're heading to Tokyo, and from there into hiding."

"Note every detail," Tom said. "Make and model, license plate, nearest mile marker, how much fuel he has, everything."

"Nissan Pathfinder," Jordan said. "Gas tank at one-half."

Hal pulled back so they seemed to be traveling backward in front of the vehicle. "California plates," he said. "Tag number: three, X-ray, Zulu, X-ray, seven-one-three."

"Okay," Tom said. "Now we just need to know where he is."

Still pacing the SUV, they climbed to an altitude of what Tom guessed was about a hundred feet and surveyed the area. "There's something up ahead," Lucas said. "A toll booth, maybe?"

"Oh, hell," Tom said. "That's the entrance to Yellowstone. Our guy's only minutes from the Wyoming border."

Jordan asked with obvious concern, "How long till he reaches the caldera?"

"Fifteen minutes to the perimeter," Tom said. "He'll reach dead center in an hour. After that, it'll be too late to stop him."

# THIRTY-EIGHT

EVERY MAP OF Wyoming and Yellowstone National
Park that Marco had been able to find in The 4400
Center's educational library was open on the cafeteria
table between Tom and Diana. It was a veritable
mountain of paper.

The NTAC team had gathered in the Center's main
commissary to come up with a plan, no matter how hasty,
for intercepting the Marked agent transporting the bomb.
Despite the fact that the building had a dedicated power
generator, the current crisis had necessitated the shutdown
of noncritical systems—which, to the group's collective
chagrin, included the air-conditioning.

"Tom's time estimate was correct," Marco said, sleeving
sweat from his forehead. With his index finger, he traced
the line of the highway leading into the park from the
west. "By now our guy is on West Entrance Road. He'll
turn south on Grand Loop Road in about twenty-five

minutes. From there, he's only half an hour from the western shore of Yellowstone Lake."

Jed returned from the kitchen with an armload of pre-made sandwiches wrapped in cellophane and thin cardboard. "All I could find was egg salad with low-cal mayo," he said, dropping the sandwiches on top of the maps. "Heather gave everything else to the wounded folks in the auditorium."

"I wouldn't care if it was shoe leather," Marco said, reaching for one of the packages. "I'd eat anything right now."

"Ditto," Tom added, grabbing a sandwich for himself. "What about bottled water?"

Apologizing with a shrug and a shake of his head, Jed said, "They went to the same place as the good sandwiches. Along with the juice and the soda."

Diana tore open a sandwich for herself and bit off a huge mouthful. Through half-chewed egg and bread, she mumbled, "God, these are terrible," but she kept on eating, just as everyone else did. It had been a long day, and none of them had eaten since before coming to work seven hours earlier. Not even the ripe odor of exhausted bodies wrapped in heavy, Kevlar-lined tactical vests was enough to put them off their appetites.

Munching on his own sandwich, Jed asked, "Can we alert the Park Service? Have them intercept the truck?"

"It's not really what they're trained for," Tom said. "One mistake and they might get themselves killed, or worse, set off the bomb. Besides, how are we supposed to contact them? We still have no phone, e-mail, or radio contact with the world outside Seattle."

Jed shrugged. "Maybe one of Jordan's people can send out a message telepathically."

Marco looked askance at the agent. "Yeah, that'll really add to the report's credibility: a mental message from the people the government's trying to kill, telling them they need to drop everything to stop a bomb in Yellowstone."

Glowering at Marco, Jed replied, "It was just an idea."

Looking back and forth between two maps, Diana asked, "How far is it from here to Yellowstone?"

"In a straight line?" Marco said. "Roughly seven hundred nautical miles. Why?"

"There's a Cessna Citation jet hangared at Boeing Field," she said. "Maybe if we—"

"It'd take us twenty minutes just to get to it," Tom said. "Besides, what if it's not fueled?"

Marco added, "Plus, the Citation's top speed is about five hundred knots. Even if we went wheels up right this second, we'd never make it."

"You're forgetting one more thing," Jed said. "How far do you think we'll get from Boeing Field before the Air Force shoots us outta the sky?"

"Fine," Diana said, flinging up her arms in surrender. "We can rule out air travel." She massaged her forehead. "God, this is annoying. Stopping bombs in trucks is the whole reason the Department of Homeland Security was created! But now, even though we know where the truck is and where it's going, there's nothing we can do about it."

They all stared at the maps, each of them wearing the same scrunched look of consternation.

Tom shot a look at Marco. "If you could teleport us—"

"Not a chance," Marco said. "Shifting myself out to the lab and back was one thing. Taking somebody with me is just too draining. I can't do that again, not this soon, and not from this distance." Frowning, he continued: "If we could just get Jordan to pull one telekinetic, or one electrokinetic, and put them in touch with that telepathic gestalt team of his, we could frag Jakes and that truck, and end this right now."

"Forget it," Tom said. "It took the threat of an apocalypse just to convince Jordan this was important enough to let us use his team to *find* the damn truck. As long as he's stuck in a shooting war with the Army, he's not taking any chances."

"In other words," Jed said, crumpling his empty sandwich package, "Jordan can't see the forest for the trees." He lobbed his trash into a distant garbage can. "He's so busy defending his backyard, he can't see the sky is falling."

Jordan's voice turned their heads toward the door. "I'm well aware of what's happening," he said, walking into the commissary. "But contrary to popular belief, aggressive abilities aren't that common among the promicin-positive. For every person who develops a talent suited for combat, there are nineteen who don't." He stopped at the end of the table and stood with his hands clasped behind his back. "My people are badly outnumbered on the street, and most of those defending this Center have to do so with guns. I have one telekinetic fighting to keep a protective force field around the building, and one bodyguard skilled in psychic attacks protecting me. So it's not that I don't *want* to task anyone with helping you. It's that I don't currently *have* anyone available to do so."

"Yeah, we get that," Tom said. "And we'll take out the truck on our own, if only we can *get* to it."

"*That*," Jordan said with a smile, "I can help with."

Several minutes later Jordan returned, stopped in the stuffy commissary's doorway, and looked back into the corridor behind him. "Kendall? Can you come in, please?"

Diana watched Jordan usher a pretty teenage girl into the dining hall. He directed her to the table with the NTAC agents and followed her in. As she drew closer, Diana saw that the girl was of mixed Asian and European ancestry. Her raggedly sheared, shoulder-length black hair was streaked with bright pink and turquoise highlights. She was attired in ripped blue jeans that had been faded almost to white; a Colbert Nation T-shirt; a leather jacket that looked as if it had endured more than one high-speed wipeout on a gravel road; and scuffed combat boots.

"Everyone," Jordan said, "this is Kendall Graves. I've asked her to help you, and she's agreed." Nodding to the girl, he added, "Say hello."

With a glazed look of boredom that seemed unique to adolescents, she lifted her chin at the agents. "Hey."

Diana had no reason to dislike the girl, but everything about Kendall—from her dismissive hauteur to the way that she radiated feral sexuality simply by virtue of her youth—made Diana fear that this was what the future held for Maia.

Finger-combing his sweat-soaked hair from his eyes, Marco asked the girl, "Are you a teleporter?"

"I open portals," Kendall said with evident pride. With

a casual turn of her head, she tossed her multicolored hair behind her shoulder. "Show me where you want to go, and I'll give you a door that gets you there."

Tom gave an approving nod. "Sounds perfect."

"Beats dealin' with the airlines," Kendall said with a smile. She planted one hand to accentuate the curve of her hip and shifted her weight to emphasize the lines of her coltish legs. "So . . . where ya goin'?"

"Yellowstone National Park," Diana said.

A befuddled look raised the girl's steeply arched eyebrows, one of which Diana saw was pierced. "Where is that, exactly?"

"Wyoming," Diana replied. "Heard of it?" Holding up a map of the United States, she pointed at the park. "Here."

Kendall nodded, apparently ignoring Diana's thinly masked, irrational hostility. "Cool. No sweat. I've done portals that far before. I can get you there."

Tom asked, "Can you move more than one person at a time?"

"I just open a door," Kendall said. "Whoever goes through, goes through. One, five, ten—makes no difference to me."

"So far, so good," Jed said. He asked Jordan, "Can we get our guns and ammo back? I'd rather not have to throw rocks at this sonofabitch when we catch up to him."

"I'll have your weapons brought down," Jordan said.

Marco interjected, "If someone could throw in a few bottles of water while they're at it—"

"Consider it done," Jordan said.

Diana spread out a map of Wyoming on the table. The

paper crinkled crisply under her hands as she said, "All we have to do now is decide where we should ambush Jakes."

Everyone gathered around the map. "At this point," Jed said, pointing, "he's probably still on West Entrance Road."

"Yeah," Marco said, "but we have no way of knowing exactly *where* on the road. If we pop in behind him, we're sunk."

Pointing at the map, Tom said, "I see another problem: not many side roads off that stretch. There's no place to set up."

Crossing his arms, Marco said, "The only place where we'd have that is the intersection of West Entrance and Grand Loop Road. We know he has to make that turn to get to his target."

"Isn't that cutting it kinda close?" Diana asked. "If we wait until he reaches the intersection, he'll already be well inside the caldera's perimeter. What if he detonates the warhead before we can disarm it?"

"Then six billion people are gonna have a real bad day," Tom said. "Jed and I can set up for sniper shots. Diana, we'll need you as an advance scout, to give us a warning before he comes into range. As soon as he reaches the intersection, we'll take the shot: kill him first, then stop the truck."

Jed nodded. "Copy that."

"Guys," Diana said with a worried frown, "I hate to ask this, but what if you miss? How do we pursue the truck?"

Tom looked expectantly at Kendall. "I don't suppose we can take a car through with us?"

"Sorry," Kendall said. "I can only open a portal as wide as my arms can reach." Striking a pose that reminded

Diana of Leonardo da Vinci's famous sketch "Vitruvian Man," Kendall added, "Nothing wider than this can go."

Marco quipped, "Anyone got a Mini Cooper?"

"Screw that," Jed said. "I'm not doin' a high-speed pursuit in a goddamn Mini Cooper."

"Relax," Marco said. "It was just a joke."

Dismayed grimaces darkened the agents' faces. Jed paced and wiped sweat from his face. Then he stopped, turned to the group, and said, "We could commandeer a car on site."

"There's no guarantee we'll find one exactly when we need it," Tom said. "Plus, the moment we start jacking rides, the park's rangers'll be all over us. And in case any of you have forgotten, we're technically all federal fugitives right now."

Diana looked at Kendall's scratched-and-patched leather jacket and had a flash of inspiration. "Motorcycles!" she exclaimed. "Tom, I know you still know how to ride, and I can handle one okay. What about you, Jed?"

"Hell, yeah," Jed said. "I used to ride a Harley."

"Narrow enough to pass through the portal," Diana said, "and more than fast enough to catch an SUV."

Tom smiled in approval. "Nice thinking." He looked at Jordan. "Can your people scare us up some cycles?"

"Absolutely," Jordan said. "We have some in the garage."

"That leaves just one little problem," Jed said. "Assume everything goes right: we clip Jakes and stop the truck. How the hell do we disarm this superbomb of his?"

Everyone cast imploring looks at Marco.

"Oh, sure," the harried young analyst said with a put-upon scowl. "No pressure."

# THIRTY-NINE

## 3:17 P.M.

Tom KEPT TELLING HIMSELF the same lie, in the hope that simple repetition would make it true: *This is just another mission, no different than any other.*

He ignored the acid burning in his stomach. The sour bile twisting its way back up his throat. The adrenaline tremors that were shaking his hands.

*It's nothing,* he assured himself, even though he knew he was lying. No matter how many times the FBI or NTAC had trained him to go after rogue weapons of mass destruction, the real thing never felt like it did in the training exercises. The people who had trained him had been able to simulate everything except the sickening sensation of real fear.

No simulation had ever made him hear his own pulse pounding in his temples, or feel his heart slamming against his sternum, or need to wipe sweat from his palms every ten seconds.

*I might never see Kyle again,* he realized. There were many things he still wanted to say to his son and not nearly enough time to say them. *I should ask to talk to him before I go*, he decided. *Just in case . . .* He didn't want to complete that thought.

As soon as Shawn's and Jordan's people rounded up three motorcycles, Tom, Jed, and Diana would drive them through one of Kendall's dimensional portals, on their way to a rendezvous hundreds of miles away, with a fanatic who was ready to end the world in a storm of fire and ice.

"All in a day's work," he and Diana had joked, both of them hiding behind thin smiles made of nothing but bravado.

For a few more minutes, however, Tom had a small office to himself as he prepared for the op. He had tightened the straps on his tactical vest, checked his Glock twice to make sure it was fully loaded, and visually confirmed that he had all three magazines for his M4A assault rifle tucked into pockets of his vest. As long as someone fetched him a decent riding helmet, he'd have everything he'd need to make a suicidal attack on a rogue Marked agent with an antimatter bomb.

*Nothing like playing for all the marbles*, he mused, downing the last few drops of water from a liter-sized bottle.

A knock on the office's door startled Tom out of his gallows-humor reverie. He set aside his rifle and lunged for the door. His instincts told him that it was Kyle on the other side of the door, here to see him in case this proved to be their last opportunity to say good-bye.

Tom pulled open the door and discovered that, as usual, his instincts were completely wrong.

Maia Skouris looked up at him with her disturbingly steady gaze. "I need to talk to you," she said. She strode into the office without waiting for his reply. "Shut the door."

Turning to face the blond teen, Tom said, "Maia, shouldn't you be seeing your mother right now instead of me?"

"There's no time," Maia said. She reached into a pocket of her dust-coated jeans and produced a needle and a syringe filled with luminous chartreuse fluid. "You need to take this," she declared, placing the hypodermic needle on the desk. "Now."

"Stop right there," Tom said, backing away from the syringe as if it contained something radioactive. He pointed an accusing finger at it. "Is that what I think it is?"

She walked behind the desk, as if instinctively seizing the power position in the room. "It's a concentrated version of the promicin shot," she said.

He shook his head. "I've been taking U-pills every—"

"U-pills can't block this," Maia said. "It'll work much faster than regular promicin, but it won't matter unless you inject it before you leave on your mission to stop the bomb."

Tom recoiled in surprise. "How do you know about . . . ?" He let his question fade away. It wasn't important how she knew about the mission. Folding his arms, he continued. "I'm absolutely not taking that shot, Maia."

"You have to," she said, her voice becoming more forceful.

He stepped forward and leaned on the desk, enabling

him to loom over her. "Why? Because of that 'White Light' prophecy book Kyle says he found? I don't care if that thing's true or not. Even if it guarantees that I survive the shot, there's no telling what kind of freakish power I'd get. What if it turns me into a living nightmare, the way it did to my nephew Danny? Or to that Typhoid Mary woman your mom and I had to chase down a few years ago? Who's to say I'd turn out any better than them?"

"Me," Maia replied. "That won't happen to you. I promise."

Pushing back from the desk, Tom shook his head. "No," he said. "Not good enough. I made a promise to myself, Maia. I refused promicin when Kyle offered it to me, and after the fifty/fifty virus killed my sister I swore I'd *never* take the shot. So I can't just take your word for *this*."

"But you need to," Maia said.

"What're you saying?" Tom asked, trying to figure out what the girl was leaving unspoken. "That you know I *will* take it?"

"No," Maia said. "What I *know* is that you have a choice."

"I've made my choice," he said.

Fury imparted a shrill edge to the teen's voice. "You're making the wrong one! You have to trust me."

"Trust you?" He almost laughed. "You've lied before, when it suited you. Made up false prophecies."

"I know," she said, looking guilty. "This is different."

"Why?"

"Because you're the one who decides whether the human race lives or dies." She met his stare. "Unless you take this shot right now, before you leave this room, every single person on the planet will die—starting with Diana."

Hearing his partner's name jolted Tom. He wondered whether Maia had invoked her adoptive mother's name because of some lingering resentment stemming from their argument a few days earlier, or if she was doing it merely to manipulate Tom.

He rounded the desk and confronted Maia. "What do you mean, 'starting with Diana'?"

The girl held her ground, not backing up even half a step as Tom marched toward her.

"Let me tell you something I've learned about the future," Maia said. "It's like a river—always moving, always taking the path of least resistance. Sometimes the things we do make ripples in the water; sometimes they make a splash. Only a few things are ever big enough to change the river's direction."

Nodding at the needle on the desktop, he asked, "What does that have to do with Diana? Or the death of the human race?"

"You and Diana are leaving in a few minutes to stop the bomb," Maia said. "If you don't take the shot, you're going to fail, and Diana will be the first to die."

"And if I do take the shot? What happens then?"

"That's not as clear," Maia said. "Right now, the future in which you *don't* take the shot is the dominant one. It makes all the others too hard to see."

"So you're saying I *don't* take the shot."

"No!" Maia growled and pulled her fingers through her

crud-encrusted hair in frustration. "Listen to me. Some events in the future can't be changed, but some can. I'm not saying you don't have a choice—you do. All I'm telling you is what the consequences of your choices will be."

Maia picked up the syringe and held it up between them.

"You can take this shot and stop a lunatic from destroying the world . . ." She set it down, without releasing him from her merciless stare. "Or you can refuse it . . . and watch Diana die."

# FORTY

## 3:29 P.M.

DIANA'S HEART RACED like the engine of the alpine-white BMW high-performance motorcycle idling between her legs. She was at the back of the formation, behind Tom and Jed, who were mounted on, respectively, a blue Suzuki sportbike and a black Yamaha supersport street cycle. Their engines thrummed, deep and loud, with every rev of their throttles resounding inside the concrete environs of the Center's underground parking garage.

Standing several yards in front of Tom was Kendall Graves. The slender, punkishly dressed, and colorfully tressed teen seemed more focused and serious now that the moment of action had arrived. She gave a two-finger salute to Tom.

He nodded in reply, then turned back to face Jed and Diana. "This is it," he said. "All set?"

Jed flashed a thumbs-up and donned his riding helmet; as he lowered it into place, it bumped the muzzle of the assault rifle strapped across his back. Diana dipped her chin to confirm that she was ready, and she put on her own helmet.

Immediately, her protective headgear muffled the roar of the bikes' engines to a moderate drone. Its polarized visor eliminated the harsh green glare from the garage's intense overhead fluorescent lights, and it cut down on the head-ache-inducing exhaust fumes from their engines and the garage's pervasive odor of mildew festering on damp cement.

Kendall stood with her legs apart and her arms raised wide above her head, shaping herself into a human X. A pinpoint of golden light formed in front of her navel and expanded outward, like the iris of a camera spiraling open.

Within seconds, it was large enough for Diana to see through it, as if it were merely an open window. On the other side was a curving, two-lane wilderness road bordered by skinny pine trees and hardscrabble land-scape. The sky above the road had the dark gray hue of tarnished tin. A blue recreational vehicle rolled toward them on the other side of the double yellow line, then it passed from view.

When the portal was open just wide enough for the trio and their motorcycles to pass through, Tom raised his arm, made a twirling motion that meant "move out," and pointed forward. He leaned forward and down behind his bike's windscreen, shifted the Yamaha sportbike into gear, and accelerated forward.

The Suzuki's engine growled mightily as Jed cruised forward, following close behind Tom.

Diana squeezed her bike's clutch, stepped down to shift

it into gear, and turned the throttle. Her BMW leaped ahead, the steady vibration of its engine pulsing with growing vigor.

It felt to her as if they were driving toward a movie screen, but then they rolled through it—and all at once the air changed. It was heavy with the scent of rain and the fragrance of pine, and it was warmer by several degrees.

In her side-view mirror, Diana saw the portal twist shut. *On our own now*, she reminded herself.

The plan was for one of Jordan's clairvoyants—probably Hal or maybe Lewis Mesirow—to monitor the three NTAC agents' progress in stopping the SUV. As soon as the agents had control of the bomb, Kendall would open another portal and send Marco through to disarm it.

*We hope*, mused Diana.

Speeding in close formation, the trio rounded a bend into a long straightaway. Far ahead was the intersection that led to Grand Loop Road. Tom raised his fist, which was the signal to stop, and he waved Jed and Diana over to the right shoulder. They pulled over and stopped parallel with each other.

Tom flipped up his visor, so Jed and Diana did the same. "That's the intercept point," he said, glancing at the T-shaped intersection a hundred yards ahead. "Quick radio check."

The three agents pulled compact walkie-talkies from their tactical vests and tested them to make sure that they worked, now that they were clear of the military jamming signals that had cut off all radio communications inside Seattle.

"Check, check," Tom said, and his voice came through clearly on Jed's and Diana's radios. "Okay," he said, putting away his walkie-talkie. "Diana, set up here, behind those trees, and watch for the white SUV. When it passes by, give us a heads-up. Jed, you'll break left at the intersection, I'll break right. We'll set up for overlapping fields of fire. Take out the truck's driver if you can. Otherwise, aim for his tires."

"Got it," Jed said, and he slapped his visor back down.

Looking at Diana, Tom asked, "Questions?"

"Nope," she said, keeping a brave face. "Let's do this."

"All right," Tom said. "Good luck, and good hunting. Last one back to Seattle buys the first round."

He lowered his visor, ducked low, and sped away on his bike, with Jed barely two seconds behind him.

Diana pulled off the main road, onto a dirt trail that led deep into the pine forest. Once she was far enough in not to be visible to traffic on the main road, she turned back and set herself in place to emerge on a moment's notice into a pursuit position. She wondered which would come first: the white SUV, or the storm that was threatening to rip open the sky.

She checked her watch. If the observations and calculations had been correct, Jakes would arrive within half an hour.

It was only 3:31 P.M. Pacific time, but already this felt as if it had been the longest day of Diana's life. She had woken up expecting just another Thursday at the office. Instead she had been forced to go rogue and fight for her life in a war zone. Now she was hundreds of miles from

Seattle, sitting on a motorcycle in the middle of Yellowstone National Park, lying in ambush for a fanatic with a doomsday fetish.

She wanted to swallow and choke down the anxiety welling inside of her, but her mouth was dry. *Nothing to be nervous about,* she told herself, hoping to salve her fears with sarcasm. *After all, it's just us three standing between the human race and total extinction. What could possibly go wrong?*

### 3:57 P.M.

Jakes watched the yellow line blur toward him as he cruised down the lonely two-lane stretch of West Entrance Road. He was less than a mile from the turn onto Grand Loop Road, which meant that his journey would draw to a close in fewer than forty minutes.

Confronted with the imminent end of his mission and his existence, he found himself in a philosophical state of mind.

It didn't bother him to know that death was so near at hand. From the first moment he had accepted his assignment, he had known that he could never return to the future he had left. Whether he succeeded or failed, he had condemned himself to die in the past. That had made many other choices much easier.

He glanced at the sky and wondered if the stormhead would make good on its promise of rain before or after he reached his destination. *There would be a certain visual poetry to standing in the rain as my truck sinks into the lake,* he thought with an expression of mild amusement. *Like something in a movie.*

There was still much that he didn't understand about his mission, or about how his masters had occasionally changed their definitions of success. Most of the inquiries he had made before being sent back had been ignored or glossed over with evasions.

One conundrum that still nagged at him, even as he moved closer to making it irrelevant, was that of the causality paradox inherent in his mission. His superiors had insisted that the reason for his mission was to stop a renegade band of scientists from altering the past by creating the promicin movement and, by so doing, destabilizing his time's last bastion of human civilization.

*But how could the promicin movement succeed if I and my peers were still able to mount a response to it?* he wondered. *Wouldn't altering the past immediately erase the world we knew?* He pondered the possibility that his leaders were deceiving him. *Might the real purpose of my mission have been hidden from me?*

The more he thought about time travel, the less sense it made to him. Watching the forest blur past on either side of his SUV, he tried to let go of all his questions, but they continued to haunt his thoughts and demand answers. *If I succeed, and I wipe out Jordan Collier's movement, will I be creating the future that I left? Or did that future vanish the moment the 4400 appeared on the shore of Highland Beach?*

He recalled a hypothesis that suggested branching temporal outcomes created new quantum universes. *If that's the case,* he concluded, *then the future I knew was never in danger at all. It would simply have continued on its course, its past unchanging, while the renegades' efforts to rewrite history accomplished nothing more than creating splinter timelines with different outcomes. But so what? What difference would it make whether parallel universes followed different paths? Why would they ask us to download ourselves into nanites and go back in time if there was no real threat to our power?*

There were competing postulates, naturally. One was the "dominant probability" hypothesis, which held that if the likelihood of a given outcome became overwhelming, then the quantum realities it favored would eventually erase less probable universes from existence. If that conjecture proved to be correct, then it might explain why his masters felt it necessary to expend resources, energy, and personnel on multiple efforts to defend their preferred version of history.

A road sign on the side of the road informed him that he was approaching the turn to Grand Loop Road. It started to rain.

*No point in obsessing over this now,* Jakes decided. *It's not as if I'll unravel centuries of contradictory temporal logic between now and when I reach the lake.*

Orders were orders, he reminded himself. His mission was to disrupt, by any means necessary, the spread of Jordan Collier's movement. The plan that he, Wells, and Kuroda had set into motion seemed perfectly suited to that goal; the fact that it also would transform the world into a very close semblance of the barren globe from which they had come was simply a bonus.

Jakes guided the SUV through an easy right turn onto Grand Loop Road. He imagined the look of shock on Collier's face as the end of the world caught him unawares. It made him smile.

The SUV's windshield spiderwebbed with cracks, pulverized glass stung Jakes's face, and a large-caliber bullet tore off part of his left shoulder, spraying blood across the backseat.

His screams of pain mixed with squeals from the vehicle's tires as it swerved wildly, back and forth across the road.

He fought to recover control of the SUV. Bullets peppered its windows and doors.

Blood poured down his numb left arm, soaking his shirt.

Nauseated and dizzy, he pressed his foot on the accelerator and struggled to see through the fractured-white windshield.

Over the rush of wind, the roar of the SUV's damaged engine, and his own labored gasps, he heard more gunshots.

Next came the growling buzz of motorcycles, closing fast from behind him.

Holes appeared in his roof. Windows exploded into shards. Slugs perforated the passenger seat.

A random shot tore into his side. It felt like a rod of fire jammed deep into his guts, aching and burning inside him.

Then a deep boom shook his vehicle, and the wheel began fighting him, resisting his efforts to steer around the slow-moving cars on the road ahead.

*Lost a tire,* Jakes reasoned. *So be it.*

He started swerving, wide left and right, and though

he felt himself dying by degrees, he was laughing. The war was over, and whoever had found him out was too late to stop it. He was inside the effective target area for the warhead; though the lakeshore had been identified as the optimal detonation site, this desolate stretch of road would more than suffice.

Jakes knew that the dead-man switch linking him to the warhead would finish the mission, even if he himself could not. It didn't bother him that he wouldn't live to see the end. One death was just as good as another.

He rammed a station wagon out of his path and kept the gas pedal pinned to the floor as more bullets flew through his SUV.

This would be the last mile of his journey, and he was determined to enjoy the ride while it lasted.


Diana kept the throttle of her motorcycle pinned wide open as she flew down the winding road, slowly gaining on Tom and Jed.

They were more than fifty yards ahead of her, dogging the white SUV, which they had riddled with bullets from their assault rifles. Now they had to rely on their Glocks, but even a semiautomatic pistol was hard to aim and fire while pushing a sportbike to its limits in a high-speed, high-risk pursuit.

Wind hammered at Diana, and it sounded like thunder rushing over her helmet. Rain pelted her and slicked the road.

Up ahead, the SUV swerved from side to side, preventing Tom and Jed from pulling forward on either side of it. Though one of its tires had been damaged by rifle fire, and Jakes had been wounded, he still had at least partial control of the vehicle.

Stuck on its rear flanks, Jed squeezed off a few more shots, which ricocheted off the Pathfinder's rear door and bumper. The right-handed Jed was having trouble aiming his weapon with his left hand—a necessity imposed by the fact that a motorcycle's throttle was located on the right handgrip.

Tom, who normally handled his weapon with his right hand despite being left-handed, was having an easier time shooting lefty. In two shots, he blasted apart the SUV's rear window.

The SUV and the two motorcycles swung wide through a curve in the road. As Jakes raced ahead, Jed and Tom braked.

Coming the other way was a massive recreational vehicle almost wider than its lane. It veered toward the shoulder to avoid the madly winding SUV, which narrowly missed a head-on collision. The RV began to tip onto its side as it rode up the slope beside the road, then slammed into a stand of pines. Two people—the male driver and a female passenger—burst through its windshield and tumbled like rag dolls to the dusty ground.

Not far ahead, the road was busy with traffic. It was a mix of SUVs, small cars, station wagons, and pickup trucks. Most of them were loaded with camping equipment, and some were hauling canoes or small boats on trailers.

*Oh, shit,* Diana thought, imagining the worst.

Her cycle's speedometer read ninety-five miles per hour.

She knew this was about to get ugly.

Jakes swerved in and out of the line of cars. He rammed a station wagon topped with camping gear off the road and forced an oncoming pickup truck to swerve into a head-on crash with a tiny hybrid vehicle that cracked like an egg.

Within seconds the road was a deadly maze of shattered glass and broken metal, bent vehicles and bloody bodies. It was all Tom and Jed could do to slalom through the obstacles without causing more damage or hurting any civilians.

Diana detoured onto the right shoulder and sped around the accident scene, fighting to keep up with the chase.

The damaged white Pathfinder continued to weave erratically down the road at nearly ninety miles per hour. More vehicles lay ahead of it, unaware of the danger heading their way.

Then the SUV straightened its course.

Jed swung wide left and pushed his bike to its maximum speed. Riding the center line, he pulled alongside Jakes's door and fought to steady his left-handed aim across his right arm.

Jakes jerked the SUV to the left and slammed Jed into the next lane—and into the path of a car that had been trying to steer wide around him. Jed's bike spun and fell sideways. Then the car smashed into him.

The impact knocked Jed from the bike, which was

mangled under the car's tires. Even as the car ditched into the trees to avoid running over Jed, the next car was unable to stop in time. Jed vanished under its wheels as Tom and Diana raced by.

Tom signaled Diana with a wave of his Glock that he was going to make the next attack on Jakes's left side, and Diana understood that her role was to make a simultaneous assault from the SUV's right. She drew her pistol, nodded her acknowledgment, and swung to the right as she opened the throttle.

Some part of Diana's mind, deep beneath her years of NTAC training, knew that she ought to be terrified—but as the road ripped by in a mad blur, and the wind buffeted her chest, all she could think about was making the kill.

The purr of the BMW's engine resonated through her entire body, but her pistol was steady in her hand.

There were cars ahead, more innocent-victims-in-the-making. Diana had no intention of letting Jakes get that far. Too many had died for this madman's cause already.

*It ends here*, she vowed.

Through the SUV's empty window frames, she saw Tom nod.

They made their move.

Together they sped forward, moving in synchronicity. As she took aim through the SUV's passenger window, Tom leveled his Glock at Jakes from the driver's side.

They fired in unison.

Jakes twitched as bullets struck his head and neck.

He slammed on the brakes, and swerved left.

Tom's motorcycle rammed against the side of the

Pathfinder as it spun out. The SUV's rapid deceleration sent it into a chaotic roll. It broke apart as it tumbled over the asphalt, shedding glass, broken plastic, and metal debris.

Diana fought to outrun the rolling catastrophe behind her, only to find the road ahead blocked by slow traffic. She stepped on the rear brake pedal, but at that speed all she could do was wipe out and get dragged across the pavement by her bike.

The wrecked Pathfinder was still rolling toward her.

She couldn't see Tom or his bike.

Ahead of her, over the scrape of her body being towed across dirt and asphalt, she heard the dull metallic thuds of cars colliding. Shouting, screaming, and tears.

But the last thing Diana saw was the smoking blur of the broken white SUV as it rolled over her.

# FORTY-ONE

JORDAN COLLIER'S FIRST WARNING that The 4400 Center had been breached and was under attack was the sound of rifle fire in the corridor outside the executive suite.

"Fall back!" shouted Marco, one of the few people in the building bearing a weapon. He locked the main entrance and pointed to an exit at the rear of the meeting room. "Get to cover! Move!"

Gary and Kyle led the retreat, shepherding Maia into a hallway that led to several offices and the restrooms. As more people followed them out, Marco struggled to push the conference table over onto its side. Jordan rushed to Marco's side to help him, and Lewis Mesirow joined them.

Working together, they knocked the long, thick-topped hardwood table on its edge. Marco ducked behind it and pulled the assault rifle off his back. To Jordan and Lewis he said, "Run! And stay down!" Then he primed his weapon and aimed it back over his impromptu barricade as the locked door was blasted in.

Lewis was at Jordan's heels as they sprinted toward the exit. A furious stuttering noise split the air. Something warm and wet sprinkled the back of Jordan's neck.

He dashed around the corner and looked back for Lewis.

The middle-aged clairvoyant wasn't there.

Stealing a peek back around the corner, Jordan saw Lewis facedown on the blood-spattered floor. Jordan palmed the moisture from the back of his neck. When he looked at his hand, it was streaked with fresh blood.

Bullets ripped a trail across the wall in front of him. He ducked low and scrambled away from the door, down the hall.

An explosion ripped through the meeting room. Fire and debris erupted through the door into the back hallway.

Lamenting the sacrifice of the NTAC agent who had stayed behind, Jordan slammed through a fire door into the emergency stairwell—only to collide with Marco Pacella, who was scuffed but definitely alive.

"Bad guys, two flights down," Marco said, adjusting his eyeglasses, which now had one cracked lens. "Head upstairs, I'll cover you." Jordan nodded to the young teleporter, then scrambled to the next floor while Marco backpedaled up the stairs behind him, his rifle braced against his shoulder.

As they reached the next landing, Marco asked, "You didn't happen to see which way Dennis Ryland went, did you?"

"Sorry, no," Jordan said, opening the door to the Center's top level, which housed the chief executive's master office suite. He stood aside and let Marco scout the path ahead.

Waving Jordan through the door, Marco said, "Don't worry about it. I'm sure he'll turn up." He added with a contemptuous grimace, "He always does."

Shawn winced at the rattle-roar of automatic weapons. He could barely see dim shapes moving through a fog that scorched his throat and stung his eyes until they watered.

People screamed in agony, ran in every direction, crawled under furniture to hide. His young friend Chongrak twitched in the grasp of crimson tendrils of electricity. Tristine, one of Jordan's bodyguards, convulsed as horrific, bloody gashes opened in her throat, her abdomen, and her back, as if she were being flensed by a great invisible blade.

Trusting in his memory, Shawn scrambled on all fours through the cubicle maze until he reached a corridor that was clear of tear gas. His lungs felt full of fire. Painful coughs racked him as he sprinted toward the closest possible exit.

As he ran, he fought to see through the toxic smoke, into the offices and meeting rooms that lined the hallway. He knew that he ought to take cover and stay there, but he had to know—

"Shawn!"

Heather leaped to her feet from behind a photocopier in a small anteroom on his right. She ran to him and peppered his face with kisses both grateful and fearful.

"Thank God," he said. "C'mon, we have to go!"

Taking her hand, he led her in a clumsy, stooped run around the corner, on a mad dash across the top floor's elevator lobby, into the reception foyer of his executive suite.

A sound like a jackhammer on crystal meth rattled Shawn's teeth and turned a wall of glass panels into a carpet of hazardous jagged shards that covered the reception area's floor.

He pulled Heather to cover behind his assistant's desk. Impacts and ricochets tore splinters from the desk and the wall.

Between bursts of gunfire, Shawn heard a high-pitched, girlish yelp of terror from the other side of the reception area. He and Heather turned their heads and saw Maia lying behind the end of the leather sofa, her back to the wall.

Heather screamed, "Maia! Stay down!"

Another spray of bullets ripped off the corner of the desk in front of Heather's face, and she flinched back into Shawn's arms. She threw a scathing glare at Shawn. "What happened to Gary and Kyle? They were supposed to protect her!"

"I don't know," Shawn protested, raising his voice above the din of bullets shredding the desk behind them.

Eyes darting back and forth from Maia to Shawn, Heather shouted, "We have to help her! Do something!"

"I can't!" he said. "I'm trying to sense their life forces, but something's blocking me—one of them. It must be the leader, Frost."

He fell backward, and it took him a moment to realize that someone had telekinetically levitated away the desk he and Heather had been using for cover.

"Move!" Shawn cried, diving through a doorway into the administrative office behind the receptionist's desk. He landed hard atop a razor-sharp mess of broken glass and fought to protect his hands and his face from harm.

Jagged chunks sliced and punctured Shawn's forearms and his back as he rolled across the lacerating debris. It was only when he stopped moving that he saw Heather wasn't with him.

He looked back as Heather made a desperate, stumbling run toward the cowering Maia—

Something invisible cut Heather down. A massive wound sliced her entire body, splitting her open from chin to navel.

She fell, bleeding and beyond Shawn's reach.

Maia let loose a scream of horror.

Shawn unleashed a scream of rage.

There was nothing he could do but watch Heather die.

Jed Garrity blinked as the car made impact, grinding him and his motorcycle against the rain-slicked pavement of Grand Loop Road. He expected to taste his own blood at any second.

But in that flash of a moment, he finished his blink to see not the road or the motorcycle or his broken body . . . but a hallway littered with shattered glass and spent shell casings, and obscured beneath a haze of dispersing tear gas and thick smoke. It took him a second to recognize the interior of the top floor of The 4400 Center. Then his ears registered the stutter of weapons firing and the sounds of panic.

He turned around and saw four men, all facing away from him toward the executive suite. They were soldiers, attired in black-and-gray urban camouflage and equipped with gas masks, night-vision headsets, body armor, and military weaponry.

From the far end of the hallway, Jed heard Heather Tobey call out, "Maia! Stay down!"

The soldiers took turns laying down suppressing fire in the direction of Heather's voice, and he heard Maia scream.

One of the soldiers extended his hand and, with a casual gesture, telekinetically flung aside the thick wooden desk behind which Heather and Shawn Farrell had been hiding.

Shawn wisely jumped for more cover.

Heather sprinted across the soldiers' field of fire.

A different soldier made a chopping motion with his arm, and a brutal wound cut Heather down in a bloody heap.

The telekinetic tossed aside a sofa, exposing Maia.

Jed stepped forward, locked his arm around the throat of the soldier at the rear of the squad, grabbed his chin, and gave the man's head a sharp twist.

None of the other soldiers heard the man's neck break.

As the body slid from Jed's grasp, he drew the man's sidearm from its holster and fired off snap shots. He dropped the psionic slasher first, then the telekinetic.

The last soldier ducked inside an office and jumped over a desk to cover, half a step ahead of Jed's semiauto barrage.

Moving past the office, Jed emptied his clip laying down fire to keep the soldier at bay.

The pistol clicked empty. Jed discarded it. He unslung the assault rifle from his back and kept it pointed back at the last soldier's position as he moved to Maia's side.

"Maia," he said, taking her hand. "It's me, Jed from NTAC. Stay behind me, honey, I'll protect you." He helped her up and nodded at the doorway through which Shawn had fled. "That way."

The girl retreated behind him as Jed guarded her, only now remembering the vow he had made to Diana hours earlier. "Whatever happens," he'd said, "I've got your back—and Maia's."

It was time for Jed to make good on his promise.

*Never let it be said I'm not a man of my word*, he thought, following Maia into what he only then realized was a dead end.

Kyle had run so hard and so blindly that he had lost track of everything else. All he had been able to see was the next step ahead of himself, the next flight of stairs, the next door, the next spot of cover. Jordan had said to run, so he'd run.

He'd thought that Gary and Maia and others were right behind him, but it was only after he'd barreled through the door of Shawn's office and saw that there was nowhere left to run that he'd looked back and realized that he was alone.

Shouts of struggle and flight reached him, muffled but not silenced by the office's walls. He heard staccato bursts of gunfire, then running footsteps drawing near.

He took cover behind a thickly padded chair in the corner of the room and fumbled to arm the semiautomatic pistol he'd been given during the preparation of the Center's defenses.

Cassie poked her head over his shoulder. "Move your thumb before you pull back on the slide," she said. "And keep it down or you'll rip it off when you fire that thing."

He scowled at her know-it-all tone but did as she'd said. Still struggling with the weapon, he asked, "Now what?"

"Release the safety," she said. Pointing at a small lever on the left side of the weapon, she added, "There."

Disengaging the safety with his thumb, Kyle extended his arm and aimed over the top of the chair. Cassie made a derisive *tsk*. "You've exposed your head," she said. "Get down and aim around the side. And use your left hand to support your right. It'll help your aim."

Glaring over his shoulder, he snapped, "You want to do this?"

"I would if I could," she snipped.

He heard footsteps right outside the door. It opened with a long creaking whine of dry hinges.

Kyle saw the muzzle of an assault rifle edge into the room. His finger tensed on the trigger of his handgun. He held his breath to steady his hand.

Then Cassie whispered, "Don't shoot," and she gently placed her hand on Kyle's arm and lowered it until the gun was pointed at the floor.

Marco Pacella stepped into view, then made a sharp pivot in Kyle's direction.

Raising his arms in a gesture of surrender, Kyle called out, "Don't shoot! It's me!"

The NTAC agent lowered his rifle and nodded to someone behind him. "Clear," he said.

Jordan followed Marco into the office and did a worried double-take at Kyle. "What happened to Gary and Maia?"

"We got separated," Kyle said. He asked Marco, "Why aren't you with Kendall?"

"I was covering the retreat," Marco protested.

They all recoiled from resumed bursts of rifle fire just outside the office's main door. Marco waved Kyle back. "Get behind the chair." Then he pulled Jordan with him behind the desk. "Get down," he said, dropping to a crouch and aiming over the desktop at the door. Jordan dropped out of sight beside him.

The door to the outer office swung inward, and once again Marco averted his aim. Maia scrambled into the room, followed by Shawn and then by NTAC agent Jed Garrity, who backed in while keeping his rifle trained on whatever might appear behind them.

"Stay out of the doorway," Jed said as he kneeled and pushed the door most of the way shut. He left it open just enough to aim through the crack. "I dropped three out of four hostiles in the hallway, but it's a good bet number four's calling in reinforcements." Glancing back, he said to Jordan, "If you've got any cavalry to call in, now's the time."

Marco stood, walked quickly to Jed's side, and said, "If I can get a look down the hall, I can pop behind them once they're in position, set up a crossfire."

"Risky," Jed said. "But worth a try." He shifted left to

let Marco look past the barely open door and scout the corridor beyond the outer office.

While the two NTAC agents whispered their plans to each other, Kyle heard choked, muffled sobs behind him. Shawn was crouched behind the desk with his face in his hands, his chest heaving with grief. Kyle went to his cousin, kneeled, and gripped his shoulders. "Shawn? What's wrong? What happened?"

"Heather," Shawn choked out, his face still hidden in his palms. "They just . . . she . . ." He inhaled with a sharp wet hiss of intake, but then seemed unable to go on.

Cassie kneeled beside Shawn and looked at Kyle. "He loves her," she said. "He thinks she's dead, but she's not—not yet, anyway." With a pointed stare at Kyle, she added, "Tell him!"

"Shawn," he said, leaning closer to him. "Listen to me. Cassie, my power, she's telling me Heather's alive. There's still time to save her."

Looking back in alarm, Jed said in a harsh whisper, "Are you crazy? He can't go out there!"

Cassie took hold of the back of Kyle's neck. Her touch was firm but also strangely comforting. She whispered in his ear, and he repeated her words to the others. "The soldier who was masking all the others is dead," Kyle said. "Jed got him. Our people can see the others now. We can *fight back*."

Everyone else was processing the news as Shawn went quiet and stood. He wiped the tears from his face. His reddened eyes took on a steely quality as he lifted his right hand.

"I can sense her life force," he said. His voice trembled as he added, "It's fading fast." Recovering his composure, he closed his eyes, lifted his left hand, and concentrated. "I can sense the soldiers, too. They're coming up the far stairs. They'll be here in ten seconds." When he opened his eyes, they had a coldness that Kyle had never before seen in his cousin. "Maia," Shawn said in a tone that would brook no debate, "get inside the bathroom and lock the door. Kyle, Jordan, take cover. Jed and Marco, guard the door till I get back."

Shawn walked to the door as Maia sprinted into the bathroom and locked herself inside. The NTAC agents blocked the exit. "No," Jed said to Shawn. "You can't go out there unarmed."

"I'm not unarmed," Shawn said. "And Heather needs me."

He stepped between Jed and Marco, who backed apart and let Shawn pass. Kyle watched his cousin step through the door.

"We'll have your back," Jed said, and he nodded for Marco to follow him as he stepped out behind Shawn.

As Marco stepped out and pulled the door closed, he said to Kyle and Jordan, "We'll be right outside. Stay down."

"Dibs," Jordan said, pulling out the chair and stuffing himself into the space under the desk. Kyle stepped quickly across the office and ducked back behind the heavy chair.

Cassie strolled cavalierly after him and draped herself over the chair's back. "This is your chance," she said.

He whispered back, "Chance to what?"

"To shoot Jordan. No witnesses. You can say one of the enhanced soldiers popped in, plugged the promicin messiah at point-blank range, and popped out. No one'll know."

If he hadn't already been backed into a corner, he would have recoiled. "No, you're crazy! Gary's a mind reader! *He'd* know." Nodding at the bathroom, "And so would Maia."

"Gary's no longer necessary to the Movement," Cassie replied. "And Maia's expendable."

Gunfire thundered on the other side of the office's door. Then came several blood-chilling, guttural howls of suffering.

"No," Kyle said. "I'm not doing this!"

She grabbed his hair and pulled it. "You have to! Dammit, Kyle, get up and be a man! Shoot!"

He twisted free of her grasp. "Really? Pulling a trigger will make me a man? Okay, then . . ." He turned the pistol toward his face and put its muzzle inside his mouth.

Cassie rolled her eyes and let out a sigh of disgust. "Now you're just being stupid, Kyle."

Shawn walked out of the office suite into the elevator lobby. Heather lay on the floor to his right, surrounded by shattered glass and tiny bits of debris blasted from the desk and walls.

From behind him, he heard Marco plead in a strained whisper, "Shawn! Come back!"

He ignored him. There was one man alive in a room on the left side of the hall leading away from Heather. More were coming up a stairwell at the far end of that passageway. All were coursing with aggressive energy and adrenaline.

Even though Shawn couldn't see any of them, he sensed their vital essences with such clarity that he knew where every one of them was. He felt their every footstep, tasted their every breath, heard their heartbeats as if they were his own.

They were behind the corner. Waiting.

"I know you're there," Shawn said, challenging them.

One man pivoted around the corner with his arm cocked, a grenade in his hand.

Shawn raised his left hand and stopped the soldier's heart.

The man gasped, twitched, and fell to his knees.

He dropped his grenade. It rolled behind him.

Someone shouted, "Fire in the hole!"

Soldiers scrambled around the corner, hurdling over their fallen comrade in a mad dash away from the live grenade. They ran almost halfway up the corridor toward Shawn before the grenade exploded, filling the hall behind them with fire and smoke. A few of the soldiers stumbled and fell.

The two in front lifted their rifles to aim at Shawn.

They froze before they finished the movement.

All five men in the hallway convulsed and turned cyanotic. In seconds they were on their knees, each of them in more pain than he had ever felt before.

Inside the office on the left, the last man tensed to strike. He exhaled and spun as he stepped toward the doorway, his sidearm in his hand—

—and fell to his knees as Shawn stopped the man's lungs from expanding to draw another breath.

Standing over Heather, Shawn held six men's lives in his left hand. He kneeled beside his mortally wounded love and felt her life slipping away. Her last spark of neuroelectricity was dying in the tissues of her brain. Her lungs were full of her own blood. Her organs had been savaged by the telekinetic assault.

Shawn placed his right hand on her forehead. He remembered the sensation from just a few hours earlier, of healing a man outside the Center without needing to touch him. The implication of that moment had been immediately clear to Shawn. If his power had grown to the level where he could heal without making contact, then the reverse was also true: he could kill without making contact.

With his left hand he took the life from six men who had come into his home to deal out death.

With his right hand he gave that life energy to Heather. He mended the damage inside her body, purged the fluid from her lungs, and replenished the vital sparks that danced between her synapses. In the span of a breath and a heartbeat, he pulled her back from the edge of death's dark frontier.

Mere yards away, six men died to make her miracle possible, but Shawn felt not one ounce of guilt, not a moment's regret.

Heather's back arched as she drew a breath, sharp and deep, the kind of greedy gasp that only the resurrected can muster. Her eyes snapped open, first in shock, then in fear, then at last in relief. She sat up and embraced her savior. "Shawn!"

He hugged her and wept with gratitude, certain that he had made the right choice. To save Heather, he would take six lives, or sixty, or six hundred, or six thousand. There was nothing he wouldn't do to protect her.

Nothing.

"The building's secure," Jed said to Jordan. "And we have a clear zone out to at least one mile from the Center."

Jordan nodded. "Good," he said. "Communications?"

"Getting there," Marco said. "Your people took out the military's jamming systems, so short-range walkie-talkies are coming through loud and clear."

More of Jordan's advisors filed into the private office. It reminded him of a time only a few years earlier when the room had been his sanctum, before his apparent assassination had left the Center and its myriad responsibilities to Shawn.

"Good news," Emil said. "U.S. forces are being routed all over the city. Madrona's clear, and the Marines are using Broadmoor Golf Course to evac their people on Black Hawks."

Lucas added, "We'll have Beacon Hill clear by sunset, and the troops that came in from Fort Lawton are on their way back."

"Excellent," Jordan said. He looked at Kyle. "Any advice from Cassie on what our next move should be?"

Kyle rubbed his temples wearily. "No," he said.

Outside the office, Shawn ministered to other casualties of the battle inside the Center. At the front of the line was Gary, the victim of multiple gunshots, who had been found unconscious one floor below, minutes after Shawn had slain the troops outside his office. The telepath jolted awake in a state of panic and shouted, "Where's Maia?"

"It's okay," Shawn said, restraining the muscular ex-athlete with a gentle hand against his chest. "She's fine." He pointed inside the office, where Maia stood beside Jordan. The girl waved to Gary, who relaxed and sat back.

Marco turned and eyed Jed with a quizzical expression. "Wait a second. What're you doing here? You were in Yellowstone with Tom and Diana."

"Got hit by a car," Jed said. "What about you? Weren't you supposed to disarm the bomb?"

Dismay widened Marco's eyes. He looked at Jordan. "Who's keeping an eye on the mission in Yellowstone?"

"It was Lewis," Jordan said, "but he . . ."

Looks of anxious confusion traveled from person to person. It became painfully clear that the need to monitor NTAC's efforts to stop the antimatter bomb had fallen off the radar during the attack on the Center.

"That's what I was afraid of," Marco said.

# FORTY-TWO

## 4:04 P.M.

IT SOUNDED LIKE applause.

On the other side of darkness, it was everywhere—a steady wash of sound, a fall of white noise, a dull random patter, a faint irregular percussion.

Tears ran across Diana's face, but they weren't her tears. She wasn't crying. Blind and motionless, numb and silent, she lay as droplets kissed her face.

Warmth and pressure attracted her attention.

"Diana," the voice said. It sounded distant, like someone calling from the far side of a large house with many rooms.

Awareness flooded back. She opened her eyes.

Everything was brighter than blinding.

Raindrops pelted Diana's face and body. She lay on her back, in the middle of the road.

Tom was on one knee at her side.

She swallowed to clear the thick, sticky sensation from her mouth, then rasped, "Tom?"

He held her hand. "I'm right here."

"What about the bomb?"

"Ticking down," he said. "Jakes must've tripped a dead-man switch that started the timer."

She turned her head toward the white SUV, which lay on its side several yards down the road. "Is he . . . ?"

Nodding, Tom said, "He's dead. I checked."

Diana felt no shame in taking some measure of satisfaction in that news. "Have to . . . stop the bomb."

Her partner frowned. "I tried. Most of that thing is parts I've never seen before. Plus, the control panel's smashed. Only part that still works is the countdown timer."

As her pulse quickened with alarm, she asked, "How long?"

He looked at his watch. "Ninety-one seconds." Cracking a rueful smile, he said, "I don't suppose you happened to bring a manual for disarming superadvanced munitions?"

"Sorry," she said. "Left it in my car."

Seconds passed as Diana regarded the lonely road strewn with wreckage and surrounded by barren landscape. She knew that they were well within the caldera's danger zone. When the bomb detonated, it would unleash the extinction event that would wipe the human race from the Earth.

*We blew it,* she realized.

Admitting the failure to herself gave her courage. All was forfeit, so she had nothing left to lose. She tightened her grip on Tom's hand. He looked at her.

"Do you remember," she asked with a trembling smile,

"when my sister April used her ability to force you to admit that you'd had sexual fantasies about me?"

Rolling his eyes, Tom said, "How could I forget?"

"Well," she said, "I think you deserve to know . . . I've had them about you, too."

For a second he stared at her as if he were in shock. Then he checked his watch again, and looked back at her, at once exasperated and amused. "*Now* you tell me."

They chuckled together at the absurdity of it. As their mild laughter tapered off, she asked again, "How long?"

"Fifteen seconds."

"Hold me till it's over. Please."

He helped her to sit up, then sat next to her and hugged her to him. She clutched him and shut her eyes, knowing that in a few seconds, just yards behind her back, the world was about to end in fire and fury.

She counted off the seconds in her mind.

*Three . . . two . . . one . . .*

Even through her eyelids, the flash was intensely bright, and the heat wave surged against her, tingling her entire body with twice the pain of the worst sunburn she'd ever had.

Then, to her surprise, the light dimmed. Not by much—it was still too bright to look at directly, but it had diminished. The heat abated quickly, as well.

She opened her eyes and turned her head.

The SUV was gone, devoured by a massive sphere of white fire that had seared a bowl out of the pavement beneath it. But the miniature sun seemed to be contained inside another sphere of energy, an amber shell that flickered as the raging inferno within pulsed against it but failed to expand.

"Thank God and Jordan Collier," Diana said, certain that one of Jordan's p-positives had intervened to save her and Tom.

Then she noticed that Tom was trembling. His jaw was clenched, and his neck muscles were taut with exertion.

He was staring into the heart of the fireball beside them.

Diana realized that he was holding her with only one arm. She looked over his shoulder.

Tom's other arm was pointed at the crackling ball of white-hot energy, his hand open, his fingers spread apart. He lifted his arm higher, and the sphere rose from the ground. Then he began curling his fingers into a fist and turning his wrist, as if he were miming the crushing of a bug.

The trapped fireball shrank in proportion to Tom's gesture. As his fist clenched white-knuckle tight, the contained blast dwindled to a pinpoint—then blinked out of existence.

He collapsed into Diana's arms, exhausted and shaking.

Rain poured down on them.

After a moment, Tom caught his breath enough to say, "Don't thank Jordan . . ." He opened a pocket of his vest and took out a syringe that was empty except for luminous traces of promicin trapped beneath its rubber plunger.

He mustered a weak smile. "Thank Maia."

# Part Three

# The Promises

# FORTY-THREE

**JULY 24, 2008**
**8:43 P.M.**

SUNSET WAS MINUTES away. The sky above Promise City had dimmed to indigo in the east, and the western horizon burned with a vermillion glow. Parts of the city were still burning, but Jordan knew that his people would soon have those blazes under control. Smoke curled from other neighborhoods that had been razed, either by artillery or by enhanced soldiers with devastating powers.

Watching him, and broadcasting with her promicin ability all that she saw and heard to every cable and frequency on Earth, was a young Israeli woman named Ilana Teitelbaum. She was a slip of a girl with long, straight brown hair. Jordan tried not to become entranced by her soulful, dark eyes as he stared into them and delivered his address to the world.

"All around me," he said, pacing around The 4400 Center's roof in a slow circle while Ilana pivoted to keep him in her sight, "you see the consequences of today's attack by the United States military against Promise City. As I vowed we would do, we defended ourselves." He stole a quick look away from Ilana at the tower of smoke and the smoldering mountain of rubble where the Collier Foundation building had stood until that morning. "As you can see, we've suffered losses of our own, and our city has taken great damage. But our casualties have been light compared with those of the forces that attacked us."

He beckoned Ilana forward and directed her view over the edge of roof, to the driveway and the main entrance of the Center. "Even now, the wounded of Promise City, p-positive and p-negative alike, know they can come to us and be healed. Unlike the soldiers who left here today maimed or critically wounded, tomorrow our people will be healthy and whole."

Ilana stepped back but kept her eyes on him as he gestured for her to turn her view toward the southeast. "By morning, the fires of Promise City will be extinguished. Our people will have clean water, steady electricity, and reliable sewage removal—all for free. In a week, we'll have rebuilt our roads, including the elevated highways that the military destroyed."

He stopped circling and stood with his back to the sunset, knowing intuitively that it was backlighting him with a halo. Every regular and high-definition video frequency in the world was showing Ilana's transmission; those who didn't see it live would almost certainly see it ad infinitum on the Internet in the days and weeks to come.

The hour had arrived. It was time for Jordan to throw down the gauntlet. He smiled.

"The United States, on the other hand, has fared quite poorly in this conflict. Its military satellites have been destroyed, crippling its ability to wage war and defend itself from attack. Because its numerous intelligence agencies had illegally hacked into several civilian satellites, their destruction has cut off much of North America's cell phone service, impaired its broadcasting capability, and knocked out its Global Positioning Systems. It might take America several years to restore these services."

He folded his hands in front of him and continued. "Taking this kind of damage to its national infrastructure so soon after the tragic earthquake that devastated much of California must be a cause for concern not only to all Americans, but to all the people of the world who fear the global consequences of a U.S. national collapse.

"Such a tragedy must not be allowed to happen. That is why I am here tonight to tell you that I and the citizens of Promise City bear no grudge against the people of the United States or its allies. You don't have to face these dark times and daunting challenges alone." Consciously echoing the final words of his speech to the city government of Seattle after the Great Leap Forward, Jordan spread his hands and said, "In this time of crisis, we stand ready to help, in any way that we can, in whatever way that you need. All you have to do . . . is ask."

# FORTY-FOUR

EVERY PART OF Tom's body was in pain.

His muscles ached, and his skin burned with abrasions. Each beat of his heart made his head pulse with agony, as if something were trying to push out his eyeballs. He lay atop a long dining table and ruminated on his miserable evening.

It had been a few hours since he and Diana had returned through a second portal opened by Kendall. Tom had carried his gravely injured partner back to The 4400 Center, where Jordan's followers had whisked her away to be seen immediately by Shawn.

It wasn't until Tom had found himself abandoned in the Center's infirmary that he had realized no one had asked whether he needed medical help. *It's my own fault*, he told himself. *That's what I get for acting stoic all the time.*

He'd gleaned from overheard conversations that there had been an attack on the Center, but that it was over, and that the principal leaders of Promise City were alive. Having been in no shape to go running all over the building looking for Kyle or Shawn, Tom had scrounged two tabs of Vicodin from an unlocked infirmary medicine cabinet. Then he'd walked across the hall to a private office, where he'd found a bottle of cheap bourbon in a bottom desk drawer. *That'll do nicely,* he decided.

In the commissary, he'd selected a juice glass from the plastic rack stacked next to the front door. Then he'd sat down at a table, crushed the Vicodin tablets into dust with the butt of his pistol, swept the powder into the glass, and poured in what he'd figured was a triple shot of his borrowed liquor. He'd stirred it with his index finger until it looked mixed, then downed it in one long draught.

A few minutes later, the pain coursing through his body had abated . . . a little bit.

The relief had almost been enough to let Tom fall asleep, but every time he began to let go of his grip on consciousness, some random sound—a distant gunshot or explosion, or a nearby footstep echoing in a hallway—had made him shudder back to full wakefulness. On one occasion it had been a scent of sulfur, like a struck match, that made his eyes pop back open.

Another dream fluttered just beyond his reach when he heard the door of the commissary open with a loud metallic clack. Overlapping footfalls echoed inside the dimly lit dining hall.

With great effort, Tom pushed himself up from the table until he was sitting upright, legs dangling over the end, facing his visitors: Jordan, Shawn, and Kyle.

At least, he was fairly certain it was them. The booze and the drugs hadn't done much to dull his suffering, but they had done a fantastic job of blurring his vision.

"Uncle Tommy," Shawn said, his voice sounding strangely deep, slow, and resonant. He reached out and gripped Tom's shoulder. "You all right? How're you feeling?"

"Like I got run over by a truck full of hooch," Tom slurred out. He pitched forward.

Shawn caught him. "Take a breath," the young man said.

Tom felt a glorious warmth wash through him, and as he inhaled, his mind and his vision cleared. Exhaling, he felt his pain melt away, as if he had breathed it out.

"Any better?" asked Shawn.

Tom grinned. "Much." He pulled his nephew to him and gave him a bear hug. "Good to see you."

"Good to be seen," Shawn said. As Tom released him, Shawn said, "Don't worry about Diana. I healed her a couple hours ago. She's resting upstairs."

"Thanks," Tom said, letting Shawn go.

Kyle stepped forward, taking Shawn's place. "Hey, Dad," he said, clearly struggling with a flood tide of powerful emotions that he still felt embarrassed to share in front of others.

"C'mere," Tom said, wrapping his arms around his son and holding him in a fierce embrace. "Thought I might not see you again. Thought I . . ." Grappling with the effort of expressing his feelings, he appreciated the irony of where Kyle had inherited the trait. Committed to changing his ways, Tom blinked through his tears and made himself continue. "Thought I might never see you again. Not get to tell you one last time . . . that I love you."

"Love you too, Dad."

Shawn put one hand on Kyle's back and the other on Tom's shoulder, and they stood together for a few moments in silence. It felt right to Tom. They felt like family again.

Then Jordan had to ruin it by speaking.

"I'm sorry to interrupt—"

"Then don't," Tom said.

"I just wanted to welcome you to the ranks of the promicin-positive, Tom. We all understand this was a big step for you."

Tom let go of Kyle and Shawn, stood, and took a step toward Jordan. "I didn't do this for your movement, or to live out some half-baked prophecy."

"It makes no difference to me why you took the shot," Jordan said. "What matters to me is what you did with it. You literally *saved the world*, Tom."

It was hard for Tom to argue with a man who was praising him so lavishly. After a few seconds of opening and closing his mouth in stymied silence, Tom said, "Maybe. But that doesn't mean I'm on your side, Jordan. Or on the government's side."

Jordan shrugged. "No one says you have to choose a side, Tom. It's my hope that one day very soon there won't be any 'sides' at all. Just people, living in peace."

He almost had to chuckle at the naïveté of Jordan's utopian vision of humanity's future. "Yeah, sure. You'll buy the world a Coke and everyone'll sing in harmony. Except for the kooks and the scumbags who'll try to use their powers to get rich, or hurt people, or take control."

"True, there will always be those among us whose

motives are less than noble," Jordan said. "Who pose a threat to us."

Nodding, Tom said, "That's what I care about, Jordan: Making sure people like you—"

"People like us," Jordan corrected.

Chastened, Tom frowned. "Making sure that people like *us* obey the law and don't get away with hurting people."

"Good," Jordan said. "Because that's exactly what Promise City is going to need: someone fair. Someone trustworthy, who'll keep us all honest." He extended his open hand. "And for what it's worth, Tom . . . I'm glad it's you."

Tom looked at Jordan's hand and realized that he was being offered more than a truce, more than simple friendship. What Jordan had proffered was a partnership in a new understanding, and a role in the shaping of the world to come. It was more responsibility than Tom had ever wanted for his life.

He reached out and shook Jordan's hand.

Jordan smiled, then let go of Tom's hand and stepped toward the door. "Shawn? Kyle? We have a lot of work to do tonight."

Shawn turned to join Jordan, but Kyle stayed by Tom's side and said, "I'll catch up in a few. I just need a few more minutes with my dad."

With a nod and a smile, Jordan signaled his understanding. Then he and Shawn walked quickly out of the commissary, talking under their breath about matters of apparent urgency.

Once the door closed after them, Kyle cast a hopeful look at his father. "Dad, can I ask you a personal question?"

"Sure," Tom said.

"I know you were against taking promicin, but now that you've done it . . . how do you feel?"

The question made Tom stop and think for a few seconds. Now that he was free of the pain that had preoccupied his thoughts for the past several hours, he was really able to take stock of himself, inside and out.

He felt the corner of his mouth turn upward in a contented half smile. "I feel good," he admitted. "Like myself, only more so." Looking at Kyle, he added, "It's almost like the promicin knew who and what I am at my core, and then it amplified it." He shook his head. "Does that make sense to you?"

"Totally," Kyle said. "Diana said you were making force fields?" Off Tom's nod, Kyle continued. "That makes perfect sense. You've always been about protecting people, so you got a power that lets you defend yourself and others." He looked away, then added, "You have other powers, too. Did you know that?"

Leaning forward and listening with keen interest, Tom asked, "What *kind* of powers?"

Kyle turned away, as if he were listening to someone else. Tom wondered if his son's peculiar ability amounted to hearing voices. "You'll be immune to mind-control effects," Kyle said. "No getting read by telepaths, or mentally attacked. Any power that works by affecting the minds of others won't work on you anymore." He grinned. "Pretty cool, huh?"

"Well, it certainly sounds useful," Tom replied, secretly reveling in his newfound sensation of invulnerability. He and Kyle started walking toward the door to leave the commissary.

"You're like that Simon and Garfunkel song Mom used to play all the time," Kyle said. "You know the one: 'I Am a Rock.'"

Tom chuckled, but in his heart he felt that Kyle was more right than he knew. Hearing the song in his head, Tom knew that for him it had become figuratively true: he was an island.

Diana opened her eyes to see Maia standing beside her.

"Hi, Mom," Maia said. She looked freshly bathed. Her hair was wet, and her natural curls were reasserting themselves despite her attempts to straighten her tresses. She wore clean clothes: baggy jeans, pink-and-white sneakers, and a borrowed Rush T-shirt that was at least two sizes too large for her.

Sitting up on the sofa, Diana reached over, gently took Maia's hand in hers, and smiled. "Hi, sweetie. Are you okay?"

Maia nodded. "The fighting's over," she said. With perfect surety, she added, "The military won't try to come here again."

"That's good news, I guess," Diana said.

She glanced around the small office, to which Shawn's people had brought her after Tom had carried her back through a portal from Yellowstone. Most of what had happened after that had been a blur. Diana remembered

Shawn leaning in the doorway and watching her for several seconds, but he had never actually laid hands upon her. Still, her pain had vanished, leaving only exhaustion, and she had passed out.

Eyeing Diana with a combination of contrition and concern, Maia asked, "Are *you* okay?"

Diana nodded. "Yes, honey. I'm all right." She stroked a wayward lock of Maia's damp hair from her eyes and tucked it behind the girl's ear. "You were very brave today." Replaying their earlier arguments in her memory, she glanced at the floor. "I know I said some angry things to you. And I didn't stop to think that maybe you are getting old enough to make some big decisions for yourself." Gathering her courage, she met her daughter's gaze. "That's why I need to say I'm sorry, Maia. It's not easy for me to admit that you're starting to grow up—and that maybe you don't need me as much as you used to."

Maia hugged Diana and rested her head on Diana's shoulder. The fragrance of soap still clung to her. "I never said I don't need you. I just want you to be on my side, is all."

Holding her away at arm's length, Diana said, "Maia, I am *always* on your side, even when I don't agree with you. That's what being a mother is all about." Pulling Maia back to her, she continued. "And being a family is about sticking together. Now that the fighting's over, will you finally come home?"

Shrugging free of Diana's tenuous grasp, Maia backed up half a step and stood, arms at her sides, chin bowed. "Not yet," she said, looking and sounding mildly abashed.

From the front pocket of her loose-fitting jeans, she removed a syringe fitted with a capped hypodermic needle and filled with a luminescent golden fluid that Diana knew on sight was promicin. Handing it to Diana, Maia added, "Not until you take the shot."

Diana looked at the syringe in her hand, dumbfounded. Years earlier, Dr. Kevin Burkhoff's early experiments with promicin—which had used Diana as an unwitting test subject—had resulted in Diana developing a natural resistance to the substance, and Maia knew that. Casting a puzzled look at the girl, Diana said, "But, sweetie . . . I'm immune to promicin."

In the uninflected, eerie monotone that she often reserved for her precognitive prophecies, Maia replied, "For now."

# FORTY-FIVE

Two minutes shy of midnight, Tom was the first of the NTAC agents to reach Shawn's office. Tom had been about to go home when word had reached him of an actual phone call from someone authorized to speak on behalf of the United States.

"What's going on?" he asked as he stepped through the door to find Shawn and Jordan waiting behind the big desk.

Shawn tilted his head at the phone. "We've been asked to wait until you're all here."

Impatient for an update, Tom replied, "Asked by who?"

Jordan lifted two fingers to his lips in a shushing gesture that made Tom want to kick him in the groin.

The door swung open behind Tom. Diana hurried in, followed closely by Jed and Marco. Diana asked, "What's going on?"

"Funny," Jordan replied, pointing at Tom. "That's exactly what he said." Before Tom could tell him to shut up and get on with it, Jordan reached down and tapped a command into a computer keyboard.

A flat-screen monitor mounted on the wall to Tom's right came alive with an image of the secretary of Homeland Security, a round-faced, balding man named Andreas Ziccardi.

"Mister Secretary," Jordan said, "they've arrived."

*"I can see that, Mister Collier,"* Ziccardi said. Turning his attention to the NTAC agents, he continued. *"You four have had one hell of a long day, haven't you?"*

The others all looked at Tom. As the ranking agent on the scene, the responsibility for answering to the Department of Homeland Security fell to him. "Yes, sir," he said.

*"Would you care to guess the reason for this call?"*

Tom felt his face tighten with anxiety. "Not really, no."

The ghost of a smile haunted Ziccardi's fleshy countenance. *"Did you ever think that maybe I was calling to commend you all for a fine day's work in the middle of a war zone?"*

"No, sir," Tom said, spotting the rhetorical trap that Ziccardi was so artlessly setting for him. "The thought never even crossed my mind."

Ziccardi's mien turned fiery. *"You're goddamn right it didn't, Baldwin! You four had direct orders to board that evac plane and report to D.C. for your new assignments. The minute you bailed from that jet you were all officially AWOL."*

Unable to suppress his ire, Tom shot back, "Yeah, 'cause that's what's important here. No need to thank me for saving the planet at Yellowstone, by the way. All part of the service, right? After all, you can't let a little thing like Armageddon get in the way of slapping my wrist for going AWOL."

The secretary frowned and nodded. *"Ah, yes. I heard about your little stunt at Yellowstone. Some tourists even got video of it. Didn't know that, did you, Baldwin?"* He held up a piece of paper packed with small type. *"Know what this is? It's a federal warrant for your arrest, for the illegal self-injection of promicin."* He quaked, as if overcome with fury. *"This, I could've fixed. And if this had just been about going back for Skouris's kid, I could've pardoned you. But guess what one of our long-range recon teams recorded earlier today?"* With a joyless smile, he added, *"Let me patch it in for you."*

The secretary typed some commands into his own computer. Seconds later, a shaky, grainy image replaced his visage on the wall screen. It was handheld video footage, shot with a long-range zoom lens, from an angle that suggested the camera operator had been on the roof of a low building.

The scene that played out was one that Tom recalled all too vividly: his and Diana's altercation with the soldiers outside the Beacon Hill Library. The video showed the soldiers shooting the p-positive child and her family, as well as Diana killing three of the four troops responsible. It also showed Tom quite clearly firing the fatal shot at the fourth soldier.

As it played on, it documented Tom and Diana turning away from the carnage outside the library to face in the direction of the scout's camera—making their faces unmistakably recognizable.

Tom bowed his head in shame as the recording ended.

Ziccardi reappeared on the monitor. *"Are either of you going to try to tell me that wasn't you?"*

Before Tom could reply, Diana shouted, "Are you gonna try to tell me those soldiers didn't murder children in cold blood? They just gunned them down, unarmed civilians in broad daylight! Last time I checked, that's called a *war crime!*"

*"And if you'd wanted to file charges against those men, the case would have been investigated through proper channels,"* said Ziccardi. *"But instead, you both attacked uniformed American military personnel in an occupied territory of the United States. The second you did that, you became illegal enemy combatants. Along with your two accomplices, you've been declared enemies of the United States of America. If any of you ever sets foot on American soil again, you'll spend the rest of your life at Gitmo, in a pit with no windows"*—he shot a pointed look at Jed—*"just like your carbon copy."*

Leaning so close to his webcam that it distorted his face into a grotesque caricature, Ziccardi added, *"Enjoy your stay in Promise City. Because the day any of you steps even one inch outside of it, your ass is mine."*

The screen cut to black. Stunned silence filled the office.

The NTAC agents turned in unison as Jordan cleared his throat. "Let me know if any of you are looking for jobs," he said.

# FORTY-SIX

IF THE PAST NIGHT had taught Dennis Ryland nothing else, it was that it was always easier to drive into a war zone than it was to drive out of one.

*Because fools rush in,* he chided himself. He shambled down the corridors of the new Haspelcorp headquarters in Tacoma. Morning sun slanted in through the southerly facing windows, bathing the hallway in golden light. It made him wince. Thanks to the tribulations of escaping from Promise City after dark, he'd had no sleep the night before, and now his eyes itched. Fatigue made his arms and legs feel rubbery and weak.

He was looking forward to a cup of coffee. Maybe a Danish.

Instead he opened his office door to a reception of stern faces and three men with drab suits, badges, and sidearms.

"Don't tell me," Dennis said in his best deadpan voice. "You're here for an intervention?"

"That's one way of putting it," said Miles Enright. The gaunt, middle-aged man stood in front of the window with daylight at his back, and Dennis glimpsed his own reflection in the man's black glasses. Miles cracked a cold smile. "Dennis," he said, gesturing at the man to his left, "this is Agent Brill of the NSA." Of the man on his right he said, "This is Special Agent Roel of the FBI. The man by the door is Agent Wilson from the CIA. They'd like to ask you some questions."

"Actually," said Special Agent Roel, "we'd like to arrest you first, then ask you some questions."

Agent Wilson added, "Which might or might not involve your head spending long periods of time being held underwater."

"Depending on how well you cooperate," Brill said with a menacing smile.

Roel stepped forward. "Mister Ryland, face the wall please." Dennis did as the man said, and continued following his instructions. "Spread your legs, lean forward, and place your palms flat on the wall."

The agent frisked Dennis quickly but thoroughly, then snapped a pair of handcuffs shut on Dennis's right wrist. The steel was cold and cut into his flesh almost to the bone as Roel pulled Dennis's right hand behind his back, forcing him to stand straight and take his left hand off the wall. Roel grabbed it and in quick, practiced motions, he had Dennis in cuffs.

"Dennis Ryland," Roel said, "you have been charged with compromising the national security of the United States of America, misappropriating federal funds, aiding and abetting terrorist enemies of the United States, and illegally transporting radioactive materials into the United States."

Miles interjected with more than a small measure of visible schadenfreude, "Oh, and Dennis? You're fired." To the men in suits he said, "Get him out of here."

The worst part of being perp-walked out of the Haspelcorp building, as far as Dennis was concerned, wasn't the gawking stares of the middle managers or the smug nods of the rank-and-file underlings who took such glee from seeing him in custody. No, for Dennis, the real disappointment of this turn of events was that he had been denied his coffee and Danish.

A few dozen cars—some marked as Washington State Police, some not marked at all—had converged outside the front entrance of the building. Dozens of uniformed state troopers were there to make sure that Dennis—with his flat feet, bad back, and desk jockey's physique—didn't make a run for it. Overhead, a pair of black helicopters pounded the morning air with the thumping of their massive rotors. It was such an exhibition of overkill that Dennis almost had to laugh as Roel pushed him down into one of the unmarked cars and took pains not to bump Dennis's head.

*This is the one thing the government's always good for,* Dennis mused. *The one thing they do best: a circus.*

Every window at Haspelcorp that faced the street framed one or more faces staring down at Dennis. He looked up and smiled back at them. He'd been down this road before.

He'd be back.

# FORTY-SEVEN

KYLE STOOD AT the closed door to Jordan's temporary residence in The 4400 Center. He felt Cassie appear behind him. Her breath was warm on his neck. Her perfume was delicate and floral.

"This is it," she whispered in his ear. "He's alone. We'll never have a better chance."

His sweaty right hand closed around the grip of the pistol tucked into the waistband of his jeans at the small of his back. With his left hand, he knocked on the door.

From the other side, Jordan replied, "Come in."

Taking his hand off the weapon, Kyle pushed open the door and stepped inside Jordan's living room. Its furnishings were spare but comfortable.

Jordan stood in front of a long window that looked out on the Center's landscaped garden. In one hand he held a saucer, in the other a teacup. He wore loose-fitting, unbleached linen pants and a matching shirt, and his feet were shod in plain leather sandals. Outside the window, the sun was setting behind the lush boughs of Interlaken Park.

He turned and regarded Kyle with a serene expression. "What can I do for you, Kyle?"

Cassie's voice was sharp with anger. "Do it now! While his hands are full!"

Beads of sweat traced paths down the side of Kyle's face as he forced himself not to react to Cassie's malevolent commands. To Jordan he said, "We need to talk."

Perhaps reacting to the urgency in Kyle's tone, Jordan furrowed his brow and asked, "What about?"

"About Cassie," Kyle said.

She stepped between him and Jordan. "What are you doing, Kyle? Don't wuss out on me now. *Shoot him!*"

Jordan set his cup and saucer on a ledge in front of the window. "Is something wrong with her?"

"She wants me to kill you."

Cassie slapped Kyle's face. His eyes blinked in shock and his head snapped sideways from the blow.

Looking confused and worried, Jordan said, "Kyle? Are you all right?"

Ignoring his dark muse's hate-filled stare, Kyle said, "She just hit me." He touched his tingling cheek and grinned. "Guess I wasn't supposed to tell you that."

Furious, Cassie retorted, "Gee? You think?"

Folding his hands together and steepling his index fingers, Jordan began to pace in front of the window. "Did she tell you why she wants you to kill me?"

"She said the Movement's falling apart. That you're not the leader it needs in wartime. She wants me to take over."

Jordan nodded. He looked calm. Pensive.

"I see," he said. Then he examined Kyle. "Did you bring

a weapon, or does she want you to kill me with your bare hands?"

There had been no anger or sarcasm in Jordan's question. His strangely sanguine reaction horrified Kyle and put an evil smirk on Cassie's face. Kyle reached behind his back and drew the pistol. "I brought this," he said, showing it to Jordan.

"Good. At least it'll be quick." Jordan stopped pacing, faced Kyle, and let his arms fall at his sides. "I'm ready."

"Well, I'm not," Kyle said.

With a push of his thumb, he released the ammunition clip, which fell from the pistol and clattered across the floor. He kept the weapon pointed away from Jordan as he pulled back on the slide and ejected the last round from its chamber. Then he hurled the unloaded pistol past Jordan, through the window. It fell in a flurry of shattered glass to the garden below.

Cassie glared at him. "That was stupid of you, Kyle."

Jordan looked out the shattered window, then back at Kyle as he asked, "Why did you do that?"

Kyle understood Cassie's reaction, but Jordan's baffled him. "What're you saying? You really want me to shoot you?"

"If that's what Cassie told you to do, then she must have a reason," Jordan said. "She's never been wrong before."

"Listen to him, Kyle," Cassie said with a smug sneer.

"There's a first time for everything," Kyle said. "The sinking of that ship? The use of force on Harbor Island? Cassie told me to make those things happen."

She punched him in the gut. He doubled over, unable

to inhale for several seconds. As he forced himself upright, Cassie said, "Shut up and do what I tell you, Kyle. There's a knife in the kitchenette, in the drawer next to the stove."

"Right now she's telling me where to find a knife," Kyle said. "Sometimes she uses me as a puppet. She speaks, but the words come out of my mouth."

Her foot slammed into the back of his knee, and she pushed him forward. He fell on his knees in front of Jordan. "You're weak," Cassie said, circling like a shark. "You make me sick."

Jordan said, "Kyle, if I need to die for the Movement to go forward, then we should accept that."

"No," Kyle said, shaking his head. "I think she's *lying*, Jordan. Killing you has nothing to do with the Movement."

Stepping closer, Jordan asked, "Why do you say that?"

"Something my dad said. He told me that promicin gave him powers that seemed to reflect who he was inside. The real him. And I thought about other people's powers. Shawn was always trying to make things right between other people; now he heals. Heather wanted to teach people; now she brings out their hidden talents."

Jordan nodded, apparently understanding. "And what was it you wanted, Kyle?"

"I thought I wanted answers," he said. "But now I see that what I wanted was attention. I wanted respect." He glowered at Cassie. "But not like this."

She locked one hand around Kyle's throat and squeezed. "You need to stop talking now, Kyle."

He tried to pull her hand off, but she was stronger than

him. Choking out his words, he said, "You have to stop her."

Jordan moved to Kyle's side. Cassie let go of Kyle and retreated. Jordan said, "What are you asking me to do, Kyle?"

"I want you to take away my power," Kyle said as he fell forward onto all fours, gasping for breath. "Please."

Jordan covered his mouth and sighed through his nose. Lowering his hand, he said, "I don't know, Kyle. Cassie's been vital to guiding the Movement. Without her—"

"Listen to me," Kyle said, looking up. "She's more than a little crazy, and she's got a mean streak. But what scares me is that she's *stronger* than me. One of these days she'll use me to do whatever she wants. I'm begging you: don't let that happen."

The request seemed to leave Jordan taken aback. "Kyle, I need to make sure you understand what you're asking for. If I neutralize your power, it'll be gone forever. *Cassie* will be gone forever. You'll never be able to get your power back, and you'll never be able to get another one. Is that something you can live with?"

"Yes," Kyle said. Recalling his possession years earlier by an agent of the Marked, he continued. "I've already been used once by a nutcase living in my head to try to murder you. I'm not letting it happen again."

"Fair enough," Jordan said. He placed his hands on either side of Kyle's head. "I won't lie to you: this will hurt."

"That's okay. It ought to."

From across the room, Cassie shrieked like a terrified child then screamed, "Kyle, stop! Don't do this! We can make a deal! I'll behave! Please . . . !"

Crushing pressure seized Kyle's skull, and all his thoughts turned red. Cassie screamed like a heretic being burned at the stake. Her howls of agony sent a chill through Kyle, who wept not only in pain but in mourning.

Cassie ceased her doleful wails long enough to cry out, "Kyle! Please! I love you . . ."

He shut his eyes and felt Jordan's exorcising power knife through his mind, cutting away every trace of Cassie with the subtle violence of a surgeon's scalpel. Her frightened cries diminished to a pitiful whimpering.

As Jordan released him, Kyle thought he felt Cassie's hand on his back. He turned his head as the sensation faded away—

There was no one there.

Wiping the tears from his face, he picked himself up and nodded once to Jordan. Then he shuffled in trembling steps to the door. As he opened it to leave, Jordan called out to him.

"Are you okay?"

Kyle looked back. "She's gone."

"That's not what I asked."

He gave a small nod. "I know."

He left and shut the door behind him.

Walking away down the empty corridor, Kyle felt the difference in his soul: Cassie was dead, and he was alone.

# FORTY-EIGHT

Tom FLOPPED ONTO Diana's couch with a satisfied sigh. "Great dinner," he said. "When did you learn to cook like that?"

"I'm not *totally* useless in the kitchen," she protested. "Though, to be honest, rigatoni Fiorentina's kind of easy. It's just pasta, chicken, fresh baby spinach, and vodka sauce from a jar." Holding up the mostly drained bottle of Pinotage, she asked, "More wine?"

"Please," Tom said, lifting his glass.

She refilled it with half of what was left, then poured the rest of the robust red wine into her own long-stemmed glass. A distinctive aroma of candle smoke still lingered from the just-snuffed tapers on the dining room table, and a faint jazz melody drifted from the speakers beside the TV as Diana settled onto the opposite end of the sofa from Tom.

Cocking his head toward the music, he asked, "What are we listening to?"

"Ella Fitzgerald," she said.

He grinned. "From Maia's collection?"

She smiled back. "How'd you guess?"

They sat back, sipped their wine, and listened to Ella's soft and sweet crooning for a while.

During a lull between songs, Tom sighed. "What a day. Did I tell you Meghan called this morning?"

"No," Diana said. "What'd she say?"

He rolled his eyes and frowned. "If the U.S. mail still came to Promise City, I think she'd have sent me a 'Dear Tom' note, instead."

With genuine sympathy, Diana said, "She dumped you?"

"Like a load of garbage," Tom said. "She actually had a list of reasons. A *list!* Can you believe that?"

Diana perched her elbow on the back of the sofa and leaned her head on her shoulder. "What was item number one?"

"She tried to make it sound like a three-way tie," he said, staring down at his stockinged feet. "Homeland Security read her the riot act and told her to end it, and that was probably part of it. The video of you and me shooting soldiers didn't sit well with her, either." Looking up at Diana, he continued. "But I think what pissed her off the most was that I lied to her in order to help you." With a dismissive wave of his hand, he added, "Anyway, it's not like we had much of a future at this point. She's out there with a warrant for my arrest, and I'm in here, playing sheriff to Jordan's insane-asylum utopia."

Raising her glass, Diana said, "Let me know if you need a trusty deputy, Sheriff."

"Consider yourself volunteered."

As Tom sipped more wine, Diana said, "I have an odd moment of my own to share with you." She shifted forward to the middle of the couch, reached over to the coffee table, put down her glass, and flipped open the lid of a cherry-wood curio box.

Inside the velvet-lined box was the syringe of promicin that her daughter had given her a few days earlier.

At the sight of it, Tom sat up and moved to the middle of the sofa, beside Diana, facing the box.

"Maia handed me this after I woke up from our Yellowstone op," Diana said. "She says she won't come home until I take the shot. When I told her I was immune, she said this was a new formula, something stronger. Is this what she gave to you?"

He nodded. "Yeah, I think it is. She wasn't kidding about it being potent. It gave me an ability in under an hour." Throwing a worried look at Diana, he asked, "You're not thinking of taking it, are you?"

"Maybe," she said, more defensively than she'd intended. "I mean, I want my daughter to come home, and if this is the only way . . ." She let her voice trail off, since she was certain that Tom understood. "Besides, you're hardly one to talk. After all your rants against promicin, and all your speeches about choosing free will over prophecy, you still stuck the needle in *your* arm." Narrowing her eyes with mock suspicion, she pointed at him and said, "What I want to know is, how the hell did Maia talk you into taking it when you wouldn't listen to your own son? Why trust her vision instead of his?"

Tom averted his gaze. Diana imagined gears turning

inside his skull as he considered his reply. Then he took a deep breath, turned his head, and looked into her eyes.

"I did it for you," he said. "Maia said if I didn't take the shot, I'd have to watch you die." His voice faltered as he added, "I took the shot so I wouldn't lose you."

Awkward silence fell between them. Staring into his eyes, Diana suddenly became aware of just how close together she and Tom were. A romantically charged, almost-magnetic sensation passed between them. As they drifted incrementally closer, Diana suddenly wasn't sad to know that Maia was miles away and not coming home tonight. She kept waiting for Tom to pull back, but he seemed to be as swept up in the moment as Diana felt . . .

She blinked and recoiled. Even though they were no longer NTAC agents, and no longer partners, a sense of taboo persisted in her mind, and it was a line she wasn't ready to cross . . . yet.

Standing and backing up a step, she pushed wayward coils of her dark hair out of her eyes and smiled politely at Tom. "Well," she said, "it's getting late."

He shot an amused look at the clock and was apparently too polite to point out that it wasn't even eight-thirty. "Yeah, I guess so," he said, putting down his wineglass on the table.

"So, I'll see you at the Center tomorrow morning?" she asked, while watching him pull his still-laced shoes back on.

"Yup," he said. Then he got up and followed her to the door, which she opened ahead of him. They did an awkward shuffle-step around each other as he slipped past her into the doorway then turned back. "G'night," he said with a friendly smile.

"'Night," she said, leaning forward. They planted chaste pecks on each other's cheeks, then backed apart. He gave her a quick half nod, then walked down the hall, toward the stairs.

She started to close the door, and had almost pushed it shut, when she surrendered to a silly impulse. Silently, she cracked the door open just a sliver, and peeked out at Tom.

At the same moment, Tom slowed for just a step and cast a look back over his shoulder at her, with a gaze of wistful consideration that mirrored her own.

Overcome with a strange glee, she grinned at him.

He grinned back, then turned and continued out of sight and down the stairs.

Diana shut her door, then spun about and fell back against it with a dopey grin on her face. She had no idea what the next day might bring, but she knew two things about it already.

It was going to be different.

And it was going to be interesting.

# FORTY-NINE

THEIR FACES HAD CHANGED, but the world had remained stubbornly the same. Something had gone wrong with the plan.

Concealed inside the bodies of a pair of swarthy Moroccan brothers, Wells and Kuroda huddled over a table tucked into the corner of a bustling Casablanca café. Outside its open façade, blinding afternoon sunlight baked the dusty street. Within the shadowy indoor oasis, the air was sultry and thick with fruit-scented smoke from dozens of burbling water pipes.

The other patrons all looked, to one degree or another, like the Marked agents' new hosts: brown-skinned, dark-haired, and garbed in desert robes whose style hadn't changed substantially in hundreds of years.

Picking at the finger food on the large metal platter between them, Wells wrinkled his nose at the cuisine. "I'd kill someone for a bacon cheeseburger right now," he said.

"You're the one who insisted we go native," Kuroda said.

Wells huffed. "Like it makes any difference now. Jakes is gone, the plan's a bust, and Collier's more powerful than ever." He cast a wary look around the room, to make sure none of the other patrons were spying on them. No one paid him any mind. "Next time, we'll have to go straight at Collier."

"Who says there's going to be a next time?" Kuroda replied. "We've got nothing, Wells. All our cash went into the warhead. And now the timeline's so fouled up, there's no way to tell what'll happen next. All those stocks you said were going to soar? They just tanked. The future that we knew is gone."

Feeling his brow knit with rage, Wells grumbled, "I don't care. I won't just sit by and let Collier win." He picked up the hose of his hookah and lifted the nozzle to his lips. "A new plan will take time," he said. Then he inhaled a mouthful of sweet, cool smoke. He enjoyed the bubbling noises that emanated from the water pipe while he smoked. After he exhaled, he said, "Fortunately, time is something we currently have in abundance."

Kuroda lifted his own hookah nozzle. "It's the *only* thing we have in abundance," he said.

The hose of Wells's hookah undulated and jerked free of his grasp, and Kuroda's did the same. The hoses swayed hypnotically, dancing between the two men with the deadly grace of serpents. Then the hoses shot forward and coiled around Wells's and Kuroda's necks, constricting in an instant to lethal effect.

All around them, the café's clientele leaped from their cushions and shrieked "Djinn! Djinn!" In a matter of seconds the place was cleared. Plates of food lay discarded and overturned, their contents scattered on the satin pillows. Knocked-over water pipes spilled into merging puddles on the dirt floor.

Only the two Marked agents remained, writhing on the ground as their own hookah tubes strangled them.

Even as his vision began to dim and lose focus, Wells saw two tall figures clad in desert robes stalk into the café. The newcomers were silhouetted against the whitewash of daylight as they came to a halt and loomed above Wells and Kuroda.

The taller man asked the other, "Are you sure it's them?"

His companion replied, "I'm sure. These are the last two."

The tube around Wells's neck coiled tighter than he would have believed possible. He felt his trachea collapse and heard his cervical vertebrae splinter as his world turned black.

In his final moment, Wells tasted defeat. The future he'd fought for was lost. The world belonged to Jordan Collier.

"Are you sure it's them?" asked Richard Tyler.

"I'm sure," Gary Navarro said, probing the minds of the two Marked agents writhing at their feet. "These are the last two."

Wells and Kuroda had never suspected that Gary had learned everything about their cover identities from the mind of their accomplice, Jakes, before his death. From the moment they had arrived in Tokyo, operatives loyal to Jordan had been waiting for them.

Every move that they had made in the weeks since then had been tracked. Not for a single moment had either of them been left unwatched.

Cracking sounds from the necks of the Marked agents made Gary wince. Despite all he had been through in Promise City, witnessing a killing firsthand still made him queasy.

"Maybe you should wait outside," Richard said, obviously having noted Gary's discomfort.

Lying to save face, Gary said, "I'm fine." Turning his back on the asphyxiating Marked agents, he asked Richard, "How did Jordan get you to come out of hiding for this?"

"Can't you just look in my mind for the answer?"

"I could," Gary said. "But I try not to do that to people who are on my side."

Richard said, "I'm not on anyone's side."

"Then why are you here?"

Sickening sounds—wet crunches and the hiss of escaping gases and fluids—from the Marked agents' bodies made Gary glad that he had looked away. He didn't want to see whatever was happening, but his ears told him more than he wanted to know.

Staring dispassionately at the telekinetic damage he was inflicting, Richard said, "I'm just finishing what I started."

Stepping forward, Richard reached inside his robes and pulled out a small glass vial filled with metallic powder. He removed the vial's rubber stopper and sprinkled the powder on the two dead bodies.

Unable to suppress his morbid curiosity, Gary turned and watched as the powder drifted down and settled over the dead men's grotesquely mangled faces. The substance seemed to absorb straight through the corpses' flesh.

Moments later, a phosphorescent shimmering consumed their eyes, and electric-blue fire engulfed their skulls and spines. Dr. Kevin Burkhoff's specially crafted radioactive nanopathogen made quick work of the Marked agent's nanites, permanently annihilating their synthetic identities. As an added bonus, it all but cremated their hosts' bodies into smoldering gray ash.

Then the glow faded, and all that remained was the greasy smoke of rendered human fat, the charnel odor of scorched flesh, and the oppressive North African noonday heat.

Gary activated a special communication device nestled inside his ear canal. Built by a promicin-enhanced genius named Dalton Gibbs, the invention permitted members of the Movement to communicate across any distance without any risk of their conversations being intercepted or tracked. Gary had no idea how it worked, and he had been assured that he didn't need to know.

He keyed the transmitter. "Jordan, it's Gary."

*"Go ahead."*

"Mission accomplished. The last two Marked are dead."

*"Good work. Come on home, and tell Richard I said thanks."*

Turning to share Jordan's praise, Gary saw that Richard was gone, already vanished into the sea of bodies outside the café.

"Will do," Gary said. "See you when I get back." He

turned off the device and slipped out of the café through
its kitchen's rear entrance. As he merged into the bustling
crowd on the street, he pondered the final thought of one
of the men he'd just helped kill: *The world belongs to Jordan
Collier*.

He almost pitied the dead Marked agents, because
he saw now that they had never really understood what
promicin represented. They had been blind to its true
promise.

The world did not belong to Jordan Collier.

Thanks to promicin, the world belonged to everyone.

# FIFTY

Tom AWOKE TO the brightest, clearest morning he had ever seen in his life. It took several seconds for his eyes to adapt from the dark haven of sleep to the glare of consciousness.

Other sensations returned first. The hardness of the surface under his back. Odors of pine and ammonia. Rubbing alcohol with a hint of lemon.

A chill prickled the flesh of his bare arms and legs.

He wasn't in his bed, or in his home.

Jolting to full awareness, he sat up and twisted left then right, taking in his surroundings: a circular room with surfaces of pristine white and gleaming chrome. Its high outer walls were dominated by windows, beyond which rolled a lush, paradisiacal landscape of rolling hills, thick forests, and sparkling rivers.

Three levels of sparsely appointed workstations encircled him. Svelte, immaculately groomed men and women in matching white clothing and shoes sat facing Tom while interacting with holographically projected displays. Low murmurs of conversation susurrated in the hemispherical chamber.

Above Tom, a transparent domed ceiling looked out upon a cloudless heaven so perfectly blue that it made him feel as if he had never really seen the sky before that moment.

"Good," a man said. "You're awake."

Pivoting about-face, Tom was confronted by a middle-aged man with brown but graying crew-cut hair, a lean physique, and an unnerving stare, which Tom quickly realized was due to the fact that the man's irises were as black as his pupils. Like the other people working in the room, he wore a long white lab coat and loose-fitting white pants, which appeared to be made of cotton, and white shoes that Tom now saw were canvas slip-ons.

Trying not to look as freaked-out as he felt, Tom said, "I'm in the future."

"Correct," the scientist said.

Tom squinted against the morning sunlight. "It looks different than I remember."

"Naturally."

Climbing down off the metal operating table, Tom asked, "What's this about? The Marked?"

"Not at all," said the scientist. "That threat is now completely neutralized."

"You're welcome." Looking up and around as he rubbed some warmth back into his naked arms, Tom continued. "So what's the problem? I did everything you told me to do. Isabelle's dead, the Marked are done, and promicin's going global." Nodding at the verdant world outside, he added, "Even the future looks brighter. So what the hell am I doing here?"

The scientist adopted a grave expression and folded his hands behind his back. "Tom, there was a reason why we never gave you promicin during any of your previous visits to the future. Even when we sent you back to confront Isabelle, with all of her powers, we didn't inject you with the drug. Didn't you ever wonder why?"

Dread stirred the acid in Tom's stomach. "Jordan always said he'd never force promicin on anybody," Tom said.

"He wouldn't, but obviously we did," the scientist said. "But not in your case. We thought you understood. But then you went and took the shot anyway."

Tom felt as if he were being put on trial for saving the world. "But Kyle, my son, he . . . he said the prophecy in the White Light book—"

"Enemy propaganda," the scientist snapped. "Lies cloaked in just enough truth to make them plausible." The scientist stepped forward and grabbed Tom's T-shirt. "No matter what that book said, you were never meant to be promicin-positive, Tom. Never."

Pushing the scientist away, Tom waved his arms at the clean, sunlit future and protested, "Okay, I took promicin! If I hadn't, the world would've been destroyed. But everything looks fine to me, so *what difference* does it make?"

There was fear in the scientist's eyes as he replied, "Possibly everything, Tom . . . *Everything*."

**Here ends the First Saga of *The 4400***

# ACKNOWLEDGMENTS

My FIRST THANKS, as always, go to my wife, Kara, who once again had to accept my absence as my deadline slipped away from me, forcing me back to my old schedule of writing during the late watches of the night and the wee hours of the morning.

I'm also grateful to my editor, Margaret Clark, who had been asking me to write a novel of *The 4400* for some time. It was a quirk of fate and of timing (also known as a series cancellation) that gave me the chance to tell such an epic tale set after the show's untimely cliffhanger final episode.

For both raising the bar and setting the stage, I tip my hat to my fellow authors of *The 4400* novels: Dayton Ward and Kevin Dilmore (*Wet Work*), and Greg Cox (*The Vesuvius Prophecy* and *Welcome to Promise City*).

Just as valuable to me are the steady encouragement that I receive from my agent, Lucienne Diver, and the many votes of confidence that I've been granted by Paula Block and John Van Citters at CBS Licensing.

I would be remiss if I didn't thank the creators of and contributors to www.the4400wiki.org, a research tool that I found invaluable while crafting this novel.

To series creators Roger Peters and René Echevarria, thanks for giving us this compelling new universe in which to play, dream, and tell tall tales. Kudos as well to the many fine writers who helped craft the saga of *The 4400* (especially Ira Steven Behr and Craig Sweeny) and to all the fine actors who brought their characters to life— in particular, Joel Gretsch, Jacqueline Mackenzie, Billy Campbell, Conchita Campbell, Patrick Flueger, Chad Faust, Richard Kahan, Kavan Smith, Jenni Baird, Peter Coyote, Sharif Atkins, Tristin Leffler, Kathryn Gordon, and Mahershalalhashbaz Ali.

Last but not least, as is my custom, I'd like to list some of the soundtracks that served as musical links to my muse as I wrote this book: *The Dark Knight* (Hans Zimmer and James Newton Howard), *Quantum of Solace* (David Arnold), *Close Encounters of the Third Kind* (John Williams), *Mission: Impossible* (Danny Elfman), and *V for Vendetta* (Dario Marianelli). Rounding out my playlist on this tale was Igor Stravinsky's 1919 *Firebird Suite*.

Until next time, thank you for reading!

# ABOUT THE AUTHOR

**DAVID MACK** is the bestselling author of more than a dozen novels, including *Wildfire*, *Harbinger*, *Reap the Whirlwind*, *Road of Bones*, and the *Star Trek Destiny* trilogy: *Gods of Night*, *Mere Mortals*, and *Lost Souls*. His first work of original fiction is the supernatural thriller *The Calling*.

In addition to novels, Mack's diverse writing credits span several media, including television (for episodes of *Star Trek: Deep Space Nine*), film, short fiction, magazines, newspapers, comic books, computer games, radio, and the Internet.

Mack's upcoming novels include *Precipice*, the fifth installment of the acclaimed *Star Trek Vanguard* series, and a new, expanded edition of *Star Trek Mirror Universe: The Sorrows of Empire*.

He currently resides in New York City with his wife, Kara.

Visit his official site: http://www.davidmack.pro.